Praise for the bestselling

WIND DRAGONS MOTORCYCLE CLUB SERIES

DRAGON'S LAIR

"*Dragon's Lair* proves a badass chick can tame even the wildest of men. . . . Not to be missed."

—Angela Graham, *New York Times*– and *USA Today*–bestselling author

"*Dragon's Lair* was witty and fast paced. A delicious combination of badass biker men and laugh out loud humor . . ."

—*Bookgossip*

ARROW'S HELL

"Redemption and forgiveness form the basis of the story, while laughter, tears, and some erotic sex scenes keep the reader engaged. Low-key violence blends well with the multiple plot lines and drama-drenched characters."

—*RT Book Reviews*

"Cheek-heating, gut-wrenching, and beautifully delivered! *Arrow's Hell* took me on the ride of my life!"

—Bella Jewel, *USA Today*–bestselling author

TRACKER'S END

"Fernando's vivid characters burst onto the page . . . pulling readers into their world immediately and completely. This tightly told tale will leave readers eagerly waiting for the next installment."

—*Publishers Weekly*

"The physical chemistry between Lana and Tracker burns up the pages."

—*RT Book Reviews*

RAKE'S REDEMPTION

"You'll find yourself sitting on the edge of your seat in anticipation of how [*Rake's Redemption*] will unfold."

—*RT Book Reviews* (4½ stars, top pick)

"*Rake's Redemption* is a story about betrayal and loss, revenge and retribution, second chances and falling in love. The premise is emotional and entertaining; the characters are passionate and energetic; the romance is fated and hot."

—*The Reading Cafe*

WOLF'S MATE

"Chantal Fernando's latest romance delivers everything MC fans could ask for—incredibly sexy men and the women strong enough to keep them, passionate love scenes, thrilling adventure, and even a laugh or two along the way!"

—*Smut Book Junkie*

CROSSROADS

"*Crossroads* is an emotional journey of discovering what will lead to lasting happiness and the willingness to go for it."

—*Always Reviewing*

SEDUCING THE DEFENDANT

The Conflict of Interest Series

CHANTAL FERNANDO

GALLERY BOOKS

New York   London   Toronto   Sydney   New Delhi

G

GALLERY BOOKS
An Imprint of Simon & Schuster, Inc.
1230 Avenue of the Americas
New York, NY 10020

Copyright © 2017 by Chantal Fernando

First Gallery Books trade paperback edition November 2017

GALLERY BOOKS and colophon are registered trademarks of Simon & Schuster, Inc.

For information about special discounts for bulk purchases, please contact Simon & Schuster Special Sales at 1-866-506-1949 or business@simonandschuster.com.

The Simon & Schuster Speakers Bureau can bring authors to your live event. For more information or to book an event contact the Simon & Schuster Speakers Bureau at 1-866-248-3049 or visit our website at www.simonspeakers.com.

Designed by Bryden Spevak

Manufactured in the United States of America

10 9 8 7 6 5 4 3 2 1

Library of Congress Cataloging-in-Publication Data is available.

ISBN 978-1-5011-7236-6
ISBN 978-1-5011-7237-3 (ebook)

For all the gentle souls out there.
The ones who love unconditionally and expect nothing in return.
Those who see the good in people, even when there is none.
You are rare, and you are beautiful.
And there is strength in your empathy.

Don't let them destroy you.

acknowledgments

A big thank you to my editor, Marla Daniels, and Gallery Books. I love every second of working with you.

To my agent, Kimberly Brower, I'm so lucky to have you! Thank you for everything you do; we make such a great team.

Arijana Karcic—thank you for always being there for me when I need you, you are one of a kind.

Natalie Ram—thank you for being the most versatile best friend ever, from helping me proofread to making me swag. I appreciate everything that is you. I know I can always count on you to have my back or help me when I need you. I kind of adore you, and I don't know how I survived before I had you by my side. You're my one-woman army, and I love you heaps.

Thank you to my parents and sisters for helping out whenever I need more writing time, I appreciate everything you do for me, and to my three sons for being patient when they know their mama has to work. I love you all so much.

Rose Tawil, I really don't know what I'd do without you. I can't say thank you enough for all the work you put in to support my dreams, and you never ask for anything in return. You truly are one of the best people I've ever met. Love you infinity.

You are so brave and quiet I forget you are suffering.

—ERNEST HEMINGWAY

chapter 1

JAXON

A BODY HAS BEEN FOUND, *dumped in the river waterfront, said police. Dental records show that it's the body of Officer Darren Melvin who has been missing for the last two years.*

I lift my head from my book and watch as the camera zooms in on the river where the man's body was found. I've been following this case ever since Officer Melvin went missing about two years ago, and now that they've found his body, the case can finally be classified as a homicide. I listen as the news reporter explains how Melvin had been shot in the head and how his body would've never been found if the city hadn't decided to gentrify the waterfront park, something that has been a hot topic of late.

I think I've been so interested in this one because my best friend is a cop and he's always given these crazy, dangerous assignments—Melvin's death could have just as easily been his. My friend and I have worked on a few things together before, but it feels like a long-ass time since I've seen or even thought about him. I've taken some time off work, but I don't think it's what I need. I should be burying myself in work, taking case after case, not leaving any time for my mind to wander.

I glance at the marble-framed photograph on my bookshelf, studying the dark-haired beauty with green eyes. I'd give anything to see those green eyes again.

My attention is brought back to the TV screen. Yeah, an idle mind is the *last* thing I need.

I need to keep busy, distracted.

I don't need to think about anything other than work. I don't need to remember.

Melvin's wife, heiress to Reyes Industries, Scarlett Reyes, has been charged with his murder, and was taken into custody after police found the same type of gun that killed Officer Melvin in her home. . . .

My phone rings, and I'm not surprised.

I'm one of the most sought-after criminal lawyers in town. I'm not bragging; it's just a fact. So when my partner, Tristan, tells me that Scarlett Reyes has requested a meeting with me, it's not a shock.

"Are you going to take it?" he asks, and I can just picture him in his office, leaning back in his chair, eyes gleaming at the prospect of this controversial case. Our firm is known for taking on high-profile cases, we usually don't turn down opportunities like this. "I know you're meant to be taking a break, but I thought since she requested you . . ."

"I want to speak with her first," I tell him. "And consider me officially off my break."

"Are you sure?" he asks. "What you've been though, Jaxon—"

"I know, Tristan, but sitting here isn't helping. I need to keep busy," I admit.

He takes a deep breath, then continues. "This case is going to be huge, Jaxon. It's going to be all over the media, and it might get messy. But if you win this . . . fuck."

If I win this case, my reputation as a criminal attorney will rise even higher. I'll be sought after—more than I already am—and I'll be paid whatever I want by those willing to do, and pay, whatever they need to escape prison time. But do I *want* this case? Normally I wouldn't have a problem defending someone whether they were guilty or not. But this case is different. Do I want to defend a woman who has potentially killed a cop, one of my best friend's brothers? I won't be able to decide until I meet her and see what she has to say for herself. I want to hear her side of the story. I'll be able to get a good read on her if I'm there in person. And if she admits that she did kill her husband . . . I don't know what I'll do.

"There's no question it'll get messy," I tell him. "But it's a challenge. . . ."

I know that shouldn't be the basis on which I accept a case, but damn, I like to be kept on my toes. I like to push myself, test myself. I like seeing how far I can bend the law in my client's favor.

"You do enjoy a good challenge," Tristan murmurs, amusement lacing his tone. "I'll handle the bail hearing. It'll give you time to look at the case and see if you're ready. I guess I'll be seeing you soon then."

"I guess you will," I say, and then tell him good-bye.

I look back at the photo, my chest suddenly getting tight. I don't have it in me to put the photo away or cover it, but every time I look at it, it hurts.

It physically hurts.

I absently rub my chest and stand, then head into my bathroom to have a quick shower, knowing I have to go to the office to do some reading. Once I'm ready, I glance around, looking for my keys. I keep my gaze down, making sure not to look in the direction of the photo. I find them next to my wallet on the kitchen counter, grab both of them and head outside to my car.

I don't need any more time off.

I have a prospective client to meet.

chapter 2

"COME IN," I SAY, lifting my gaze from what little information I have on Scarlett Reyes. A woman walks through the door, and I instantly stand, buttoning my suit jacket. She's beautiful. That's the first thing that enters my mind. Light hair and eyes, creamy skin, and a femininity I don't see that often anymore. She's dressed in a pale ice-blue loose blouse and denim jeans, her hazel eyes a striking contrast. *This is Scarlett Reyes, the husband killer?* Not what I was expecting. At all.

"Ms. Reyes?" I ask, walking toward her and offering her my hand. She looks so young, mid to late twenties maybe; I was expecting someone older.

"Yes," she says, loosely shaking my hand, then quickly dropping it.

"Have a seat," I tell her, pulling out the chair for her. I then walk to my own, opposite her, and we both sit down. "Can I get you something to drink? Tea or coffee?"

"No, thank you," she replies, glancing around my office briefly before returning her gaze to me. Tristan got her out on bail, and now it's up to me to decide if I want to be involved. If I don't take on this case, he will, so I need to decide what to do with her. As good of a lawyer as Tristan is, he knows I'm better at the murder cases. Tristan's more of a white-collar criminal lawyer.

"I'm just going to jump right into it," I say, getting straight to the point. I open the file in front of me. "You're being charged with the murder of your husband, based on the grounds that the gun used to kill him is the same kind of gun that was found in your home and that you were the last to see him alive." I pause to skim the file, making sure I'm correct. "You fled the country around the time he went missing, and you started to withdraw money out of your joint account in the days leading up to your departure. All suspicious activity." I put the file down and pick up my pen, ready to take notes. "Let's start with the gun situation. A Glock 22 was found in your possession," I say.

"I have several licensed guns, a Glock being one of them," she says, squaring her shoulders and lifting her stubborn chin. Her eyes are cold, empty, completely void of emotion. "My husband was a police officer, so our household was obviously pro-guns. I don't see why that's an issue. Practically everyone in this country owns a gun."

She's defending herself to me, instead of giving me what I need so I can defend her. There's a difference.

"It's an issue because the same make was used to kill Darren," I remind her, arching a brow. "So if that's your weapon of choice, and it was used to kill your husband, you can see why it won't look good in court."

The woman actually rolls her eyes at me.

I've gotten attitude from clients before, sure, but I don't think she realizes she's treating me like the enemy instead of a tool that can save her.

Okay, that wasn't the best metaphor, but if she works with me, I can do my job better. I don't know why I'm talking like I've already agreed to accept the case when I haven't yet. The truth is, I don't know if I should take this case. I mean, there are challenges, and then there's this. . . .

"Anyone can pull a trigger, Mr. Bentley. Just because I have the same gun doesn't automatically make me guilty. Yes, I have a Glock 22. Lots of people have Glocks. I prefer it since I have small hands and the recoil isn't as bad as others. I actually have many guns like the one that killed Darren. No, I did *not* use any of those guns to kill him. Forgive me, Mr. Bentley, but isn't it your job to prove to the court that coincidences don't equate guilt?"

I study her for a moment, contemplating her words. So she *is* claiming innocence. She's right—there are many different variables, and this could be one big coincidence. For all we know someone could have stolen one of her guns and used it, or bought one similar knowing that she owned one. However, Scarlett registered the gun about six months before Darren's death. But because the force of the river's current washed away the bullet, there is no way to run ballistics and match the striations of the bullet to the gun.

Without being able to prove that Scarlett's gun was not the one that killed Darren, it doesn't matter. In the jury's eyes, her husband was murdered with a Glock 22, and months before she left the country, she bought a Glock 22. It doesn't look good.

"I'm here to help you, Ms. Reyes," I tell her, leaning back in my chair. "But I need complete honesty to do that."

"And you'll get it," she says instantly, pursing her pink lips.

I look her in the eye, trying to determine if she's lying. I can generally tell by body language whether someone is telling the truth—I've become good at that over the years.

"All right, let's discuss the fact that you fled the country the last day he was seen alive. That's two strikes against you."

"I didn't flee. My aunt was ill, and I planned a trip to visit her. Darren knew about my trip to Paris."

I perk up at that. "Do you have any proof that he knew you were leaving?"

"Two years later? Uh, no." She looks at me like I'm an idiot.

"Well, I'll make sure to ask his friends and colleagues to see if he mentioned your leaving." I make a note in the file, realizing again that I'm talking like I already took this case. "And what about the withdrawal of close to thirty thousand dollars from your joint bank account before you left?"

"Look, I took the money because it's mine to begin with, it wasn't 'our money' "—she made air quotes before continuing— "I had every right to that account. But I was also leaving Darren and wouldn't dare leave him with one cent of my father's money," she bit out. "I needed it for my fresh start," she tries to explain. "I didn't kill him, Mr. Bentley. I stopped loving him way before I left, but I also didn't wish him dead. The local cops are all his friends, and they're out to make someone pay for his death. And that person happens to be me."

Now the cops want his death pinned on her? Sounds like a bit of a conspiracy theory. Without evidence, that's definitely not something I can say in court. Accusing cops of such a thing would not be looked upon favorably.

"No one can pin anything on you without evidence, Scarlett. But I have to admit that from where I sit, it's not looking good, so why don't you give me some more information to work with?" I ask, my gray eyes trained on her.

People usually squirm under my glare, but again, she gives me no reaction. She takes me in, from my face to the pant legs of my navy suit, while I watch her. What is she thinking?

"Are you going to take my case, Mr. Bentley?" she asks, raising her gaze to mine. "Because if my own lawyer doesn't believe me, what chance do I have? I'm paying you to believe me."

"What I believe is irrelevant. It's what I can *prove*, Ms. Reyes. It doesn't matter how good I am; they aren't going to let you go free because I say they should," I tell her, inwardly surprised at her comment. She called me out on something I don't want to admit. I still don't know if I believe her. I do know that if I decide to work with her, I will do everything I can to help her win.

"Are you sure you're the best lawyer to help me win this case, Mr. Bentley?" she blurts out, swallowing hard. "I don't want to be rude, but this is my *life* at stake. I'm not going to go to prison for a crime I didn't commit. I know it doesn't look good, but that doesn't change the fact that I didn't do anything wrong other than fall in love with the wrong man many years ago."

Finally, a little emotion flashes in her cold depths.

Fear.

Underneath she's scared, and she has every right to be.

I study her closely, and something in my gut tells me I should take this case. I don't ignore my intuition, because it's never let me down before.

"You came to me, Ms. Reyes. I'm sure it was because you were advised I was one of the best." I pause, and then add, "And I am. I'll do what I can to keep you out of prison, but you need to tell me *everything*. No detail is too small." I glance back down at the file, admitting to myself that Scarlett Reyes will be my next client. Something won't let me say no, although I don't know what it is exactly. "It says you were the last person to see him alive. Is this true?"

She purses her lips again. "I'd assume the person who killed him was the last person to see him alive, Mr. Bentley."

"Okay, I need a timeline of everything that happened the last time you saw him," I tell her, ignoring her sarcastic response.

She tells me what she remembers—what time she saw him, what he was wearing, and what they spoke about—as I write it all down.

"Anything else that can help this case in any way, or shed light on anything that might make a difference?" I ask her, feeling like there's something she's not telling me. "I'm your lawyer, Ms. Reyes; you need to trust me. If there's anything else I need to know, you have to tell me. Now."

She doesn't acknowledge the fact that I suddenly decided to be her lawyer; instead, she looks down at her hands. "I'm innocent; that pretty much sums everything up."

I decide to change the subject a little.

"So you got married five years ago," I summarize, tapping my pen on the notepad. "You might have brought the money into the relationship, but you realize since you were married, the laws say that money was his too, right?" She grimaces as I continue. "Why didn't you divorce him if you were planning on leaving him?" I ask, brow furrowing. "And why didn't you have a prenuptial agreement to protect yourself?"

"Young love equals stupid decisions, Mr. Bentley," she mutters, jaw going tight. "Darren took what was mine and made it his own, yes, but that doesn't mean that I wasn't allowed to take money out of our joint account. There was plenty more in there. Besides, do you know who I am? The money I took was nothing in comparison to what I have in trust." I look down at the balances, seeing that she's right. She takes a deep breath. "And as for the divorce . . ." She opens her mouth, and then closes it. "That wasn't an option."

"Why not?" I ask her, leaning forward in my seat.

"Because he would never agree to one," she says, shaking her head. "He was a man who was used to getting what he wanted. So full of pride. He'd never have given me a divorce."

I'm silent for so long that she continues speaking.

"You wouldn't understand. You're a man. I was just . . ." She trails off, and I don't like the look on her face.

Hopelessness.

I hate the words I say next, but I have to see where she stands.

"I need to be honest with you. I don't know if we'll be successful in getting you acquitted. Would you consider a plea deal?"

"No," she says instantly.

"Okay," I tell her gently, making a note. "All or nothing, right?"

"Something like that," she replies, and our eyes hold for just a little too long to be polite.

I look down, knowing I have my work cut out for me.

"I'm going to do everything I can to help you, Ms. Reyes."

She nods once and glances toward the door, like she can't wait to escape.

"Let me see what I can dig up. We have to move fast, the DA is looking to try you as soon as possible because of all the publicity surrounding the case," I finally say, standing and offering her my hand. "I'll do everything I can."

She stands and takes my hand; it's small and cold against my large, warm one.

"Thank you," she says, voice clear and sincere.

"I'll be in touch," I say. "And, Ms. Reyes?"

"Yes," she replies, her tone cool.

"Call me Jaxon," I say. She needs to trust me, and I want her to feel like she's able to come to me and be open.

"Jaxon," she repeats, as if testing the name.

She moves to leave my office, but then hesitates, like she wants to say something more. But she must change her mind, as she sighs and heads to the door.

She's hiding something.

And I'm going to find out what it is.

chapter 3

J WALK INTO TRISTAN'S OFFICE, where he's sitting at his desk, texting on his phone.

"Working hard, I see," I tease, taking a seat opposite him. I've known Tristan since law school, where we quickly became close friends. We made a plan that we'd open a firm together, and six years later that's how Bentley & Channing Law was born. We've both worked our asses off to be what we are now, which is one of the top law firms in the city, even though we're small. Tristan and I decided when we started that we'd run things differently—taking fewer cases than a normal firm but truly handling everything ourselves, from beginning to end. We don't have secretaries; instead we hire law students to help us research case law. But we do have one secret weapon—Yvonne, who is pretty much our go-to person when we're in a jam. While we each practice criminal law, we've recently realized that we needed to start branching out, so we also hired a family-law attorney and an associate fresh out of law school. We also have a competitive intern program, allowing us the ability to work with the best and brightest of new talent and have our pick on who to hire. We're a small firm, but we're kind of a big deal.

"My client's late," he says, glancing at his watch and putting his phone down. "Everything okay?"

"Yeah," I tell him, studying him. "It's just that something isn't sitting right with me with this case. I feel like there's more to it."

"Tell me," he says, giving me all of his attention.

"I looked into her claims, and she didn't lie about her aunt. Her mother's sister, Leona, has lung cancer, and Scarlett did fly out to see her," I tell him. "She says she was home during the time he was murdered, but there's no witness to testify to that. I have nothing to work with here besides her word."

"Do you think she's guilty?" he asks me straight out.

"I don't know," I tell him honestly. "The evidence all points toward her pulling the trigger, yet . . ."

"Yet what?" he asks, waiting patiently for my answer. "Go with your gut, Jaxon. You know it doesn't let you down."

I can't explain to him the reason I want to help her, because I wouldn't admit this out loud to anyone. There's something familiar about Scarlett Reyes. I couldn't put my finger on what it was, but when I replay the interview in my mind, it hits me.

Her eyes.

She reminds me of *her*. Those hazel eyes hold something that Olivia's green eyes did.

Pain, helplessness . . . and a gentleness that brings out my protective side.

Eyes that have seen much more than they should have.

"I know," I tell him. "I just need to keep searching until I find something I can use, you know? What she's giving me isn't enough, and I know she's keeping things from me. I'm going to start looking into Darren, see if he had any skeletons in his closet."

"You want information to make his character look weak?" Tristan asks, brow raising. "It better be something good. You know how messy shit gets when cops are involved."

"I know," I say, cringing. "It's a starting point though. If she killed him, I won't find anything to help her case. If she didn't, I need to find out who did. I know he's a cop, and people aren't going to like this, but I'm missing something, and I need to know what it is."

"And what if she's lying?" Tristan asks, crossing his arms over his chest. He says it without malice, just curiosity. "You can still try to get her a good deal if she pleads guilty."

"She won't take a deal," I tell him. "I gave her that option as a backup, but she refused."

"Some clients don't know what's best for them," he says.

"I know, but they're the ones who have to do the time, not me."

"Let me know if you need any help," he says, standing up and slapping his arm on my shoulder.

"You got time on your hands?" I ask, smirking, knowing very well that his plate must be full since I haven't been here. "Don't worry, if I need help, I'll go to Kat. She's better at her job than you are anyway."

He playfully slaps the back of my head.

"Ha-ha, very funny," he muses, leaving his office. Kat is Tristan's girlfriend, who happens to be an associate here in the firm. She was the first associate we hired directly from law school, and started here working with me, learning the ropes. Tristan didn't want to be bothered, but when I needed to take some time off, she really stepped up and he finally realized what an asset she was. I like to give him shit about his falling for someone who works for him—how cliché is that?—but Kat is a good woman, a hard worker, and a damn good lawyer. As her mentor, I can see the potential she has in law, and as a friend I can see how happy she makes Tristan, who isn't always easy to be around. Realizing he left his office and I'm now sitting alone, I grab my files and head out.

Time to do some investigating.

I'M SITTING WITH KAT when Callum, an intern who is still in law school, comes into the conference room with his hands full of paperwork. "Here's everything you requested. You know you can just access all of this stuff online, right? You don't need me to print it out." He runs his hand through his dark hair and smirks. The kid has an ego on him, and he's one hell of a smart-ass, but he knows his shit. He's tall—really tall, at about six foot six—and when I met him, one of the first things he told me is that, no, he doesn't play basketball.

"Jaxon is old-school," Kat inserts, grinning, her brown eyes dancing with amusement. "I don't think he even knows how to use a computer."

"Hey," I mock-growl at her. "I know how to use one, okay, but why should I when I have interns to do that for me?"

"Oh, is that why you started hiring interns? For slaves to do internet research for you?" she fires back, not missing a beat. Today her long black hair is tied up on the top of her head, and it looks like Callum has stuck a pen in there and she hasn't noticed yet. Due to her current comments, I'm not going to tell her either.

"Of course it's why," I reply, pointing to her laptop. "So keep going."

She laughs, then makes a big show of pressing some keys. Callum places the paperwork in front of me, grabs a pile, and moves to sit down across from Kat.

"Well, this'll only take me several hours to get through," I grumble, picking up Darren's phone records for the last six months before he died. "Let's just hope we can find something, anything. We need leads."

"On it," Kat says, her tone now serious. "We're not leaving this office until we find something."

We sit like that for three hours, stopping only for bathroom breaks. When Yvonne brings in lunch, I finally find something.

"Holy shit," I mutter to myself, glancing up at Kat and Callum.

"What is it?" Callum asks, closing the folder in front of him and coming over to me.

"Look at this," I tell him, pointing to a phone number I've highlighted. "I kept seeing this number pop up, so I ran a search on it, which gave me the name of a woman. Then when I went onto his property documents and utility bills, her name came up again on one of the properties."

Kat comes over and looks at the name of the woman I've written down, her eyes widening. "I saw that name too. And you ran a search? By yourself?"

The woman has a sass problem.

She rushes back to her laptop and brings it over. "She was an additional cardholder on one of Darren's credit card accounts."

"So they shared a house together, utility bills, and credit cards," I say, arching my brow. "Mistress?"

"Looks like the cop isn't so clean after all," Kat murmurs. "Still not a reason to be murdered, but it's a lead. Do you think

Ms. Reyes found out Darren had a mistress and decided to kill him?"

"I don't know," I say, although that does make a lot of sense. Still, in my gut, why do I feel like she's not guilty? Maybe my radar is off after Olivia. Losing my sister has messed me up in ways I don't know will ever heal. Maybe I have no fucking idea what I'm doing anymore. I need to look at this from all angles and be realistic about the fact that Scarlett Reyes may indeed be a murderer. "Can you both run searches and find anything you can on this woman?"

They scurry off to do just that.

"Valentina Sullivan," I say out loud. "Let's hope you have some answers for us."

MS. REYES MEETS ME at my office. She looks put together, dressed in all black with big sunglasses on top of her head. Her blond hair is down and flowing to her shoulders.

"Ms. Reyes," I say, greeting her with a handshake.

"Please, call me Scarlett," she says. She has the same blank expression as the last time I saw her, and again, when I look into her eyes, there's something there that reminds me of Olivia. It both kills me and stops me from wanting to look away.

I pull out her chair, and she takes a seat.

"How have you been?" I ask, opening my file. "Any run-ins with the media or anything like that?"

She shakes her head. "I haven't left my property much, and it's gated, so no one can really bother me there. You said you have some news for me, but you didn't say whether it was good or bad."

I'm going to go with bad.

I'm normally a man who is very open and forward with my clients, but for some reason I'm having trouble telling her the bit of information I've found. Then again, maybe she already knows. And maybe she killed her husband after she found out. Still, I wouldn't want to tell any woman the next words that come out of my mouth.

"I did some research," I tell her, clearing my throat uncomfortably. "I found some other accounts in Darren's name, and the trail led me to a person." I paused, wishing I didn't have to say the next few words. "A woman. Valentina Sullivan. Does that name sound familiar to you?"

"No," she says, confusion in her gaze. "Should it?"

I study her for a few seconds, and her reaction seems genuine. Did she really not know that Darren was having an affair? One for too long of a time to call it that; it seems more like he was leading a double life.

I take a deep breath and force myself to push the words out. "Were you aware your husband was having an affair, Scarlett?"

Hazel eyes widen as she shakes her head. "No, I was not."

She doesn't show any other emotion, and although I know that's not a good thing, it makes it easier for me to continue. "It seemed like he was living a double life. He had another house, bills, everything. I'm sorry to have to tell you this."

That's an understatement.

"It's fine," she says, lifting her chin. I don't know how it can be fine, or how she can be so emotionless over something that has to hurt. Maybe she just has complete control over her emotions and is good at hiding her reactions, I don't know, but either way, I'm getting nothing from her right now. "He mentioned a high school girlfriend to me once, now that I think about it. Obviously I assumed that was where it ended, but as usual, Darren loves to prove me wrong."

She has fight in her, even after everything, and I like that. I respect it. "What does this mean? Does this help me?"

"I'm going to find out everything I can. To be honest, I don't know whether this will help you. It can either lead us to the real killer or it could give the prosecution a motive for your killing him," I tell her. "Any questions you have, or if you think of anything that can help, please give me a call. Until then, do you have a safe place to stay?"

She nods. "I'm safe where I am, yes. Did you need to bring me in for this? I mean, you could have just told me this over the phone."

I could have, yes, but I wanted to see her reaction. She's so cold that I think a phone conversation would've been monotone. I want to find out more about this case, about the woman I'm defending. I want to put the pieces together, and I couldn't have done that over the phone.

"I find it more personal to speak face-to-face," I tell her, which is half true. "I also want you to feel comfortable coming to me with any information."

She hesitates before saying, "Darren was *not* a good man, Jaxon. That doesn't mean I think he deserved to die, but what I should've told you before is that just because he was a cop doesn't mean he was good."

"What does that mean exactly?" I ask her, keeping my tone gentle. "He didn't treat you well?"

Her cheeks suck in, like she's biting the inside of one, then she closes her eyes as she says, "There was a reason I was finally leaving him. I wanted to for so many years, but I was scared. He'd threaten me, and . . ." She trails off, then stands up. "You said I could tell you anything, that no detail was too small, so there it is. Darren wasn't the hero cop his friends made him out to be." She moves to leave, and I know it's because she's trying to escape the words she said out loud.

"He'd threaten you, and what?" I push. I know she doesn't want to talk about it, but I'm here to help her win her case, not to be mindful of her feelings.

"He wouldn't let me go" is all she ends up saying, and the lift of her chin tells me she isn't going to elaborate much more today.

I sigh. "Thank you for telling me that, Scarlett. Call me if you need or think of anything," I tell her again. I stand and walk her to my office door. "You're a strong woman, Scarlett."

She turns and studies me, tiling her head to the side a little. "I'm tired of being strong, Jaxon. For once, I just want to be free."

Free.

Did Olivia just want to be free?

I stand there for a moment, then return to my desk and pick up my phone. Did Darren abuse Scarlett? Is that what she was getting at? She said he wasn't a good man, more than once—did that mean he put his hands on her? Emotionally abused her? The thought makes my blood boil. No man should ever lay his hands on a woman, especially a cop, who should be leading by example how women should be treated.

There are a few things I didn't tell Scarlett—one, because I didn't want to worry her, and two, because I want to find out more information before I do. It seems Darren's mistress, Valentina, has ties to the Wind Dragons Motorcycle Club, a well-known local biker gang. This would normally be a very bad thing, because no one wants to mess with the Wind Dragons, but luckily I have a contact on the inside.

The phone rings four times before he answers.

"Hello," he says into the phone.

"Hey, it's Jaxon," I say quickly. "Just have a question for you. Are you free to talk?"

"Yeah, is everything okay?" he murmurs low into the phone.

"Yeah, it's fine. I'm just working on a case," I say, pacing the office. "What do you know about a woman named Valentina Sullivan and her ex-boyfriend, Darren Melvin? He was a cop."

There's silence on the other line for a few moments, but then he says, "You free to meet me today?"

"Yeah," I say instantly, brow furrowing in concern. "Why, is there a problem?"

"Not yet there isn't," he says with a deep sigh. "I'll be at your house around ten."

"See you then."

When we hang up I stare at the phone, wondering why he'd want to see me in person instead of just telling me. I trust him though; he's a very smart man, and he knows what he's doing.

Let's hope the same goes for me.

I HEAR THE RUMBLE of his bike before I even see him, so I stand outside and watch as he hops off his black Harley.

"Jaxon Bentley," Demon says, grin on his face. He pats me on the back and walks past me.

"Demon," I say, lifting my chin. "Come on in. Can I get you something to drink? A beer?"

"I'll grab something," he says, heading straight to my fridge and opening it. I watch as he acts like he lives here, grabbing a beer and then some chips from the pantry. "You want something?" he asks, sitting down when I shake my head.

"You going to tell me why this had to be a face-to-face conversation? Isn't this dangerous for you? My imagination is running wild right now." I sit down opposite him.

"Yeah, about that," he says, taking a long draw of the ice-cold beer, then giving me his full attention. "I don't know what case you're working on, but you need to get the fuck out of it. You know I won't give you WDMC information, Jaxon, and this is crossing that line. You need to stay out of this."

"You're not going to give me *any* information? I need something more than a warning, Demon," I say, keeping a close eye on him for anything he might unwillingly give away. I know this man well, and I can tell from his body posture that he doesn't want to share anything with me. Why is he hiding something? Is Demon covering for this Valentina chick?

"Darren was a dirty cop. He was a piece of shit—into drugs, and all sorts of things. I'm sure if you dig deeper you'll find it," Demon says, muscle ticking in his jaw.

My eyes widen. "Wait, you knew him? Fuck, Demon. You need to tell me everything. I need to find out who killed him or his wife is going to do time for it," I say, my eyes pleading with him. He knows more; I know he does. He might not have been there, but Demon always knows what's going on.

He continues as if I didn't say anything. "I also know for a fact that he was an abusive asshole, so I feel for his wife, but I can't help you here, Jax. Like I said, you should stay out of this," he says, shaking his head. "I'm sorry, but that's all I can tell you. My hands are tied. I'm sorry I couldn't be of more help."

He stands, slaps me on the shoulder, and goes toward the door. Before he reaches it, he sees the photograph on my bookshelf. After a pause, he's gone, leaving my brain spinning.

Scarlett was abused. That's what she was trying to tell me.

Darren is not a good man.

She couldn't say the words, because of her pride or because of something else I don't know, but that's what she meant.

I picture her, all feminine and poised.

And anger fills me.

No, Darren was not a good man, and I'm going to make sure everyone knows that.

chapter 4

SCARLETT

DARREN HAD A MISTRESS. He knew her longer than he knew me. They were together longer than we were. Does that make *me* the mistress? Why did he marry me instead of her? Was he with her the whole time? Did he treat her better than he treated me? Or was he an asshole to the both of us?

How many ways can a man mistreat a woman?

I don't have any feelings for Darren, at least not any good ones, but these thoughts still run through my head. He was away a lot, of course, on work and such, and those times were good for me because I was left alone. I never thought he was living a double life, having two homes to go to and two women to sleep with and make their lives miserable. The sad thing is he most likely financed this other life with *my* funds. Darren didn't come from money, and living on a modest cop wage there's no way he could support another household without the money I brought into our marriage. My father was a very wealthy man, and when he passed away he left me with cash, property, and his construction business, Reyes Industries, which I sold shortly after his death. I met Darren when he was just starting at the Police Academy. I worked in the college library on the weekends, and he came in one day and introduced himself.

"Hello," he says, and hands me a book that had fallen down from the shelf. I'm on the ladder, reaching up to put away some books.

"Hello," I reply with reserve, then return to my stacking.

"Can I help you with those?" he asks me.

"Pretty sure that's my job," I tell him, narrowing my gaze on him. "What do you want?"

"Nothing," he says, but then he grins. "Except maybe your number."

I consider it, but then reply with a no.

So every weekend after that he'd come in to see me. He'd chat me up, help me carry books, and sometimes he'd bring me little gifts, like flowers or cupcakes. This went on for three months before I finally gave him my number.

And a few more months after that I fell in love with him.

He wasn't always bad. The first few years were actually pretty good—he was charming back then. Too charming, clearly. He was obviously a master manipulator and a narcissist. I fell for it, and so did this poor other woman. Or maybe she was the lucky one, and he treated her well. I find myself hoping so, because I wouldn't wish what I'd been through on anyone. The emotional abuse was almost worse than the physical. He would be nice to me one moment, then so cruel the next. He'd be loving and caring and then he'd come home and push me around. Sometimes he'd go days without talking to me if I did something he didn't like. He'd tell me I was worthless and that no other man would ever want me. He did everything he could to put me down. Toward the end, he got more physical with me, but never enough to draw attention. A shove here, a push there, a smack across the face when I talked back to him. Nothing to ever leave a mark. He knew better.

I wasted years on the man—years. I don't know why I stayed as long as I did. I think, for a while, I actually started to believe the horrible things he said to me. I became a shell of a woman, alienating all my friends. And I finally got away, leaving the country for two years, staying with my aunt and escaping his torment. It was during those two years that I finally felt a little bit like my old self. Only to return and be pinned with his death. The bastard couldn't even stay alive so I'd be left in peace. The cards I've been dealt haven't been fair, but I'm still standing. I'm still here, and I'm still fighting.

I won't stop fighting.

My mind roams to Jaxon.

I know there are some things I need to tell him about Darren, but I don't want to. I mean, I tried, but I don't think I was direct enough. I'm embarrassed, and I don't want to see the pity in his eyes, or anyone's eyes for that matter. However, I know if I don't tell him, it'll be that much harder to win this case.

My freedom should trump my pride.

Then how come my lips couldn't move?

Next time. I'll tell him next time.

I may have thought about a hundred different ways to kill Darren, but I didn't do it. Some other lucky bastard had that pleasure. And as grateful as I am that he's gone, I'm not going to take the fall for it.

I don't know how I've managed to get into this situation. I just wanted a fresh start, to be free, and away from Darren, but now it looks like there's a chance my life is going to be even worse than before. I didn't think that was even possible. I don't deserve this. I know there's no point feeling sorry for myself; I need to fight. I'm lucky enough to be able to afford a good lawyer, and now I just need to prove that I'm innocent.

Even if I have to do it my damn self.

I'm putting my faith—my life—in the hands of a man I just met, in a lawyer. They don't have the greatest reputation for being the best kind of people, but I hope I can trust this man.

He seems like the type who wouldn't want to lose, so maybe he says what he means?

I really hope so. I turn on some music to clean my house to, and even start to dance to the song a little. I'm out on bail for now, but it won't be long until my fate is decided and I might not be able to do simple things like this. I need to enjoy life as much as I can, while I can. There are so many things I'd like to do that I never got the chance to. I turn the music louder and sway my hips from side to side. I'm not the best dancer, but that doesn't mean I shouldn't be able to do it. Actually, it was Darren who told me I wasn't very good at it, made me believe it, but he's not here anymore, and his words no longer hold any power.

Maybe I'll find someone one day who will dance with me in my kitchen, who will taste my cooking without complaint. Someone who will tell me that I'm beautiful, instead of pointing out all of my flaws, and laugh with me when I make a mistake instead of yelling.

Laugh *with* me, not *at* me.

After finishing cleaning, I decide to do a little research of my own. I go through Darren's filing cabinet, the one he kept all his important documents in, and look for anything that could potentially help my case. The police searched the house but surprisingly left his files alone, so when I put that house up for sale and moved into a new one I brought them with me. I'd had a feeling once they found my Glock they'd stopped searching. I pull everything out, then glance over it all to see each paper's relevance so I don't miss anything. I'm halfway through when I find something that has my blood boiling. I now know why Darren married me instead of this Valentina girl. I feel like an idiot. It should have been obvious.

My money.

Darren was always interested in the properties my dad left me when he passed, and took them under his control. He told me that he didn't want me to have to worry about handling everything and he knew people who could help him renovate so we could eventually sell them for more money. I never questioned it. Darren was a very practical man, and he seemed to know about these kinds of things, while I was happy to work, now, in the bookstore and look after the household. I was content with my simple life. He said the properties were all rented out to tenants, but I haven't even thought about what has been happening to those properties or what might happen now? I suppose I should take care of that. I've always wanted to donate a property to a charity, so maybe I should organize that before anything starts with the trial. I feel stupid. And angry. How did I let it go so far that a man controlled what belonged to me? I've never been very materialistic. All I cared about was being happy; I was a hopeless romantic back then. An optimist. Old me would look at who I am now and cringe.

Maybe one day I can go back to who I was when I lived in Europe. Maybe that will be my goal. After this is all over I'll head back overseas and live a quiet, peaceful life, away from everything. A fresh start. Just like I'd always wanted. There's such a hurdle to overcome before I get there though. I have to prove that I'm worthy of freedom, that I didn't do this crime against a man who I tried to make happy but failed.

After putting all the files back, I decide to go see my properties. There's no time like the present, and I don't really have anything else to do for the rest of the day. I grab my sunglasses and wide-brim hat, along with the paperwork, and jump in my car.

Some sun and fresh air is just what I need.

AFTER HEADING TO THE bank first, only to find my joint account with Darren frozen, I thank God I was smart enough to reroute all the money that comes from the properties into my personal account shortly after I left to be with Aunt Leona. After taking out the initial $30,000 before I left, I forgot about everything. I didn't use the joint account out of fear Darren would find me. Because I alienated all my friends during my marriage, I didn't have anyone here to check in with. Hell, I didn't even know Darren was missing! When I left, I left and never looked back.

I'm going to empty the joint account when I gain access to it, not that he's going to need it from beyond the grave. I'm not going to need any of that money either, but some lucky charities will definitely benefit from it. I'll send my aunt some of it too.

Knowing I probably can't just show up and look around without raising suspicion or alarming the tenants, I decide to simply drive past the different properties to see how they look and maybe plan what to do with them. By these records, there are four.

The first one is familiar to me: it's my childhood home. I want to give this house to any children I'll ever have, even though I'm not sure if that will ever happen. Still, it's sentimental to me; I have nothing but good memories here, of me as a child, playing hide-and-seek with my father and riding my own pony, Belle. I had a wonderful childhood. I wanted for nothing and was treated like a princess. I will never sell this house, ever. When a little girl comes running outside with a smile on her face, it makes me smile too. At least more happy memories are being made here.

The second property is a little outside the city, but I enjoy the drive. When I arrive there though, I can tell something isn't right. The entire place is fenced off, and there are several cars parked out front.

And dogs.

They have pit bulls and rottweilers out front, as if guarding the property. Not sure what else to do, I leave, but send Jaxon a quick text asking him what I can do about it. The other two houses are fine—residential properties with tenants. After viewing them all, I stop at a diner on the way home to grab some food.

"Aren't you a pretty thing," a man says to me, smiling as he gives me a once-over with his dark eyes. He has those holes in each ear, the ones that you use to stretch out your ears on purpose. Ear gauges, I think they're called, but I'm not sure. I don't usually like them, but they look good on him.

I try to force a smile, but I'm afraid it comes out as more of a grimace. I take a step back and cross my arms over my chest, trying to shrink into myself. I don't like attention, and I don't dress to get any. I'm wearing black jeans and a loose black top that covers my bottom. Even my jeans aren't overly fitted, just enough that they don't hang off me.

"Leave her alone, Preston," another man says, eyeing me. He has green eyes and longish black hair that's tied at his nape.

He's a handsome man, but it's his friendly eyes that comfort me. He grabs Preston by the T-shirt and pulls him back. "Ignore him, sweetheart; he won't come near you."

I almost feel like apologizing. Why can't I be normal? Accept a compliment, and know how to handle situations like this without shrinking into myself. I glance down at my feet.

I need to be stronger.

Lifting my head, I look the man in the eye and say, "Thank you. For the compliment. Even though I don't exactly appreciate being called a thing. I assume you meant it in a kind way."

"He did," the green-eyed man says, grinning.

"I did," Preston says at the same time. "Maybe you should give me your number so I can clear that up for you a little." He pauses. "On a date, or something."

Green Eyes throws his head back and laughs. "When have you ever taken a woman on a date?"

"I take women on dates all the fuckin' time, Parker. You follow me around and know my every move?"

"You know how women talk," Parker replies, amusement written all over his face. "I would've heard about it."

"Well, maybe she's beautiful enough that I want to take her on a date," Preston announces, squaring his shoulders and looking back to me. "So what do you think, miss? Can I take you on a date?"

"Oh," I say, nervously shifting on my feet. I shouldn't have said anything . . . why did I open my mouth? Oh, right, the whole strength thing. "I'm sorry, but I can't. I appreciate the offer though."

"Rejected," Parker calls out, chuckling. "Harsh, dude, harsh."

I flash him a look, silently asking him to stop being so mean, and then turn back to Preston. "Not that there's anything wrong with you . . . you are lovely . . . but, well . . . I'm kind of out on bail and could end up in prison soon, so dating probably isn't the best idea."

"Did she say prison?" I hear Preston ask Parker. "And did she just call me lovely?"

"Yeah," he says, sounding shocked.

It's this moment that the news comes on the TV in the corner of the diner and broadcasts a preview for tonight, featuring my case. They both glance at the screen, and then look at me, eyes wide.

I shrug, in an *I told you so* kind of way. I don't know what else to do—it's embarrassing, but it's my life right now. There's no point trying to deny it. I'm innocent, and I know the truth. I can't change what people think about me, but *I know the truth*.

I know my heart. I know I'm good. If they can't see that, then there's nothing else I can do; let them judge. When it's proved I'm innocent, let them all know they were wrong.

The waitress calls out my ticket number, so I step to the counter and grab the bag. "Nice meeting you both," I say as I turn to exit.

"It's always the ones you least suspect," Preston says, waving 'bye to me, his expression one of shock and confusion. "Is it bad that the prison thing only makes me want her more?" are the last words I hear.

I smile on my way to the car.

If I can't find humor in the situation, I have nothing.

It's smile, or cry.

chapter 5

JAXON

AFTER DOING SOME RESEARCH on the property Scarlett was asking about, I've found out that not only had Darren been using it as a drug lab but also he'd changed the ownership for this property, and the others, into his name. I don't know how the hell he did it. It's a property she was given by her father, and she doesn't even know what's happening with it. Darren's a total piece of shit.

I inform the police of my findings, and hope that they shut the operation down. It's something else I can use against Darren's character in court, to really paint a picture of the true person he was. It shows the type of dangerous people he was associated with, and that any of them could have been the one to take his life. I make a note to ask Hunter, our family-law attorney, to look into what we have to do to get everything back in Scarlett's name. Luckily they were still legally married when he died, so she inherits everything.

I don't know why Scarlett went to that property, but I have a feeling she's a woman who tends to get herself into trouble. I know the type—good intentions, but somehow trouble always finds them. They're usually beautiful too. And although she's my client, I'm not blind. Scarlett has a classic beauty not many could deny, including me. She dresses to hide her figure, but she has that natural hourglass shape—wide hips and a narrow waist—that can't be hidden. Not that I've been looking, or anything. It's just a little hard to miss.

"What're you thinking about?" Tristan asks, making me jump a little.

"Nothing," I say a little too quickly. "Found an operating meth lab in one of Ms. Reyes's properties. Her husband apparently was a heavy user as well. Just another day on the job."

He barks out a laugh and leans back against the doorframe. "Why do you always get the fun cases? You should've let me take this one."

"We must have a different opinion on fun," I mutter, sighing heavily.

"I think we must," he replies, amusement in his tone.

Kat comes up behind him and wraps an arm around his waist. "Is there anything you need me to do before I leave, Jaxon?"

"Thanks, but I'm good," I say, knowing she'll stay behind and work late without hesitation. "You two go home to those beautiful kids of yours."

"It's late, Jaxon. You should go home and get some rest too."

I glance out the window, and it's now dark outside. I don't know where the time goes. "Shit, yeah, I will. I'll see you both tomorrow."

I pack up my things slowly, not in any rush to leave.

The truth is, I don't like being at home. I don't have anyone to go home to. It's just an empty house. Yes, it's beautiful, but it's still empty. Just sitting there and giving my mind time to over-think things isn't good for me. For a while Olivia was there and made it feel like home again.

I like to stay busy and distracted. Since taking time off, I've started building things, from tables to bookshelves, just to give me something to do. I don't need much sleep, and I'm not one to laze around in bed unless there's a woman in there with me, which, to be honest, is rare these days. I've always preferred quality over quantity, but recently there's been none of either. There was one woman I was casually sleeping with, before everything happened with Olivia, but I haven't seen her in a while. Maybe I should message her. I could really use both the distraction and the release. As I go to text her though, my fingers linger over the SEND button without pressing it. I don't actually want to see her, if I'm being honest.

I don't know why, but I'd rather be alone. I think having meaningless sex would just make me feel even emptier at this point. I haven't been the same since Olivia died. I withdrew and started looking at life in a whole different way. She was everything to me, my only family, and someone I've loved from the moment I laid my eyes on her. Will the pain of losing her ever go away? Will the guilt of not being able to save her ever lessen? That was my job.

To look out for her.

And I failed.

I head home, but only to do more work.

I might as well just stay at my office.

A FEW HOURS' WORK and one hundred push-ups later, I jump into a lukewarm shower. Hopefully after this I'll be able to relax a little. I'll eat something and then watch a movie and fall asleep. For some reason, my mind roams to Scarlett. I wonder what she's doing right now. As I look down at my cock, which has somehow gotten hard, I consider it nothing more than an inconvenience. As I run my hand along it, I groan a little, the feeling of it so good. I've always had a healthy sex drive, but lately I've been trying to ignore it. Tonight, however, it looks like it needs to be taken care of. If I had called someone over, she'd be here on her knees in front of me, her mouth on my cock, looking up at me. When I picture that though, it isn't blue eyes looking up at me—they're hazel.

Fuck.

I begin to stroke harder and faster, water streaming down my body, my hand pumping away, bringing me closer and closer to orgasm. I brace myself against the tiles as I come, each jerk bringing more pleasure than the last. When I come back to myself, and to reality, I cringe.

Did I just jack off to my client?

To Scarlett? A woman accused of murdering her husband?

Fuck.

I'm so inappropriate, it's not even funny.

I finish showering and hop out, grabbing a towel, unable to even look at myself in the mirror. Never in the history of my career have I ever thought about one of my clients like this, and I've represented many beautiful women before. It was a line I've never even thought about crossing. It's wrong, I know, but I can't seem to help the fact that she's beautiful. Her eyes are haunting, and her soul—which is begging to be free—simply calls to me, but I need to fight this. It doesn't matter how fucking stunning she is, it's not right, and it's not going to happen. She needs me right now, and not in any other way than to save her from what she's been accused of, and maybe to be someone she can trust.

I guess I should be careful what I wish for, because I wanted another distraction, and I got one.

chapter 6

SCARLETT

$\mathcal{I}$ FEEL LIKE THE MORE information we find out, the worse it gets. Jaxon told me how Darren has changed mostly everything into his name, from my properties to a secret bank account where he was pulling money out from our joint account and funneling it into his own. Jaxon also just told me what he found out about Darren's other woman.

"So she's part of a motorcycle gang?" I clarify, thinking that she also must have bad taste in men. Then again, maybe I'm wrong. I personally don't know any bikers, so I shouldn't judge.

"Yes, the Wind Dragons," he explains, pushing his glasses up on his nose. I don't know why I find that cute, but I do. Today he's wearing a crisp white shirt, sleeves folded up to his elbows, and black tailored pants. He has expensive taste, judging by the quality of the pieces. I know designer goods—I grew up wearing them and saw them on my parents every day. He must make a lot of money, not that it matters, but when I needed a lawyer, his firm was the one recommended to me over and over again. He has a reputation as a sharp-witted, quick-thinking lawyer who will do whatever it takes to win. He's known for going above and beyond, and giving each case his all. I think he genuinely likes to help people. I don't think it's all about money or his ego, though I'm sure some of that is a part of it.

When I first saw him, dressed in that navy suit, reading glasses on, gray eyes focused on me, trying to see through me, I couldn't help but notice how handsome he is. The man is good-looking, there's no doubt about it. I had no idea what the best and most expensive lawyer in town would look like, but I didn't expect this. Maybe someone older and not looking like he just stepped out of a *GQ* magazine.

"Unfortunately the only information I got was that Darren was a dirty cop and he didn't treat her right either. I don't think any of the MC will stand up in court and testify to that though, so we're going to need to find another way."

I'm not surprised, but I don't like hearing that he made another woman's life hell too. No one deserves that.

I tuck my hair behind my ear, wondering how exactly I'm going to get out of this. It's not looking good, every lead is a dead end, and although it seems like Jaxon might now believe me, proving it to the world is going to be an issue. I'm in an even worse predicament than I thought I was, and I already thought that I was pretty damn screwed. Deep inside though, I thought justice would prevail. I didn't kill Darren, so naturally I couldn't go to prison for it. The truth always wins, right? I am so naïve.

As if Darren didn't torment me enough in life, he's still putting me through hell from beyond the grave.

Apparently I'll never escape him.

I'm not even lucky enough to get the "till death do us part" vow.

I take a deep breath and look down at my hands. "Darren wasn't always bad, but after he started taking drugs, he completely changed. He started taking things out on me, emotionally destroying me until I didn't know who I was anymore. He tried to break me, Jaxon. He tried to take everything I was and destroy it. I wasn't enough; it was my fault everything happened. And then, when that wasn't enough, when he wasn't happy with the amount of pain he was causing me, he started using his hands. He'd push me, slap me. He tried to strangle me once. He'd bully me with his size, try to intimidate me. It took everything I had left to escape all of that, and now it looks like I'm going to, once again, pay for something I'm innocent of. How is this justice? You don't know what it's like, living with someone who makes it their life goal to make you feel as small as possible every day. Like you're nothing. Like you wish you didn't exist."

I grit my teeth, hating that I just blurted all of that stuff out to a stranger. But he needs to know the extent of everything that happened to me up until this moment. What brought me here. And although I feel weak and vulnerable after having admitted this to him, it was necessary. Right now, Jaxon is the only person who can help me.

I need to trust him, and I need him to trust me in return, but that still doesn't make it easy for me to look into his eyes after what just came out of my mouth. Jaxon Bentley is a strong, powerful man, and I don't want him to see me as weak.

Or worse, as a victim.

I don't think I could handle seeing pity in those gray depths. Not now.

After a few tense seconds, I manage to lift my head and look at him, but I find that his eyes aren't even on me. I let out a slow breath of relief that he's giving me a little space and not staring at me, but then I see the look on his face.

He looks far away, lost in his own thoughts. His brow is furrowed and pain is etched all over his too handsome face.

"Jaxon?" I say, keeping my voice soft and even. "Is everything okay?"

He shakes his head, as if clearing it, and slowly looks at me. "I'm sorry you had to go through all of that, Scarlett." His eyes are gentle, but there's no pity or judgment in them. "But I don't think you should be giving up so soon. I've worked with less and won. It's not over just yet. I'm going to fight, and I need you to do the same."

He sounds confident, sure. Is that his ego talking? Or does he really think we can win this?

"Did they fingerprint the gun?" I ask him. "I know it was found in my house, but I wasn't even in the country then, anyone could have put it there. Can you even test a firearm for fingerprints after two years?"

"Apparently prints can be preserved if the firearm wasn't in an open environment or in contact with weather or water, and yes, the police ran the prints and said . . ." He trails off, looking contemplative, then turns those eyes on me. "Does Darren have many police buddies?"

I nod. "They'd come to the house now and again, and he always bragged that they'd have his back in any situation, no matter what."

"Do you even know how to shoot a gun, Scarlett?"

"Of course I do," I admit, nodding. "Darren taught me when we first met. But I've never actually shot a gun anywhere other than the shooting range. I've never had a reason to. All the guns in the house were his, even the ones registered to me."

I don't think I would pick up a gun even if I needed to.

Does he think that maybe Darren's colleagues had something to do with this? That he associated himself with corrupt men, just like himself? It's very likely, if I'm being honest. The few things I overheard are not what upstanding men of the law would say.

"Do you think they lied about the results?" I probe.

"I never said they found your prints on the gun. They said the gun had been wiped clean and had no prints," he says, leaning back in his chair and studying me. "What if they were covering for someone?"

"Who?" I ask, brow furrowing. "Another cop? And if the gun was just in my house, shouldn't the fingerprints have been preserved, since there was no water or bad weather to affect them?"

"Exactly," he murmurs, then makes some quick notes. "And I don't know, I just feel like there's more to the story, something we've been missing. I want to look at this from every angle, consider every possibility. There has to be an answer for all of this, and I'm not going to discount anything. The trial is set for two weeks from now."

What he just said shocks me. "*Two weeks?* Our time is running out. I don't know what else can be done. No one is going to believe me!" I hear panic rising in my voice.

"We'll find a way," Jaxon says, strength in his tone. "It always comes back to the MC or the police force. Someone there knows exactly what happened the night of Darren's murder, and I'm going to find out who."

His confidence makes me relax a little. "Okay, well let me know if there's anything I can do to help."

"You can stay out of trouble and not drive alone to meth

labs," he chastises, but then shakes his head and smirks. "Maybe you should stay with some friends. The more I push the MC and the cops, the more backlash is possible. I'm not saying that to worry you, just for you to be alert at all times."

"I don't really have any friends," I admit, cringing. "I lost contact with all of mine after I married Darren, and then I left to be with my aunt. There's no one I'd feel comfortable calling anyway. Don't worry, I'll be fine. The security is good at my place."

He doesn't look convinced. "How would you feel if I send a security guy to check it out? I know someone who's the best in the industry."

"Sure," I say, nodding. "That sounds good."

"Good," he says, eyes softening. "If there's nothing else, I'm going to have a chat with Valentina Sullivan and see what she has to say about all of this. If she'll vouch for the abuse and Darren's involvement in illegal activities, it'll be good for our case."

"Do you think she will? Is it safe trying to talk to her, with her MC ties?" I ask, not wanting anything bad to happen to him. "Can't you take a police officer with you?" I pause, then add, "if you know one who isn't corrupt, I mean."

"I can't take a cop because we aren't making any arrests and because she doesn't have to talk to me if she doesn't want to," he gently explains. "I'm hoping her hate for Darren will win out and she'll help us."

I nod. "Good luck."

Does he actually believe that I'm innocent, or is he just really good at his job? I don't know, and maybe I don't want to know. He's acting like he believes me, but I guess I'm paying him to, right? I mean, he has nothing to lose, it won't be him going behind bars, and he gets paid no matter what the verdict is.

He walks me to the door, pressing his hand on the small of my back. I'm unable to hide my flinch as he does so, and I know this, even though I don't look up at him, because he quickly removes his hand. Over the last two years I've gotten much better with letting people touch me, but sometimes, if it catches me off guard, I can't really help my reaction. It doesn't necessarily mean that I don't trust or like the person. Feeling like I should probably address the situation or say something about it, I turn to him and am about to explain when he shakes his head.

"It's fine, Scarlett. You don't have to explain."

I close my mouth.

Understanding.

He walks me to my car in silence, opening the driver's door for me after I unlock it.

"Thank you," I tell him, looking him in the eye.

I want to say more, but I don't, and I don't even know why I want to or what I'd say. I shouldn't have to explain myself to anybody, and I don't usually, but in this case I want to tell him. Maybe it's because he's a good listener, or maybe it's because of the way he reacted when I opened up to him. It's been a long time since I felt like someone's equal.

He nods and steps back, and I hesitantly get into the car. He waits until I pull out, then heads back into his office. I don't know how this is going to play out, but it's all we have for now, so I hope it goes well. I can't beat Darren alone. I don't know who killed him, and I feel a little bad that someone has to do time for making the world a better place, but I shouldn't have to pay for a crime I didn't commit.

And I won't.

On the way home I notice a car following mine. At least, I think it is. Something just doesn't feel right. I purposely change my course and head to a fast-food restaurant where there are lot of cars and people around.

The car continues straight ahead.

I wait until it's out of sight, then drive home.

Must have just been my paranoia.

chapter 7

JAXON

"VALENTINA SULLIVAN?" I ASK the woman as she walks to her car. She pushes back her hood, exposing a mane of red curls. Her green eyes narrow on me.

"Who's asking?" she replies, arching a brow and cocking her hip. She gives me a once-over, then crosses her arms over her chest.

"Jaxon Bentley," I say, offering my hand, which she ignores.

"What do you want, Jaxon Bentley?" she asks, glancing around the parking lot. "I can tell you're not a cop, so who are you?"

"I'm a lawyer," I tell her, handing her my card. "And how do you know I'm not a cop?"

She points to my shoes. "Cops don't wear fancy designer shit. Those are Armani. And what does a lawyer want with me? Perhaps you should speak to my lawyer, instead of following me like a creep."

"It's about Darren, your ex-boyfriend," I tell her, noticing her grimace. Yeah, that seems to be the reaction I get whenever his name is mentioned. The man sounds like a bucketful of sunshine.

"What about him?" she asks, keeping her expression deceptively neutral. "I saw the news, his body was found and they have a suspect. What does that have to do with me?"

"You don't have anything to say about the fact that he was married for all those years when you two were together? Or that Darren's wife is going to do time for a crime we both know she didn't commit?"

I'm bluffing here.

I don't know if she knew or not, and I don't know if Scarlett did it or not, and I don't know if she knows who might have killed Darren if Scarlett didn't.

Basically I don't know much, but I do know how to get information out of people, and I know body language. I also clearly know how to talk myself in and out of a lot of shit.

She looks down, avoiding my gaze. Yeah, she knows something.

"Valentina?" a woman calls out, exiting the store with bags in her hands. "Are you okay?"

"I'm fine," she calls out, then turns back to me. "I didn't know he was married, no. But Darren, and my time with him, feels like a lifetime ago. I don't have anything to do with what's going on now, all right? So yeah, it sucks for his wife, but that's not my problem. If you need to talk to me again, contact Faye Black." She turns to her friend and says, "Come on, Shayla, let's get out of here."

"Valentina—"

She opens her door, climbs in, and slams it behind her. She can't get out of the parking lot fast enough. All I can do is hope that my words stick with her, play in her mind, and that maybe she'll be willing to cooperate in time.

I'm not giving up just yet.

OVER THE NEXT FEW days I try to talk to Valentina again, but she's never alone. The MC club has clearly gone into protection mode, but I have to wonder why. I'm no threat to her, and I didn't harm or threaten her in any way, so why are they acting like I'm the enemy? What are they trying to hide? The whole thing is quite puzzling. Do they think I'm trying to pin the murder on Valentina? When talking in person doesn't work, I attempt to reach them on the phone. I leave a message. I leave three. I want to try to do this without Faye Black in my face, but if that's the only option, then I'll have to take it.

Faye Black is a force to be reckoned with. I've never met her personally, but every time I ask someone about her, they visibly cringe. Apparently she's a pain in the ass, and not someone one would want as an enemy. Not only is she a lawyer, she has ties to the feds and is married to the former Wind Dragons president before he stepped down.

I wish Valentina would just talk to me though, so I can ask her more about Darren. I have nothing. Scarlett never reported the abuse to the police, and with Darren being one of them, I can understand why. The hospital didn't have any records to help either. Quite frankly, I don't know if that's a good or bad thing. If I were to prove Scarlett was an abused woman, the prosecution could then argue that she killed him as revenge. It gives her a motive and could actually play against her. The only thing that'll save her now will be finding out who actually did kill Darren.

When she told me about the abuse, she couldn't even look at me. That hit me, hard. It explains the coldness that comes off her, and also why she recoils to touch, something someone else might not think anything of. It killed me to see her flinch when I led her out with my hand on her back. I didn't mean anything by it, but I won't do it again. I don't want her to feel uncomfortable in any way. It's clear she's been through a lot. So far, everything she's said has been the truth. Demon confirmed that Darren was abusive and corrupt, so even though I'm still working on proving it, I know that to be the truth. The way Scarlett behaves is a huge indicator. She's very standoffish, and clearly isn't comfortable with certain things that wouldn't faze others. And now with the way Valentina and the Wind Dragons are acting . . . Something isn't right.

I believe Scarlett, and in my gut I truly don't think she did this.

Now I just have to prove it.

I LIFT MY HEAD when someone knocks on my door. "Come in."

"Hey," Hunter says, closing the door behind him and taking a seat. My gaze goes straight to the artwork on his forearm, since his sleeves are rolled up to his elbows. He's the only lawyer I've ever met who is covered in tattoos. I've seen him cover them up before, when he's meeting with a client or in court, but most days they're on display. No one in the firm cares, but I know other places that would. All I care about is that he's one of the best family lawyers I've come across. It's why Tristan and I enticed him to join our firm. We needed a good family-law attorney to round out our practice, and he was our first choice.

"I've been looking into this property stuff for you. It looks like Darren forged Scarlett's signature, or he might have even brought someone in with him to pretend to be Scarlett, and gotten her to sign," he explains.

My jaw goes tight. "What can we do?"

"Well, we can prove it wasn't her signature by doing a comparison between the real and the fake, and then we can start working to get everything back into her name. But because they were married, everything he owns will revert back to her anyway. He didn't have a will; I looked into it. Apparently he thought he was so untouchable even death wouldn't come after him. So I'll just file the paperwork with the court to get everything put back in her name."

"Thank you, Hunter. What did I do before you joined the firm?" I ask him, stretching my neck from side to side.

"Your own work?" he jokes, blue eyes full of amusement.

My lip twitches. "How are you liking it here so far?"

He tilts his head to the side, considering. "I love it here, to be honest. I have the freedom to work on my own time and schedule, and the receptionist wears stripper heels."

I chuckle at his description of Yvonne. "Be careful. She won't hesitate to stab you in the eye with one if you piss her off."

"Oh, I know." He smirks, then sighs. "Anyway, I'll let you know if I have any updates on the case."

"Thanks. This one just keeps getting deeper and deeper, doesn't it?"

"Looks like it," he murmurs, then smirks at me. "But at least you get to look at Scarlett Reyes all day while you're working on it."

He sees the look on my face, which I'm sure is extremely unimpressed, and laughs. "What? You have to concentrate on the pros. Anyway, leave this with me; I'll handle it. It looks like your plate is full right now."

"Thanks, man," I tell him, meaning it. We have a support system here, and help is always available when needed. "I appreciate it. I promise to be your lawyer when a woman finally sues you for sexual harassment and you're looking at doing time."

"I'll hold you to that," he replies, not missing a beat. He glances at his watch. "Want to head out for lunch? There's this new place that just opened around the corner I want to check out."

My stomach rumbles just as he says that. "Sounds good actually."

I pack up my things on my desk, placing the paperwork and file neatly on the right-hand corner, then stand and walk out of the building with Hunter. When we stop at a bar called Riley's, I come to a standstill. "This is a bar."

"I know." Hunter grins, opening the door and stepping inside. I follow him, glancing around. "When you said new spot, I assumed you meant a lunch spot. I'm not on the same liquid diet you are, Hunter."

"I'm sure they have pub food here." He shrugs, then sits down at the bar. He grabs a menu and hands it to me. "See? They have food. And beer. Lots of beer."

"How did I hire a functioning alcoholic?" I ask myself, glancing over the menu.

A pretty brunette walks out from the back, a red bandanna wrapped around her hair. "What can I get for you?" she asks, while Hunter's head snaps up at the sound of her voice.

"Hello there," he says to her with a smile. "Knew I wanted to check this place out for a reason."

"That reason better be a beer and a meal," she tells him, brow arched. "Because that's all that's on offer. For you anyway."

I can't help the laughter that spills out of me. "Could I please order the steak?"

"Sure," she says, pulling out a mini notepad from her pocket. "How would you like it?"

"Medium rare, please, and with pepper mushroom sauce."

"Perfect. Fries or mashed potatoes?"

"Fries," I tell her, then glance at Hunter. "What do you want?"

"Just a beer, please, darlin'," he says to her, not at all fazed by her recent rejection. In fact, he seems to enjoy the sassier, bolder women. It's like they amuse him to no end, no matter how mean they are.

"Gotcha," she says, then disappears into the back once more.

"Fuck, she's hot," Hunter exclaims, running his hand down his beard. "She wants me."

"Seriously?" I repeat, shaking my head at him. "Something's wrong with you, you know that?"

"Yes," he states, pointing to where the woman disappeared to. "And that something is that she isn't mine yet."

"Hunter—"

"This place is going to be our new local," he declares, rubbing his hands together with glee.

"If this place is our new local, you're going to have to stick to your 'don't shit where you eat' motto," I point out.

"That motto isn't compulsory. Come on, it's a pretty sweet setup. It has a pool table, the menu looks good, and lots of alcoholic beverages to try." He grins. "And the waitress is a fucking babe."

"Actually, I'm the owner," the woman says as she moves back in front of us. She looks to me and says, "I'm Riley."

Riley's.

This really is her place.

"Jaxon," I say, offering her my hand. She takes it and gives it a quick shake.

Hunter's eyes widen. I can tell he's liking her more and more with each second that passes. "I'm Hunter," he says, kissing her hand. "We work down the road, at the Bentley and Channing law firm."

"Appropriate name," she replies, rolling her eyes and pulling her hand away. She pours him his beer and slides it over to him. "Never seen a lawyer covered in tattoos before."

"I'm one of a kind," he smoothly replies.

"Probably a good thing," Riley tells him with a smirk, then disappears again.

"Probably is a good thing," I agree, grabbing his untouched beer and taking a sip. "Changed my mind. Maybe I will have a beer."

Hunter sighs and looks for Riley to order a replacement.

A man suddenly comes into the bar and glances around. "Is the owner here? I'm late for work and she's a she-devil."

I nod. "She's in the back."

"Fuck me dead," he groans, slowly walking out the back, accepting his fate.

Riley walks out again and almost bumps into him. "Preston, you're late."

"I know," he tells her. "It's a long story. One I'm sure you don't have time for, so I won't bother explaining."

She sighs, her hand on her hip. "How the fuck are you the best bartender in town?"

"I have skills," Preston replies with a smirk. "In the bar and in the bedroom. And I'm a mixologist, not a bartender. Don't make me sound average."

"Don't be late again, Preston. Fancy bar skills or not, I'll fire you without hesitation," Riley tells him, ignoring his rant.

"Noted," Preston grumbles.

She leaves, and he turns to us. "See? She-devil."

"I can hear you, asshole!" Riley calls out from the back.

Hunter and I share a glance and then start laughing.

"If you can hear from back there, can you get me another beer?" Hunter calls out to her.

And that's how Riley's became our new place.

chapter 8

SCARLETT

"I DEFINITELY DIDN'T SIGN ANYTHING," I tell Jaxon, exhaling slowly. "Why would I sign over my legacy to him? I can't believe he did all of this."

"My associate is taking care of everything," he assures me, leaning back in his chair, gray eyes pinned on me. "Everything will revert back to your name, so don't stress. The money will all go back to you once the accounts are unfrozen too, it's just a matter of time."

He's in another navy suit today, and I wonder if that's his favorite color. He's wearing a crisp white shirt underneath, and I can't help but notice his smooth skin peeking out beneath the two undone buttons.

"Okay," I reply, crossing my legs and running my hand down my beige pencil skirt. "I guess I won't need money and houses if I'm going to prison anyway, right? Will you send me cigarettes so I can trade them for security?"

Jaxon arches a brow. "Have you been watching prison movies?"

"Consider it studying for my potential new life," I reply in a dry tone, letting my head fall back before composing myself. "It's hard not to think of it when it's a possibility, you know?"

He reaches out his hand to touch me but then pulls it away. I think he's a naturally affectionate, caring person, but he knows that I don't always feel comfortable with touch, so he's stopping himself. I don't know if that makes me happy or sad at the reality of it. He can't even touch me like he would anyone else. I'm too messed-up.

"You need to stop thinking like that and instead focus on the solution, Scarlett," he says, tapping his hand on the paper in front of him. "Have a little faith in me, all right? I have a few ideas, and I know one of them is going to pay off and give us something to work with."

I puff out a breath. "Trust isn't the issue here, Jaxon. Like you said, if we don't have the evidence to prove anything, it doesn't matter if I'm innocent or not."

"Did I say that?" he asks, wincing.

"Not in those words, but basically," I reply, shrugging. "At least that's what I got out of it."

"What did you do in the two years you left the country?" he asks, and I get the feeling this has nothing to do with the case but rather his own curiosity.

"I helped my aunt," I tell him, picturing her house in my mind. "She lives in this two-story house—in Paris. I cooked for her, took her to her appointments, and did anything I could to help. I went for walks and soaked up the culture. I guess I kind of took the time to heal, you know? To remember who I was and figure out who I want to be. I helped my aunt, but she helped me too. She helped me remember my worth, my goodness."

He nods, our eyes connecting and holding. "I'm glad you had that time to find yourself again."

"Me too," I say, flashing him a small smile. "I've changed in that time. And unless something catches me off guard, I'm mostly normal."

His gaze drops to my hand resting on the table. "So if I touched your hand while you saw it happening, you wouldn't react or flinch?"

I swallow hard, and nod once. "I don't think I'd flinch, no."

Because I'd be expecting it, and I can brace myself.

Slowly he reaches his hand across the table and, as I watch, gently squeezes mine. My first reaction is to pull away, but I don't. I let him hold my hand, glancing up at him. We watch each other as we share this moment.

"Your hands are cold," he tells me, gray eyes on them.

"I'm cold," I whisper back to him.

"No, you're not," he says instantly, lifting and shaking his head. "You're warm, Scarlett. You just need someone to show you that."

We look into each other's eyes for longer than is appropriate.

I don't want to look away, but one of us needs to.

His hand is still touching mine, his warm skin mixing with my cool, lines and temperatures blurring. I start to feel a little light-headed, and a little confused that I don't mind his eyes on me. When other people look at me, I want them to look away, but not Jaxon, which is exactly why *I* need to look away. I clear my throat and drop my gaze to our hands, then gently slide mine from his and place it on my lap under the table.

We had a moment that we shouldn't have, and now I'm going to pretend it doesn't exist.

I'm good at pretending.

A FEW NIGHTS LATER I go out to dinner and see a movie alone. I know it sounds sad, but it beats staying in the house and doing nothing. I've never been much of a social person, but for the first time ever I feel like being out and around people. I stop by the supermarket on the way home to grab some coffee, since I ran out this morning. When I see Jaxon standing there, still in his business attire, I have a moment where I want to flee. I'm about to give in and turn around when he sees me and smiles. He's obviously not as awkward as I am, and knows how to act in public settings.

"Hey," I say, walking closer to him. I want to ask about Valentina, if there's been any progress, but I'm not sure if it's okay to ask right now. "Did you only just finish work?"

He nods, wincing. "I'm a bit of a workaholic."

"I can see that," I murmur. It's almost 9:00 p.m., and he should've finished work hours ago. "I guess you didn't get to where you are today just sitting around."

This is the first time I've seen him when he's off the clock, and I don't know how to act. He's still my lawyer, and I'm still his client, but we're in a completely different setting. A normal one. And it's a little weird.

"That's true," he says, grabbing a few oranges and placing them in his cart. "What did you do this evening?"

"I went to a Vietnamese restaurant for dinner," I say, walking next to him as he grabs a few more items. "And I saw a movie. A horror. It was a rookie mistake."

He stops in his tracks, and turns to me. "You saw a horror movie alone?"

"Who said I was alone?" I tease, arching a brow. I don't know where this playful side has come from, but I like it. I can't remember the last time I had banter like this.

"Your earlier description of your lack of friends," he says, amusement written all over his face. We start to walk down the next aisle side by side.

"Okay, yes I saw a horror movie alone. It wasn't that scary," I say, grabbing a jar of coffee as we pass it. "It was pretty good actually, you should go see it."

"I can't remember the last time I saw a movie in the theater," he admits, looking beyond me. "It's been a while."

"It had been a while for me too," I tell him. "That's why I wanted to go. Something different, you know? Plus I wanted to get my mind off things and get out of the house. The movie gave me an hour and a half of pure escapism. I usually read for that, and I'll probably go home and finish my book now."

"And drink coffee?" he asks, smiling. My gaze drops to his smile.

"It seems you have me pegged," I reply, looking down as I grin. "Did you eat anything for dinner? It's kind of late."

I want to look at him more, memorize his face, but I don't. I'm attracted to him, yes, but we have more important things to handle right now. He's my lawyer, and he's here for one reason and one reason only, to get me out of this mess. My track record with men clearly isn't a good one, and I think I just need to stay away from men in general, no matter how handsome they are, or how dreamy their gray eyes are. There's nothing left for me here, and after I hopefully win the case, I'm leaving and I don't think I will ever return. There's no point getting close to Jaxon, or any man for that matter. I'd hate to think that Darren turned me into a cynic, because that would mean that he won, but I'm definitely a realist now.

That doesn't mean I can't make a friend out of Jaxon though. I don't have any of those. I know he's my lawyer and I'm just his client, but I feel safe around him. And comfortable. It's a feeling I'm not used to, and one I'd like to hold on to. I don't know if that makes me a bad person or something, but I don't think I can be blamed. It's been a long time since I've felt like this.

"Not yet," he admits, looking down at his cart. "I was hoping to grab a few things and make something simple."

"Can you cook?"

"I try," he replies with a deep chuckle. "I can make manly food."

My eyes widen. "I didn't know food was gender-specific. Are you a food sexist, Jaxon?"

He laughs, then cringes. "Okay, that's not what I meant. I just meant I live off a diet of steak and potatoes, and if I'm eating healthy, chicken and broccoli. And eggs. Lots of eggs."

"So you can fry, grill, and boil," I surmise, rolling my eyes. "So, can women eat those foods, or no?"

He smirks, shaking his head in amusement. "Feeling sassy tonight, hey?"

"Something like that, but you walked into that one." I sigh and glare up at him. "Manly food."

"How long are you going to hold this against me? It was terrible word choice."

"You're a lawyer; you aren't allowed to use terrible word choice as an excuse," I point out, lifting my chin up.

"I'm off duty," he says, nodding toward checkout. "Come on, do you want to get a coffee or something?"

I hold up the jar in my hand. "I can always make us some?"

He hesitates for a moment, but then nods. "Lead the way, Scarlett."

chapter 9

JAXON

I'M IN HER HOUSE.

In.

Her.

House.

What the fuck am I doing?

This is not professional at all, and it's a stupid move to blur the lines of our relationship. Sure, there's no rule against us being friends, but anything more is a conflict of interest. We shouldn't even be friends.

Why am I not treating her like I would any of my other clients? If I ran into them at the store, I'd say hello, ask them how they are, and move on. I wouldn't linger and chat with them, joke with them, and then follow them back to their house for coffee. I have no idea what I'm doing.

She places a giant mug of black coffee in front of me, and it smells so good, or maybe that's her.

Fuck.

"Thank you," I say, bringing it toward me by the handle. "Your house is beautiful."

It's spacious and decorated in mainly white and nude colors, with a splash of color here and there. It has a warm, welcoming feeling to it.

"Thanks," she says, smiling and sitting down opposite me. "I've been redecorating ever since I got back. I like the country feel it gives now."

It's simple. Classy. Elegant.

Just like her.

There's a picture of what must be her and her aunt on the fridge, and I look at it and smile. They're both on the beach, and Scarlett is wearing a wide-brim hat and a smile.

"Any updates on the Valentina thing?" she asks me.

"I keep trying to speak to her, but it's not going so well," I explain, shaking my head. "But don't worry, it just means I'm going to have to go through a more official route and speak to her with her lawyer present." I pause. "If they ever decide to call me back."

"And if they don't?" she asks, amusement passing through her eyes. "Stake out in front of the MC clubhouse and stalk her until they either give in or try to do something to you?"

"If I have to," I say simply. Not like I haven't done much worse than that in my time. I don't like to lose a case, especially when I know my client is innocent. It's my job to do whatever I need to, and I take my job very seriously. I didn't get a good reputation by always playing by the rules, or by sitting around and waiting for good things to happen. I go out there and make it happen. I use my contacts, I ask for help when needed, I call in favors, I do anything in my power to get what I want. And most of the time it's legal.

Scarlett looks troubled all of a sudden, her brow furrowed and her lips twisted. "That can't be safe though, can it? I mean, they are a motorcycle club after all."

I'm trying to save her from prison time, and she's worried about me doing something she's paying me to do?

Fuck, she's cute.

I can tell she's a person who genuinely cares about people before herself, which makes me want to dig Darren up and kill him all over again. People like her are rare in today's world and should be protected. We need more beauty in the world like hers, but unfortunately most people damage it instead. Ruin it. It makes me angry just thinking about it.

"I'll be fine, don't worry about me," I say gently, taking a sip of coffee.

"Can I make you something to eat? I know you haven't had dinner yet, and it wouldn't be a problem to make something," she says, looking down as if she's feeling a little nervous, shielding those eyes from me. Her eyes give so much away, and it's as if she's aware of that, which is why she's always ducking her head.

"That's okay," I say quickly, not wanting to offend her. I feel like her cooking for me is crossing even more boundaries, and I don't want to do that, even though I'm starving. It's nice to have her offer though. "I'd better get home. I have the groceries in my car that I need to put away, and biker old ladies to stalk tomorrow," I say, trying to keep things light.

She grins at that, and a dimple pops up on the right cheek. "At least finish your coffee first."

She puts some cake on the table, slyly slipping it my way. "I made this today."

"You keep busy, don't you?"

She shrugs and sits back down. "I used to work in a library, and then a bookstore. When I went overseas I didn't work because I was looking after my aunt, but now that I'm back, I don't know what to do with myself. There's no point getting a job until this whole ordeal is over, but I'm not used to sitting around all day. So I've started baking and cooking new recipes. Started gardening. It keeps my mind busy too. I don't want to overthink right now, it only makes things worse. I've also started doing some volunteer work. I like helping people."

Right.

She's on fucking bail. I almost forgot. For a moment, it felt like two people hanging out, just enjoying each other's company. She's easy to be around, and when there is silence between us, it's comfortable.

What the fuck am I doing here? I shouldn't be forgetting how we met and why we're here. It's not to hang out and have coffee. I should regret coming here, but I don't. I like being around her.

She looks down at the cake. "It's good."

My lip twitches as I reach over and take a piece. As the lemon flavor hits my tongue, I have to agree. "It's delicious."

She beams, so happy over such a small compliment. I guess she didn't hear them a lot when she was with her ex. It makes me want to compliment her until she's no longer foreign to hearing them. "Best cake I've had in a long time."

Probably the only cake I've had in months because I don't have much of a sweet tooth. I think the last time I had cake was at someone's wedding earlier this year. And I mean it: hers is better.

"Thank you," she says, ducking her face, and she smiles wide. "I don't know about all that, but I'm glad that you like it."

When she looks back up, our eyes hold and something passes between us. Something I'm going to pretend didn't happen. Nope,

I definitely didn't see that in her eyes, and she better not have seen it in mine. We have a professional relationship, and there is no room for attraction. We need to bury that shit right now.

I clear my throat and stand. "I should go home, it's late. Thank you for the coffee and cake."

"Okay. Thanks for the company," she says, standing and walking with me to the door.

Fuck.

She thanked me for my fucking company. She's obviously alone and doesn't have anyone to talk to or hang out with. I have my work colleagues, and I can always call my parents for a chat. Hell, if I really wanted, I have a few friends I could call and they'd be there. It seems like she has only her aunt, who is overseas. She hasn't mentioned any other family. I almost don't want to leave her alone here. I don't like the thought of it. That reminds me.

"I forgot to tell you. A man named Joshua will be here tomorrow at ten a.m. to check on the house security. Do you want me to be here so you're not alone in the house while he's here?"

I don't know where that offer came from. I said it before my own brain could even wrap around it.

"I'd like that," she replies, looking genuinely thankful. She reaches out and touches my arm. "Thank you, Jaxon. For everything. I know you don't have to do all these things for me."

I want to tell her someone like her should know kindness. Should expect it. I want to tell her that if she ever needs anything, I'm only a call away. Instead, instinct brings me close to her, and my lips place a gentle kiss on her forehead. She doesn't flinch. "Lock up. I'll see you tomorrow."

I leave, making sure the door is closed before I get in the car and drive home.

What the fuck am I doing?

chapter 10

SCARLETT

JAXON ARRIVES BEFORE JOSHUA does, and I'm grateful to have him in the house while a random man walks around it. I made some ham-and-cheese croissants for both of them, along with a fruit platter, just in case they got hungry.

"You didn't have to do that," Jaxon says, as Joshua helps himself.

"It's no problem," I say quickly, appreciating having someone to actually cook for. Jaxon takes one, and I like watching him enjoy eating it. Is that weird? Probably.

"The place is pretty secure," Joshua tells Jaxon. I don't know why he tells him and not me, but I stand next to Jaxon and listen anyway. "Just a few windows I'd put new locks on, and remember to change the password regularly on the system."

"When can you do the locks?" Jaxon asks. He's in all black,

pants and a T-shirt. He looks more casual than usual, and I wonder if it's because he's going to try to talk with Valentina again today. I really hope she'll help us.

"I can do them today, I just need to head to the store and grab a few things," Joshua says, then looks to me. "Will you be home? I can be back here in an hour."

I nod. "Yes, I'll be here."

"Perfect," Jaxon says. "Just send the invoice to my office."

"You can just give it to me," I tell Joshua, wondering why Jaxon would want it sent to his office when I'll be right here as he does the job.

Joshua smirks and leaves, getting into his truck and driving off.

"Will you be okay with him, now that you've met him and know what he looks like?" he asks me, scanning my face. "I can stay if you like, but he's a good guy. You can feel safe around him."

"I'll be fine," I say, smiling gently. "Thanks for being here."

"No problem, call me if you need anything," he says, then flashes me a smile and leaves.

I'm not going to lie, I check out his ass. It's a good one—tight, round, and totally grabbable.

Except then he turns around and catches me looking.

Crap.

I awkwardly wave, grimacing as he smirks and slides into his car.

"JAXON IS TAKING CARE of the bill," Joshua states, refusing me as I bring my purse out.

"What do you mean?" I ask, wrinkling my nose, and shifting on my feet. I open my purse and grab my checkbook. "Don't be silly. Please, let me know how much it will be."

"It's taken care of, sweetheart," he says, smiling and walking out the front door.

I'm still standing in the open doorway in confusion when my phone rings. I don't even check who the caller is. "Hello?"

"Scarlett," comes the smooth tone on the other end. "Did everything go okay?"

Jaxon.

Just the man I need to have a word with.

"Yeah, besides the fact he didn't let me pay," I say, closing my front door and locking it. "Any idea why that is?"

Jaxon ignores my comment and says, "Good. I have some news."

"You spoke to Valentina?" I surmise, moving to sit on my couch. "And are you going to ignore everything else I just said?"

He hesitates, and then says, "Yes to the latter, and not exactly to the former. Valentina doesn't want to talk, and the MC is making it impossible to reach her without going through all of them first."

"Then what?" I ask, wondering why he's calling if nothing has transpired.

"I came up with a plan B."

"You going to tell me what this plan B is?" I ask, eyebrows rising. "Or are you going to leave me in suspense?"

I don't know when the two of us became partners in crime, but I like it. I like knowing what's going on, and being a part of the decisions. I trust Jaxon and the choices he makes—he knows what he's doing after all—but he didn't have to call me and update me. The fact that he treats me like an equal, not a criminal, means more to me than he will ever know.

"I'll tell you, but it has to be in person. Come to my office tomorrow?"

"I'll be there," I tell him.

Not like I have anything better to do.

EVER SINCE I LEFT Darren, I've tried to hide who I am, to be invisible. I've dressed in loose-fitting clothes, and at the start I even stopped wearing makeup or putting any effort at all into my looks. I never wanted people to notice me. I didn't want any attention. I learned that blending into the background was safe, and even after I left Darren that kind of stuck with me.

After more than two years now I've finally started becoming who I was meant to be. A woman who makes her own decisions, an independent woman. One who controls her own destiny. Today though is the first time I've worn a fitted dress in a very long time. It's black and ends just below the knee, but it shows off my chest and slim waist. I don't question why I've put it on today, but I feel good in it. My hair is down and has a slight wave to it. I haven't put much makeup on, just some powder and a little blush on my cheeks. I'm learning to love who I am and accept myself, flaws and all. Before, I used to think about my flaws. But I'm proud of myself, I really am.

It would really be hell if I was sent to prison, just when I'm getting my first taste at freedom, at what life can truly be. Deep inside, I know somehow justice will prevail and I'll be acquitted. I'm holding on to that, and that's what is getting me through and why I'm not freaking out as much as I could be right now. I'm slowly becoming stronger, more outgoing, and coming out of my shell, and it's an indescribable feeling. I'm like a butterfly, just breaking free from its cocoon. One that happened to be stuck in there longer than others.

"Is Mr. Bentley in?" I ask the woman at the desk as I walk in, my car keys still in the palm of my hand.

She lifts her head and smiles. She has platinum-blond hair, but her eyes are dark and mysterious. "He is. What was your name, ma'am?"

"Scarlett Reyes," I say, listening as she picks up the phone to call Jaxon.

"I have a Scarlett Reyes here for you at the front desk," she says into the line. "Okay, no worries." She hangs up and says, "He said to go straight in."

"Thanks."

I walk toward his office and am about to knock when the door opens. "Good morning."

"Good morning," I say, flashing him an easy smile.

He's in a blue shirt today, another one that's rolled up at the elbows. I don't know what it is about that that makes him so much sexier. He shuts the door while I take a seat.

"What are you up to today?" he asks, claiming his own chair and studying me. "You look . . . nice."

I smile at the compliment, which turns into a smirk when I catch him staring, as if he's unable to look away. "I thought I'd donate some of Darren's money and belongings to a charity today, and then I'll probably go home and finish the garden. I want to turn it into a nice outdoor area where I can read and hang out. My own little space."

Anything to keep me busy. It's sad that this is what my life has become, one huge distraction to get me through, and that I have to spend the day dealing with Darren's things. However, if a charity can benefit from it, if I can do a little good in the world, at least that's something.

"That sounds nice," he says, tilting his head to the side. "You could put some furniture out there, or maybe one of those seat swings."

"That's the plan. What news do you have to tell me?" I ask, getting to the point.

"Right," he says, rubbing his hands together. "I pulled a favor and I have something in the works for your case. I'm going to need a few days, so I don't want you to worry or think that nothing is happening, okay? Try not to stress. I know it's hard, but as soon as I find out any information, I'll give you a call, okay?"

"You wanted me to come all the way here to tell me that?" I ask, crossing my arms over my chest.

"No," he says, sliding me over a file. "I actually need you to read and sign these. As you know, our family-law attorney, Hunter, has been working on your case as well. We need you to sign these to move probate along."

"Oh. Do you want me to do it now, or can I take it home and bring it back?" I ask, wanting time to read through it all.

"You can take it with you."

"Anything else?"

"Just one more thing."

He grins, a smug look plastered on his face. I don't know why he looks smug, until he reaches down and pulls out a bouquet of beautiful white flowers.

"Happy birthday, Scarlett," he says, handing them to me.

I take them, my eyes widening. I was going to ignore my birthday. I have no one to celebrate with, and nothing to celebrate about, so I was just going to pretend it was any other day.

"How did you know?" I ask softly, smelling the beautiful flowers. Peonies are mixed into the bunch, and those are my favorite flowers in the world.

"Came up on my file," he says, shrugging. "I was going to get them delivered to you, but I wanted to see your face."

"Thank you, Jaxon," I say, leaning over the table and kissing his cheek, the light stubble on his face prickling my lips. "Today was just another day until now."

"You're welcome, Scarlett," he says, gray eyes as gentle as I've ever seen them.

"I'm going to go home and put them in a vase," I say, knowing he has work to do. And I have somewhere to be: today is my first day of volunteering at the animal shelter. I've been wanting to do something productive while I'm waiting for this trial to be over, and since I have a soft spot for animals, I couldn't think of anything better to do than give back to animals in need. They told me that they needed help walking and transporting dogs to foster and prospective adoption homes.

"I'll be in touch," he calls out after me.

I turn and flash him a happy smile, then head back home to drop the flowers off before driving to the shelter.

chapter 11

JAXON

THE LOOK ON HER face.

Fuck.

It was like no one has ever given her flowers before, or even remembered her birthday.

Twenty-seven years old today, but has seen and experienced more than people twice her age. I'm glad to have put a smile on her face, and to have seen her on her birthday, even if it was just for a little bit. If I was being honest, I'd love to take her out for dinner or something, but that's not a good idea. I need to concentrate on the case, and I need to forget about how I felt when I saw her face light up.

When it was lit up because of me, because *I* made her happy.

Consider that shit forgotten.

I was going to tell her more information I dug up but decided against it. If something goes wrong, the less information she knows the better. Working with my private investigator, I've managed to get the Wind Dragons MC lines tapped. I know it can backfire if they find out, but it had to be done. It's not legal and probably won't hold up in court, but I need to know if they're involved in this or if they're a dead end. Valentina was never going to talk to me. Her boyfriend, or whatever they call male biker partners these days, is as protective over her as I'd be over my woman.

I'm going to win this case. Regardless of who I have to turn against.

HUNTER WALKS INTO MY office and hands me some paperwork. I haven't known Hunter nearly as long as I have Tristan, but the man has definitely grown on me over the last few years. He brings with him a lighthearted energy that the firm needs, because if you get too caught up in everything here, it can start to suck the life out of you.

"Some guy named Peterson is trying to get a hold of you," he lets me know.

I take the papers and thank him. "You playing receptionist now?"

He grins and runs his hand down his long dark beard. "Kat and Yvonne are on their lunch break, so I'm holding down the fort. Who says men can't multitask?"

"Women," I reply with a smirk, then nod at his forearm. "New tattoo?"

"Yeah," he says, glancing down at it. "It's still healing."

I'm about to reply when Kat sticks her head in. "I'm back. You can go have lunch now, Hunter."

"I'll be back," he announces, then disappears.

When Kat lingers, I know she has something to say.

"Is my office the new lunchroom hangout?" I tease, beckoning for her to come in. "What's up, Kat?"

She sits opposite me, an odd look on her face. "Where are my flowers?"

"What?" I ask. "What flowers? You pregnant or something?"

"No," she says, smirking. "Scarlett Reyes got flowers. I saw them. So where are mine?"

I lean back in my chair, my expression now blank. "Is it your birthday today?"

"No," she says, dragging the word out.

"Then you don't get flowers," I say, wondering why she's giving me shit about this.

"Was it her birthday?" she probes, which is when I've had enough. Kat and I have a good friendship, and we've had a few deep chats in our time, but this is crossing a line. I don't have to explain my actions to anyone. "You like her!"

"Tristan!" I call out, knowing he can hear me from his office next door. He comes in a rush, probably thinking that something is wrong.

"What is it?" he asks, eyes scanning Kat, making sure she's okay.

"Kat's crossing lines," I say, narrowing my eyes on the little she-devil. "Don't you have any work to do, associate?"

"I'm on top of everything, actually," she says, lifting her chin and staring me down.

"What are you harassing him about?" Tristan asks, sounding curious instead of angry or annoyed on my behalf.

"I've never seen Jaxon buy anyone flowers before," she says, glancing back at her man. "And he bought some for Scarlett Reyes."

"It was her birthday," I say, jaw going tight. "I don't have to explain myself."

"Yet you just did," she muses, making me want to strangle her.

I glance up at Tristan, who has the nerve to chuckle before grabbing Kat and escorting her out of the room. Just as he shuts my office door the bastard says, "For the record, I think you like her too."

Fucking hell.

"Is no one going to point out that it's a fucking ethical violation instead of giving me shit over it?" I ask.

So much for this place being a professional environment.

The door opens again and Tristan's head pokes in. "You're a grown man, Jaxon. You'll figure it out."

I call Peterson back, hoping he has some good news for me. He's my PI, and the one I have keeping an eye on the MC phone lines.

"Hey, it's Jaxon," I say into the line. "What have you got for me?"

"More than you could have hoped for," he says, excitement hitting me. I stand up and grab my keys. "Where are you?"

"At my office."

"I'm on my way," I tell him, hanging up, practically sprinting through the office.

Please let this be what I've been waiting for.

"THE LAWYER IS TRYING to contact Valentina over Darren's death," an accented male voice says. It sounds Irish, or maybe Scottish. It's the voice I heard when I tried to call Valentina myself.

"They probably want her to testify," a woman replies. "Scarlett Reyes has been charged with Darren's death; it's been all over the news."

"What proof do they have for that?" the man asks. "We all know she didn't do it."

"The gun was planted at her house, and she was his wife. She left the country pretty quickly, and the cops need to pin it on someone. Some of them were there that night, remember? They won't want anyone to know that. If they tried to drag us down, we'd bring them with us."

"So the cops planted the gun?" the man asks, sounding surprised. "Fuck, Faye. I feel like shit knowing this woman is going to go to prison for a crime I committed. As if being that dickhead's wife wouldn't have been bad enough."

"I know," the woman, Faye Black, says. "But what else can we do? You doing time is *not* an option, and we don't have anything to do with her being a suspect. That's on the cops."

They chat some more, but I already have all I need.

Valentina's boyfriend is the one who killed Darren.

And the cops knew about it.

And to save everyone's asses, they pinned it on the sweetest, most gentle woman I've ever met.

There was one variable they weren't counting on though, and that was me.

And I'm going to bring them all down.

I ASK TO MEET with the man named Irish, who arrives with his attorney. It's nice to finally meet Faye Black, but it's a shame it's under these circumstances. The only way I got her to agree to this meeting was by saying that I have some damaging evidence she's going to want to hear before I take it public.

More bluffing.

I'm not dumb enough to release this recording and have every Wind Dragon member, including Demon, breathing down my neck. But she doesn't have to know that.

"Have a seat, Mrs. Black," I tell her, then look to the large, dark-haired man next to her. "You too, Mr. Irish."

Faye smirks at that, but doesn't give anything else away. She's an attractive woman, with long auburn hair and sharp hazel eyes. She doesn't look like an old lady. In fact she's dressed in business attire I'd expect from any female lawyer—black pants with a black blazer, a white shirt underneath. Irish looks like I'd expect a murderer to, covered in what looks like a knife scar along his neck, the darkest of eyes narrowed on me.

"I'm not going to beat around the bush here," I tell the two of them. "My client Scarlett Reyes is innocent, and we all know it. However it's my job to prove it."

I hit PLAY and let them listen to the recorded conversation.

"*How* did you get that?" Faye growls, her nice demeanor gone.

"I don't believe that's the biggest issue here," I say, staying calm and focused. "Now I might not be able to use that in court, but now I know the truth of it. We all know the type of man Darren was, and that it's no loss he's gone. However, a woman who was victimized by him should not be doing time for something she didn't do. I understand, Irish, that you were probably protecting Valentina, but tell me, what other outcome is there than you doing the time for a crime you did commit, whether it was justified or not? How can you go to sleep at night knowing an innocent woman who was abused by Darren is going to be sitting in a prison cell, wondering what the fuck she did to deserve the sentence she'll get?"

"Fucking hell," Irish snarls, looking to Faye. The next move is obviously her call—she's the lawyer. I slide her some papers. "There's lots more information about Darren that has come out, from his meth lab to his cop buddies covering up all his illegal activities and abuse. We can try to get your client a reduced sentence if he pleads guilty to involuntary manslaughter. It's the only way."

"Don't try to do my job for me, Mr. Bentley. I'm very aware of the situation we have before us," she says, lifting her chin and looking me in the eye.

"How much time will I be looking at?" Irish asks Faye, a muscle working in his jaw.

"I have to take it to the prosecutor to exonerate my client," I tell the man. "It's nothing personal, but Scarlett deserves to go free and you know it. You said so in the audio."

"Best outcome would be two to three years," Faye guesses, which would've been my guess too. "Worse case, maybe up to seven."

"Fuck, I need to see Valentina," he mutters, gripping the table, knuckles white.

Faye says one thing, and with that word, I know she knows I'm right, and that there's no other way around it. "Fuck."

chapter 12

SCARLETT

"YOUR HONOR, I REQUEST that all charges against my client be dropped," Jaxon says as he looks at the judge. "The prosecution has no case, and my client's arrest was premature. All the so-called evidence against her is circumstantial. The gun found at her house had no prints and there is nothing definitive to confirm that gun was the gun that actually killed Detective Melvin," he summarizes.

I hear a chair scrape against the floor and the prosecutor, an older man with salt-and-pepper hair and an ill-fitting suit, stands up. "Objection, Your Honor. Mr. Bentley is out of line. Not only did we find the gun, but Ms. Reyes emptied her bank account and fled the country—"

"My client left the country to help her sick aunt, not because she was fleeing. She has been in France for the last two years caring for her aunt and returned the moment she was asked to, instead of remaining there or going into hiding. Her aunt sent me her medical records showing that Ms. Reyes was indeed with her during her two years abroad."

"This is ridiculous, Your Honor—"

"That's enough, both of you," the judge says sharply. She's younger than I expected, but she oozes authority. "Mr. Nguyen, does the prosecution have any evidence against Ms. Reyes other than the gun?"

It's been a long day, and it's been hard to listen to everything everyone is saying I must have done when I know the truth. But I've sat here, my chin up, hoping that Jaxon's words will be enough to keep me from being wrongly convicted. As I've watched him in his element, I've noticed how much power and confidence he exudes, and that's not something that's taught, that's just him. He was born to do this job.

"Since this is only a preliminary hearing, the police are still working—"

Jaxon interrupts the prosecutor again. "Your Honor, while it's not my job to do what the police are supposed to do, I have proof that my client did not kill Detective Melvin."

I stare at Jaxon with my mouth open. He didn't tell me this. As there is a murmuring all throughout the courtroom, the judge bangs her gavel.

"Order in the court. Mr. Bentley, what are you talking about?"

At that, the back door opens and a woman enters with a man and another woman. The first woman is in a suit, with her long auburn hair piled on top of her head, wearing a stern expression. The man looks a bit rough around the edges and has a scar across his neck. He'd look dangerous, except he has his arm protectively around the second woman. I notice her thick red hair immediately. The woman in the suit eyes Jaxon, but walks toward us.

"Your Honor, my name is Faye Black. Can the four of us"— she indicates the prosecutor and Jaxon—"go into judge's chambers for a brief discussion?"

"This is completely out of line, Mrs. Black, but I'm curious to see what this is about. My chambers. Now."

I watch the four of them go into a secluded office while the couple takes a seat in the back.

WRINGING MY HANDS NERVOUSLY, I shift my feet. The woman Darren was with for all those years, Valentina, is absolutely beautiful. Her red curls bounce as she leaves the courtroom after me. Considering the outcome, that her boyfriend, Irish, admitted he killed Darren while defending her and will do two years in prison, I'd think she would hate me, and I brace myself for such. But as she approaches me, there's no hate in her eyes. No animosity whatsoever.

She puts her hand out, and I give her mine. "I'm sorry for everything you've been through."

"You too," I say softly. "I'm sorry about Irish."

She takes a deep breath, and I can tell that it pains her that he'll now be doing time. "I just wanted to tell you that I had no idea he had a wife all those years. If I had known, things would've been different."

"I didn't know about you either," I whisper, squeezing her hand. "I'm so sorry things have to be this way, Valentina."

She smiles sadly and lets go of my hand. "You didn't kill Darren, Scarlett. Don't be sorry." She pauses, debating on what to say next. "I want you to know that when your lawyer came to see me, I didn't know what Irish had done. He kept it from me for two years and I don't think he ever intended to tell me. So what I said to your lawyer about not knowing anything, I was telling the truth. I'm sorry you got brought into this. Go and enjoy your life now, like I have been ever since I met Irish."

A few men come to stand behind her.

Great, I put one of their biker friends behind bars, and now they must all hate me.

"I'm sorry," I blurt out, feeling tears hit my eyes.

"You okay?" Jaxon asks, coming to stand next to me and placing his hand on the small of my back. I don't react to his touch like I normally would. It's like my body has accepted it now. "Come on, let's get out of here."

He leads me outside to his car and opens the passenger door. I'm thankful he drove me here because I don't think I should be behind the wheel right now. So many emotions are hitting me at full force—relief, thankfulness, but now also guilt. I hate that Irish has to do time, and that Valentina has to lose him for a couple of years. This is all Darren's fault. How many people can he keep hurting, even from the grave?

"Are you okay?" he asks me again. "They didn't say anything to you, did they? Because if they did . . ."

"No, they were nice. She was . . . really nice to me, and showed no malice whatsoever," I say, taking a deep breath. "I guess I feel a little bad if I'm being honest. I know I am innocent, but . . ."

"He did the crime, Scarlett; don't feel guilty. His actions caused him to be in the place he is now, not yours," he says to me. "You should be celebrating. All of this hell is over for you now. You can go on with your life; you can be happy."

"I know," I breathe, nodding to myself. "I'm finally free of him."

Darren was an evil man, and now that this is all over, he can no longer cause me any pain.

It just sucks it's at the expense of Valentina's newfound happiness.

"What would you like to do to celebrate?" he asks, glancing at me before looking back at the road. "Anything at all."

I don't really feel like doing anything except going home to my bed and not leaving it for the next few days, but he's trying to cheer me up, and I'd never take that effort for granted.

"I don't know," I admit. "Maybe we could go to the beach. I've been wanting to go since I returned but never got around to it."

"The beach it is," he says, glancing down at his suit. "Are we going to stop and get changed, or are we just going to wing it?"

"Wing it," I say, grinning. "Let's be spontaneous." I pause, and then add, "Or at least my version of spontaneous. Maybe we can stop and grab a few beers, or something."

"You drink beer?" he asks, sounding surprised. "I thought you'd be more of a wine kind of girl."

"I like wine too," I explain to him. "But I think the beach calls for some ice-cold beer."

"Beer it is," he says, and just like that, he gives me what I want.

I've never had that before.

I put the window down, letting the breeze hit my face, and smile.

I can't save Irish, but I can enjoy the second chance I've been given. A fresh start. A new beginning. Now I just need to decide what it is I want, what will make me happy, and then go after it.

My journey is only just beginning.

"EVERYONE IS STARING AT us," I notice, even though it doesn't really bug me. I'm just pointing out a fact.

"Probably because we're extremely overdressed for the beach," he muses in a dry tone. He's taken off his jacket and tie and rolled up his sleeves, while I couldn't do much except unpin my hair and remove my shoes. So we're sitting on the beach, with me in a navy-blue knee-length dress, beers in our hands, enjoying the sunlight and the sound of the waves.

"We are, aren't we?" I say with a smile on my face. I bring the bottle to my lips and take a sip. "I just realized I never said thank you."

"For what?" he asks, turning his head to look at me.

"What do you mean 'for what'? For getting the charges dropped, for going above and beyond your duties," I start, reaching my hand out to touch his. "For showing me that there's good in the world. For being a person I can trust. For the flowers. For everything."

I'm probably not explaining it well, but I just want him to know that he didn't have to be so amazing. He could have done the bare minimum in defending me, or not believed me at all, but he didn't. I had so much going against me, I wouldn't have believed my story. He didn't have to go out of his way to do what he did, and it shows what a great human being he is.

Not only is he handsome, but he's also kind. Smart. I'm only now letting myself admit this attraction I have toward him. I know I'm not meant to think of him like this, but that doesn't stop my mind from going there.

"You don't need to thank me, Scarlett," he says, squeezing my hand. "You're due to have some good in your life, don't you think?"

"Yes, I do," I reply boldly. "You didn't have to give it to me, but you did, and I don't think I can thank you enough."

He tucks my hair back behind my ear. "You're welcome."

I want him to kiss me, but at the same time, is it too soon? We literally just left the courtroom. Who am I kidding? It's definitely too soon, and I shouldn't even be thinking about it.

Think of something else, Scarlett.

How about the fact that my life can finally be normal?

I smile at the thought, my eyes closing, but when they open he's right there in front of me, and I'm clouded once more.

I don't know what the rules are, or if he even wants to kiss me, but I know it's not the best idea. He doesn't kiss me though. Instead, he takes his hand away from me, and looks back to the sparkling blue water. I always said that after this I'd leave straightaway, but with Jaxon next to me, I don't want to.

Maybe there is something here for me after all.

Neither of us has addressed this . . . this thing between us though, and we're acting like we're friends. That's fine for me. Besides, I don't know if I'm ready to dive into something serious yet. Two years seems like a long time to heal, but I don't know if I'm completely healed yet. I've never really had the option to explore my freedom, both with men and with my daily life. So getting into something right now might not be the best option for me. For now, I'm just happy being with him, feeling safe and knowing I have someone I can rely on. That isn't something I've ever really had, and it's a beautiful feeling.

"Will you let me cook for you tonight, or are you going to be stubborn?" I ask, being a little forward in assuming he'd want to spend more time with me after this. I don't know what's come over me. I'm not a woman who is usually forward, ever.

His deep chuckle makes me feel warm inside. "If you want to cook for me so badly, I'm not going to say no. I could take you out for dinner though."

"No, I'd like to cook for you," I say, taking in his features.

I've never seen eyes as gray as his, surrounded in thick dark lashes I could only dream of. His nose is straight, his lips perfectly full and firm.

Kissable.

The stubble on his cheeks is getting darker every day, and I wonder if he's growing it out. I think he'd look good either way. I don't know why I'm checking him out so much now, maybe it's because before I'd only look at him when I had to. I didn't want him to catch me staring, but now something is changing. I'm free, and there are possibilities all of a sudden. The cloud of uncertainty that followed me around has vanished; my future is now something I can actually contemplate.

I can do anything I want, be whoever I want, without restriction.

Freedom.

What an underrated word.

And Jaxon . . .

I can look at him; I can admire him. I don't have to hide it anymore, or be afraid of my future.

I don't have to be afraid of anything.

Except his response to me.

"Home cooking it is," he murmurs, eyes dropping to my mouth. "I think you should stop looking at me like that, Scarlett."

I swallow hard. Our faces are close, but not touching. It would only take me leaning toward him a little to have our lips touch.

"You smell good," I blurt out.

He grins, flashing his straight white teeth. "So do you."

"I don't think I want to stop looking at you," I admit, laying my head on his shoulder. "I don't think I'll ever forget today."

He wraps his jacket around me as the wind picks up. We

finish our beers, then take a long walk on the beach, the sound of the loud crashing waves relaxing me.

He doesn't take my hand, but we walk with our arms casually brushing every now and again, and that tiny bit of contact sets me on fire.

chapter 13

JAXON

I LICK MY LIPS, WHICH are suddenly dry, and shift in my seat. It's hot in here, so I open my window a little, letting some fresh air in. The car is filled with tension, the air so thick that the open window isn't even helping. She's quiet, and I wonder what she's thinking. I want to look over at her but force myself to concentrate on the road as I try to sort my thoughts out.

It's too soon.

Scarlett and I shouldn't be anything other than friends. I shouldn't be thinking about her the way I am—she needs more time; *we* need more time before we become anything more.

I want to touch her, but I can't.

I won't.

I don't know how everything changed the second we won the case, but it's like a switch flipped. The excuse I'd been using in my mind is now gone, but that doesn't mean there aren't other issues at hand here. Scarlett has just been given her freedom after being in an abusive relationship, and then accused of murder—I don't think one comes out of that unscathed. I don't know what she wants, or if she even knows what she wants, and I don't want to get attached to her if she's just going to leave. It's too early to even have that conversation though, so I don't know what I'm meant to do. I also don't want her to look at me like I'm her hero and for that to be the reason she wants me. In a way I feel like I'm almost preying on her. She's so vulnerable and I don't want to take advantage of her or her situation. But I like her. I don't know what it is, but I like being around her, and I want to get to know her better, away from all of this mess.

I want to kiss her, taste those juicy, pouty lips, but I'm not going to, at least not tonight. Too much has happened today, and I never want her to feel obligated to me or regret anything that's happened between us.

I'm a patient man; I can wait until she's ready, or until she knows what she wants.

I just want to get to know her and let her get to know me. For now, that's all I can offer, and I think it's all she's ready for.

"Should we stop at the store for groceries?" I ask her.

"I think I have everything," she says, looking like she's mentally ticking things off a list in her head. "We should be good. Unless you want a particular wine or something?"

"I'm good," I tell her, absently bringing my hand to her thigh.

I remove it the second I realize what I've done, and I hear the intake of her breath. Not in a bad way, more like a soft gasp of pleasure.

Why did I do that? Friends don't do that. They don't do casual thigh touches. It was so natural though, and I don't know where it came from. What is she doing to me? She's making me fucking crazy.

I clear my throat, and say, "Maybe another night this week you'll let me cook for you."

"Let me guess, the menu will be something 'manly'?" she asks, flashing me a side look, and then laughing to herself.

I love the sound of it. I could listen to her laughing all day.

"You're never going to let that go, are you?" I grumble, turning onto the road to her house. "I'll whip something up, just don't judge my cooking against yours."

"So no cook-offs then?" she teases, and I can feel her staring at my profile. "Don't worry, I'll take it easy on you."

"If we're having a cook-off, I'm going to need some notice so I can practice first."

So I can actually learn a recipe, for starters. Maybe I'll call Mom up and see if she can tell me how to make one of her many delicious dishes. I can just see how that conversation will go, and the million questions I'll be asked.

"Shape of You," by Ed Sheeran is playing on the radio, and I notice her mouthing the words to the chorus.

If only she knew how I felt about her body.

And the things I want to do to it.

"CAN I HELP YOU do anything?" I ask from behind her as she fixes our dinner. "Chop the vegetables or something?"

"No," she answers, turning to face me. "I've got it under control. Can I get you something to drink?"

"I'm good," I say, closing the space between us and placing my hand on her hip. Her breath hitches at the bold contact, and she looks down at my hand before raising those hazel eyes to mine. "Are you sure I can't help in any way?"

"You're already helping," she answers, and I know we're no longer talking about the food. "I can't believe how today went . . . and now you're here."

"Why didn't you trust that I'd keep you out of prison?" I tease, trying to lighten the mood. "You know I wasn't going to let anything happen to you."

"I know," she replies, licking her lips. "Which is why I kept thanking you today."

"I told you that you don't need to thank me. I did my job. I just happen to do it very well," I say, tucking her hair back behind her ear. She always has one errant lock that falls on her cheek, and I love using it as an excuse to touch her. Her hair is so soft and silky, I want to bury my face in it to smell it, and tangle my hands in it. I want to explore every inch of her, but I know that I need to go slow. Rushing into things won't keep her around—I know that. I don't know what I'm doing, if I'm being honest, but I want to try to make all the right moves here. There's no fucking map for this though, so I just need to go with my gut.

"If that's the story you're going to stick to," she cheekily replies, arching her brow at me. "I hope you like chicken."

"I love chicken."

I think I'd love anything she cooks. I'm not a fussy eater, so there's not much I wouldn't like. Who am I kidding? I'm just happy to be around her.

"Good," she says, turning back to the stove, my hand dropping from her waist. "Now go sit down and let me do my thing."

I feel my lip twitch as I move back against the counter. I like when she shows her attitude, the one I know she taught herself to hide. The more it comes out, the more I know she's being her true self and not trying to be someone Darren wanted her to be. The first time I met her I thought she came off a little cold and impersonal.

Olivia came off that way too, but I knew her, that her heart was pure gold and that she wasn't cold at all. Never once did I think that she was being abused.

Never.

And even though the asshole who did that to my sister is now behind bars for domestic abuse, I will never forgive myself for not noticing the signs. For not being there for her or making an effort to see her more. I was always too preoccupied with work. If I had been around, perhaps then I would've seen something and I could have saved her.

Why didn't she come to me?

I'll never get the answer to that.

And it kills me.

The what-ifs kill me every damn day.

"What are you thinking about?" Scarlett asks me. I didn't even notice her move closer.

"Nothing," I say quickly, which is my default answer to anyone who asks me that question.

She nods, studying me. "Are you always so closed off?"

"Are you?" I fire back at her.

"I'm learning not to be," she answers with pure honesty. "But it's hard, you know? It's a little scary to put yourself out there and trust people." She pauses and takes a deep breath. "And it's even scarier to be vulnerable, or give someone the power to hurt you."

"I know what you mean," I tell her. "I hope the next man you trust deserves it."

"That's a nice thing to say," she murmurs, stepping forward.

This time when her lock of hair escapes she tucks it back herself. "I hope you're hungry, because I'm making a lot of food."

"I'm starving."

And for more than just food.

I'm hungry for her.

chapter 14

SCARLETT

I MADE A CREAMY CHICKEN pasta, beef ribs, garlic bread, and a salad. I figure it covered anything he could be craving, and I hope he likes it. I've never cooked for any other man besides Darren. Before I started dating him I'd had only one boyfriend, and I didn't know how to cook then, nor would I have wanted to at that age. I place everything on the table while Jaxon washes the dishes that have accumulated. I told him not to, but he didn't listen. It's kind of hot, watching him, still in his white shirt and dress pants, washing up.

Really hot, actually.

Not only am I not used to being around such a good-looking, put-together man, but I'm not used to a man helping around the house either. Today has been the craziest day, from the courtroom to the beach to my house. It's hard to even process it.

And now my lawyer is in my house, scrubbing a pan, with

his sleeves rolled up, looking sexy and making me wish that he'll use those hands on me next.

Goes to show you never know what will happen in life.

I set the table with plates, silverware, wine, and water—not sure which one I feel like having with this meal. I know Jaxon has to drive home, so he probably won't consume any more alcohol. Once I'm happy with the layout, I wait for him to finish up, then sit down.

"Everything looks amazing," he murmurs, eyes going wide. "You weren't joking about a lot of food."

"We can eat some tomorrow," I say, then realize that sounds like I expect to see him tomorrow. I quickly try to backtrack. "I mean you can take some home tonight and take it to work for your lunch tomorrow. If you want to, that is."

And this, among a million other things, is probably why I'm single.

His lip twitches, letting me know of his amusement. We eat the food, chat, and make each other laugh. It's natural, and I notice how much I like being around him. He helps me clean up, and I pack him some food to take home.

But when he leaves, I only get a kiss on the forehead, which is sweet, but I find myself wanting a taste of his lips.

Maybe next time.

"WHEN ARE YOU COMING back?" My aunt Leona asks me when she calls me the next day.

"I'm not sure—I have a few things I need to sort out here before I can leave," I say, referring to the properties, Darren's money, and, most of all, Jaxon. I'm not ready to leave him yet. I know it's stupid, and I know I should just go and not look back, but something is telling me that I should wait and see what happens with him. Maybe the hopeless romantic in me is returning a little, and I don't know whether to embrace it or tell it to shut the hell up. Maybe it means old me is returning to some degree I don't know, but I'm listening and trusting that gut feeling I get when it comes to him.

"Okay, honey," she says, coughing a little. She beat lung cancer once, but there's a high chance of it coming back. I pray every single day it doesn't. "I'm just glad the whole court thing is over. I don't know what I would've done if they'd put you in prison. Your mother would roll in her grave."

"You don't have to worry about any of that," I tell her, rolling my eyes at her comment about my mother, who passed away when I was fifteen. "I'm fine, I'm safe, and I'll let you know when I'm coming back."

Not that I know when that will be. I have the freedom to do whatever I want now; I just need to figure out what that is exactly.

Now that the case is over, I don't have an excuse to see Jaxon. Who will initiate the next time we see each other? Will we see each other again? We don't have a reason to, really. What if he leaves my life now? I guess I'll just have to let him go, although I know I'll never forget him. He's really left his mark on me, and I know that whenever I think of him, I'll smile. I think it's because I've let him in. He made me stronger, and it's nice to know that a man can do that. He believed in me. He helped me, and I like the way he makes me feel.

"Good-bye, I'll talk to you soon. Take care of yourself, okay?" I say, then hang up the phone before heading out to my garden. Today I'm going to plant some flowers. I don't know where this green thumb is coming from, but I'm thankful for the distraction. I hate that I've been bringing my phone with me everywhere I go, just in case I get a call or a message from him. I hate that I keep checking it compulsively. I don't know what else to do though, because he's always in the back of my mind. I don't want to make the first move, because this needs to be a two-way street.

And Jaxon Bentley is a man who fights for what he wants, so if he wants me, he'll come and get me.

There's another issue I have, one that I don't think will be a problem for a little while, but it still plays on my mind. I haven't been sexually intimate with someone in a long time. Three years to be exact, and the last time was with Darren, and it wasn't an experience I want to remember. After he finished, he rolled off me and told me that I was terrible in bed. Cold and frigid, and that he was surprised he managed to come at all. He never bothered with making me come. I know Darren was an asshole and would say things to hurt me, but in the back of my mind I still wonder if some aspect of that was true. What if I sleep with Jaxon, and he doesn't like it or I do something wrong? The thought makes me nervous. A man like him would have women throwing themselves at him. He's good-looking, has an amazing career and a kind heart. I know that he'd never say anything mean to me, ever, but what if I can't satisfy him? Sex with Darren was boring, and he'd blame that on me but maybe it was him? Maybe I should watch a video or something, to see what sex *should* be.

I finish planting the flowers, then head back inside and take a quick shower before opening my laptop. What do I search? *Good sex? How to have good sex?* I try that one. Many links pop up, and I find myself watching a video of two people making love. Or should I say fucking. Porn. I'm watching porn for the first time ever, and to be honest, I'm a little excited about it. I feel rebellious. I grab a notepad and pen and start to make notes. I realize porn is not a realistic vision of sex, but surely I can learn something from it. Good blow job techniques? Maybe I should've searched that instead. I make a note to study blow job techniques, with and without a foreskin, because I need to be prepared. I don't know what I'll be working with.

"Oh, wow," I mutter when I see the size of the man's penis. It's huge.

I wonder how big Jaxon is. I bet he's massive. Even if he's not, I don't mind. I'm not going to discriminate. But I'm betting on him being absolutely perfect. I turn the volume up and sit back on my pillow, watching these two go at each other, the man fucking her from behind. There definitely wasn't any of this heat in my bedroom. None. I don't want to think of how much of an idiot I was to stay so long, but there's no point looking back now that time has passed. I can't get it back, so I just need to learn from it.

"Oooooh!"

The woman starts moaning really loudly, in a bit of a fake way, so I roll my eyes. However, I can't deny that I'm a little turned on. I want Jaxon's hands on me, and I want to see him naked. I want to explore his body, and I just hope I can be confident enough to be what he wants. No, not even that, I want to be confident enough to be who *I* want to be. I want to own every move I make, my sexuality, and I know it's going to take a little time, but I'm going to get there. I make another note on the list to buy some new lingerie.

"Scarlett?" I hear Jaxon say, making my head snap up. I glance up to see him standing in my room. What the hell? "Your front door was open, I got worried."

He glances down at my laptop, and I want to die.

No, seriously, is it too late to go to jail?

"Are you watching porn?" he asks, trying to keep a straight

face. I slam my laptop closed, my notepad going flying, and of course he picks it up. It's just that kind of day. He reads it out loud. "Blow job techniques." He lowers it and arches his brow. "With and without foreskin. Sexy lingerie."

I cover my face with my hands. "You had to read that out loud?"

"Aw, come on now," he says, sitting down on my bed like he's been in my room a million times before. "Don't be embarrassed. It's cute." He pauses and grins. "And a little hilarious."

I give him a death stare. "We're going to pretend this never happened, *okay*?"

"Okay," he murmurs, ducking his head, probably because he can't stop smiling. He looks at me then, expression contained, and says. "Everyone watches porn."

"Yeah, but not everyone gets caught by the guy they like during their first time watching it," I blurt, groaning with self-pity. He wraps his arm around me and brings me to his body.

Safe.

Warm.

He's teasing me, but he's not belittling me.

This is a safe place.

I squint up at him, daring to look him in the eye after this whole ordeal. He just grins, kisses me on the forehead and whispers, "No foreskin over here."

I groan, and fall back on the bed.

I need a do-over.

chapter 15

JAXON

_D_IDN'T SEE THAT ONE coming.

When I found her door unlocked and a little open, I panicked. I didn't think; I just rushed in to make sure she was okay. When I saw her on the bed watching porn, a little notepad next to her . . . Fuck, she's so cute. Was she taking notes on how to be a better lover? Does she think she isn't one? Now I'm the one making a note to make sure she's comfortable in anything we do—if we get to that point—and to pay attention to her closely. I want her to feel like she's the most beautiful woman on earth, and I don't want her to be shy or question herself. She has a sensuality about her I don't think she's aware of. And if she learns to use it, it could be a deadly weapon.

"Is there anything you want to talk about?" I ask her, as we stand from her bed and head into the kitchen. The reason I came here in the first place is because I was going to surprise her with lunch I got from a really nice restaurant near my office.

"No," she says quickly, color heating her cheeks.

"Okay," I reply, not wanting to push her. "If you ever want to talk, I'm here, and it can be about anything. No judgment, all right?"

She nods, still looking miserable. I hope the food cheers her up. "I brought you lunch."

"You did?" she asks, eyes widening.

"I did. I ate your leftovers for breakfast so I decided to get something for us to eat together while I'm on my break."

A break I'll probably be late returning from. And then no doubt I'll be getting more shit from Kat and Tristan. Soon I'm sure Hunter and Yvonne will get on board too.

She opens the bag, smiling. "It smells delicious. I love Chinese."

"I'm glad. It would've sucked if you hated it."

She grabs two plates and forks and serves the rice onto the plate for each of us. "How has your morning been?"

"Not as good as yours," I snicker, unable to help myself. I know I shouldn't tease her, but that's my nature. I'm quite playful, and I enjoy banter, so she needs to learn that I don't mean it in a spiteful way. She needs to give me shit back, and know it's just for fun.

"Jaxon!" she groans, then squares her shoulders. "Fine, I was looking for tips I could use in bed. The last man I had sex with was an idiot, so sue me."

There's my girl. She's growing bolder, and I like it.

I grin and nod. "Exactly. You're going to be perfect in bed for the right guy, Scarlett. You have nothing to worry about."

She pauses, considering my words, then says quietly, "Darren used to say that I'm cold and frigid in bed. What if you think the same?"

Anger fuels me over her words about Darren. "Let me tell you something, sweetheart. There's no way that's true. Darren was a coward. He tried to keep you down because he knew you were better than him. If there were problems in the bedroom, it was because of him, not you." I take her hand and bring it to my lips, placing a kiss there.

Her hazel eyes widen. "Thank you for saying that, Jaxon."

"It's the truth," I tell her, then add, "you sound a little confident that we're going to end up in bed together. Do you know something I don't?"

She sighs and groans, "And you were doing so well."

I can't help the deep chuckle that escapes me. "I'm just playing with you. It's fine. I like that you want to be good at that craft."

"Thought we were going to pretend this never happened?" she reminds me, her tone dryer than ever before. I've never seen her get angry or lose her temper; her emotions are always held tightly inside. I wonder if or when she will snap. The more time we spend together, I'm sure the more of her I'll get to see. She can't be so poised and perfect all the time . . . I want to see her rough edges too. And I want to let her know that it's fine to be that way. It's normal. Human.

"Right, I forgot," I say, taking a bite of the food.

"How convenient," she mutters, tasting her own. "This is amazing. Where is it from?"

"A place near my office. I go there for lunch sometimes. Pretty good, isn't it?"

She agrees with a moan, and a nod. "So good. Thank you for bringing me some."

"Anytime."

Especially because I got to walk in on her watching porn.

One thing I'll never mention to her is the sight of her watching made me hard as a rock. I don't think she noticed, she was too busy being extremely embarrassed at being caught, but fuck. I don't even know how I walked out of that room when all I wanted to do was show her a firsthand lesson.

"Jaxon," she croons after a few more bites.

"Yes," I reply, lifting my head to her to give her my full attention.

"When's the last time you had sex?" she asks, keeping her eyes on me.

My eyebrows rise. Not a question I thought she'd be asking. "I think it's been about six weeks now. Why do you ask?"

"Just curious," she says, licking her fork. "Who was it with?"

"Just a woman I was seeing," I tell her, wondering where she's going with this. "She wasn't my girlfriend, or anything, it was just casual. I'm usually too busy with work for anything more than that."

"Yet you're at my house in the middle of the day having lunch with me," she points out, a cute smirk on her face. "I think you could make time if you wanted."

I bark out a laugh, loving her boldness. "I guess you're right. Maybe all it takes is the right woman."

That either satisfies her questions, or just shuts her up, because she eats the rest of her food quietly. I check my watch and curse. "I'd better get going."

"Okay," she says as we both stand, and wraps her arms around me. "Thank you for lunch."

I kiss the top of her head. I have too much work to see her tonight, but I ask her what she's doing tomorrow night.

"Nothing," she says, glancing up at me. "Why?"

"I thought I'd take you out for dinner and a movie. What do you think?"

I always remember that night she went out by herself, and I want to take her on a date. Who knows when the last time she's even been on one. I'll let her choose the movie. Shit, I'm even willing to sit through some chick flick for her. I must really like her. I know there's this whole conflict-of-interest issue, but technically her charges were dropped and I'm not her lawyer anymore, right? Right? Fuck, I'm even trying to justify it to myself.

"Sounds perfect," she beams, her eyes lighting up.

"I'll come get you about seven," I say, cupping her cheek, smiling at her, and then leaving. She probably thinks I'm being a tease or giving her mixed signals, but I just want to take things slowly. I want her to be sure about what she wants. We have all the time in the world; there's no rush to the finish line.

"You can continue what you were doing before I got here," I call out to her. "And just so you know, I'm a fan of blow jobs."

I can hear her mutter, "Oh my god," making me laugh.

I can't remember the last time I felt so light, so happy.

I think I'm onto something here.

chapter 16

SCARLETT

I'LL NEVER ADMIT IT, but after he leaves and I clean up, I do keep watching the video. And I watch one on how to give good head, and I mentally remember exactly what to do.

I'm going to blow him away.

Literally.

I'm going on a date with him tomorrow night, and I'm so happy I can hardly contain myself. What should I wear? I haven't been on a date in years. Darren stopped taking me out when he started doing drugs. I don't know how he got into them, but eventually he became addicted to meth, which is when the abuse really began. He changed into a person I didn't know anymore. I push thoughts of Darren out of my head and concentrate on the present.

On Jaxon.

Will he kiss me tomorrow night?

I touch my lips and wonder what his lips will be like. I don't mean to sound ridiculous, but the word *magical* keeps popping into my head.

I know his kiss is going to make me weak.

"YOU LOOK BEAUTIFUL" IS the first thing he says to me.

He thinks I'm beautiful.

I smile.

"You're early" is the first thing I say back. I then add a "thank you," to not sound so rude.

"I know," he says, eyeing my black dress, from top to bottom. "Perhaps I wanted to catch you off guard."

I roll my eyes and smile at the same time. "Come on in. I just need to finish doing my makeup."

"You don't need any makeup," he says, taking my chin between his fingers and gently turning my head from side to side. "Perfect as you are."

"I know I don't need it, but I want it," I say, cringing when I realize how that sounded. "I haven't been on a date in a long time, so I want to look pretty for it and put in a little more effort than usual."

He runs his thumb across my lower lip. The man is clearly trying to kill me.

"Take your time. We're in no rush," he says, winking at me. "I'll just answer some work emails while I'm waiting."

He sits on the couch and pulls out his phone.

"Can I get you something to drink?"

"Nope, I'm good," he says, waving me off. "Don't worry about me."

Not possible.

I rush back to my room and finish with my makeup, then grab my bag and put on my heels. When I walk out to meet him, he stands up and gives me another once-over. "I take that back. You're more than beautiful tonight, Scarlett. You look absolutely stunning."

Darren never gave me his attention like this, never complimented me. He never bothered trying to make me feel special at all. If anything, he would've criticized something about my outfit, or would have told me I need to cover up more because I looked like a whore.

But Jaxon, he looks like he means it. Every kind word.

I duck my head, not used to hearing compliments, feeling the heat hit my cheeks. "Thank you. You look pretty amazing yourself."

He offers me his hand, and, without question, I take it.

For someone like me who has been through what I have, that one action is *everything*.

We walk to his BMW and he opens the door for me like he always does, then closes it once I'm in safely.

I personally think every woman needs a man like Jaxon, because it feels so good to be treated like I'm worth something. It's indescribable. I don't know if other women are just used to it so they take it for granted, but I know that I never will. I know what it's like to be on the other end, and I think it's just going to make me appreciate all the good things life has to offer even more.

"You never told me what restaurant we're going to," I say, glancing at him, feeling a mixture of excitement and nervousness. "What type of food do they have? Or what movie are we seeing?"

"We're going to see whatever you want to see. There are about five that start at the same time. And for dinner I'm taking you to my favorite Italian restaurant," he explains, reaching over and gently holding my hand as he drives. I'm not used to this casual affection, so I never thought I needed it. But Jaxon is showing me that there is so much that I want and need. "You don't like surprises, do you?"

"I liked when you surprised me with the flowers, so maybe I do," I say, smiling at him. "I'm just curious, that's all. And excited."

"Good," he murmurs. "How was your day?"

"It was good. I did a little shopping, then did more work in the garden. How was yours?" I ask him back. I know he's probably not allowed to talk much about his cases or anything like that, and I wouldn't expect him to.

"Not bad. Got two new cases. Should keep me busy."

"Do you ever take time off and go on vacation or anything?" I ask, wondering if his life is just his job. He's clearly a workaholic, and I don't know what he does in his free time to relax.

"Not recently," he tells me. "The firm has been busy, and they've needed me there."

I wonder if that's true, or if it's him who needs them. I don't think he likes being idle; he's always on the go, always working.

"What do you do when you're not working?" I ask. He's never mentioned any family or friends. Maybe he doesn't have any, like me, or maybe they live somewhere else.

"Go to the gym, take care of things at home," he says, glancing at me. "Normally I'd hang out with friends, but we've all been busy lately, so I've kind of just been going between work, the gym, and home."

"What about your family?" I ask, eyes on his profile. I hope he doesn't think I'm being too nosy, I just want to get to know him. Everything about him.

"My parents live about four hours away," he explains, parking the car. He turns to me with a cheeky grin on his handsome face, and says, "Stay here, I'll be right back."

"What? Where are you going?" I ask, as he gets out of the car. I look at the place we've parked in front of, and it's a bar called Knox's Tavern. What exactly are we doing here? It's not like he's going to have a drink while I'm in the car. Curiosity getting the best of me, I decide to not listen to him and get out of the car. I walk to the front of the bar and pull on the push door.

"Crap," I mutter to myself, pushing the door, hoping no one saw that, and walking inside. I glance around, taking the place in. There's a live band playing, and the bar has a nice atmosphere.

"Thought I told you to stay in the car?" Jaxon says as he approaches me.

"And I didn't want to," I reply, lifting my chin.

He simply smirks and takes my hand. "I just needed to pick something up, and now we can go."

"What did you pick up?" I ask, looking at his hands, which are empty.

"You don't make it easy to surprise you with something, do you?" he asks, shaking his head. "Do you want to have a drink while we're here?"

I nod. "This place is great."

The bar and all the tables and chairs are made out of a dark wood, and they have circle lantern lights hanging above the tables.

"It is," he agrees, pulling out one of the barstools for me to sit on. "What would you like to drink?"

"Is there a cocktail menu?" I ask the handsome blond man at the bar.

"Of course," he says with a smile, grabbing one and sliding

it over the counter to me. He then turns to Jaxon and gives him a smirk. "How did you manage to get her?"

"Always a pleasure, Ryan," Jaxon says in a dry tone. I can tell the two of them are cool with each other though, because there's no tension between them.

I scan the list, trying hard to choose from their large selection. "I'll have a Bloody Mary, please."

Ryan smiles at me and nods. "Awesome. And for you?" he asks Jaxon.

"I'll just grab a beer. The usual," he says, pulling his wallet out and placing some money on the table.

The usual? Just how often does he come here? And let's not forget the reason why he came in here in the first place. What did he want to pick up? I don't want to be nosy, but he said he was trying to surprise me, and now I really want to know what it is.

"Will you let me pay for dinner?" I ask him, pressing my pink lips together. "You always pay, and for once I want to."

"No," he says, softening it with a gentle smile. "You won't be paying for anything when I'm around, so you should probably get used to it."

My eyes narrow. "How is that fair? This is the modern world, Jaxon. It's not like I'm stingy or don't want to spend my money."

He cups my face with his warm hand. "I never said you were. I just like treating you. It's how I am and how I've always been. I remember when I was a young boy, my mom would take me out on a little mini date, and I'd open doors for her, pull out her chair, and then pay for the meal with my pocket money. Instead of arguing with me, why don't you just enjoy it?"

"Because it's ridiculous," I state, smiling as Ryan places my drink in front of me. "Thank you."

"No problem. Besides, don't forget you're going to be getting a very steep legal bill in the mail soon," he says, flashing me a wink.

"Worth every penny," I say as I give him a wink. "What do you think about the man always paying?" I ask Ryan as he gives Jaxon his beer. "Don't you think the woman should pay sometimes too?"

"No," he says, smirking. "Sorry, darling, I'm with the lawyer this time. I like to look after my woman too. She doesn't even need to bring her purse if I'm there, and we're married, so my money is hers and vice versa."

I sigh and bring the glass to my lips, taking a sip. They're all Neanderthals. Don't get me wrong, I think it's sweet and chivalrous, and I do think the man should pay on a first date, but after that I don't mind paying, or us taking turns. I don't expect a man to pay for everything, and I have my own money, so it makes no sense. I'm here with him because I want to be, because I want to spend time with him, and that's all he needs to give me. "It's delicious, thank you," I tell Ryan, who watches me try it.

"You're welcome," he says, smiling and then moving to serve another customer.

I turn to look at Jaxon, whose eyes are already on me, watching me sip my cocktail.

Time to get to the bottom of whatever he's up to.

chapter 17

JAXON

I JUST NEEDED TO COME to the bar to pick up some tickets one of the bar owners got me to a sold-out music concert I want to take Scarlett to tomorrow night. I thought I'd take her out for a picnic and then we could go check out the concert, which has a really good lineup. I want her to experience different things with me. I want to learn who she is; I want her to do the same. I want us to create memories. Reid said I had to get the tickets tonight because tomorrow the bar is closed. I told her to wait in the car, but she didn't. As much as I didn't want the surprise to be ruined, I really like that she did what she wanted; it shows that she's becoming more confident, more of her own person.

"So are you going to tell me what you came in here for?" she asks, arching her brow at me.

I pull out the tickets and hand them to her. "I was going to surprise you tomorrow night. I had to come and pick them up tonight though, and we had to pass this bar on the way to the restaurant. Kind of messed up the surprise factor," I grumble.

She reads the tickets and lifts her head. "I'd love to go to this concert; it looks amazing. I haven't been to a music concert since I was in high school." She hands me the tickets back, stands up, and hugs me. "I'm sorry I ruined the surprise." She pulls back and winces. "It's been so long since anyone tried to surprise me with anything. I think the last time was when Darren and I were first dating. He used to bring me flowers and gifts to the library where I was working."

She doesn't have much to compare me to, nor do I have much competition, considering her late husband, but I do want to make her happy. That's my new goal, just to see her smile and to give her the happiness she always deserves but never got. I don't know what's going to happen with us, it may be something or it may be nothing, but at least I can make her life a little better. Or at least I hope I can.

Do I want her?

Undoubtedly yes, but her happiness comes first, and it's her decision if that's with me or not. We haven't known each other long, and I don't know how the fuck this happened, but it did, and I just want to be around her. I want to protect her, and—fuck—I want her to be mine.

She pulls back and presses her lips against my cheek, a chaste kiss. "For the first time in so long, I'm excited about what the week, the month, will bring."

"Good," I rasp, resting my hand on her waist. "We'd better hurry or we'll be late for our reservation."

We finish our drinks, get back in the car, and head to our next stop.

I hope she's hungry.

THE NIGHT WAS GOING so well.

So fucking well.

Too well.

"Who is that?" Scarlett asks me when she sees a woman waving at me from the other table.

It's Rebecca.

I see her eyes move to Scarlett, and her expression instantly changes, her eyes narrowing as she sends a filthy look in Scarlett's direction.

Shit.

Rebecca is the woman I was sleeping with for a few months, and the last woman I've been with. What are the chances of her being here? There are so many restaurants in town, so it seems fate is out to get me. Maybe Scarlett won't care. I mentioned this yesterday at lunch when she asked when the last time I had sex was, so she might just blow it off.

"Umm, a friend," I tell her, taking her hand from across the table. "How's your pasta?"

"It's really good," she says, then looks back over at Rebecca, who is still staring at Scarlett.

Fuck.

"Why is your friend looking at me like she hates me?" she asks, bringing her eyes back to me. "Is she an ex-girlfriend or something?"

I grit my teeth and decide to just come out with the truth, hoping she lets it go after this. Some women can, and some women can't. I'm not sure which one she will be, but either way, I'll handle it. "She's that woman I told you I was sleeping with before."

Her eyes widen. "Oh." She glances at her again, then back at me. "I see."

She doesn't say anything else, and I wonder what she's thinking. Is she comparing herself to Rebecca? Because there is no comparison. Scarlett has so much class and natural beauty; I don't see anyone in a room except her. Rebecca is beautiful, and I won't deny that, but that doesn't mean anything to me, because I only have eyes for the woman sitting in front of me.

"Are you okay?" I ask her quietly, not wanting her to be upset, because she has no reason to be.

"Yeah," she says, nodding. "Why wouldn't I be?"

But she doesn't look at me, she's still looking into her plate.

I study her, not sure if she's doing the whole *I'm fine* thing even when she's not—which will probably result in her exploding sometime soon—or if she really is fine.

"Okay," I say casually. "Do you want anything for dessert?"

I can see that Rebecca is on a date too, so hopefully she won't come over and that will be that.

The woman has no shame though. . . . One of the reasons I used to fuck her.

Not that I'd ever admit anything like that out loud.

"Are you going to get anything? Maybe we could share something," she says, rubbing her flat stomach as if she's full. "What do you think?"

"Why don't you choose something, and we can share it," I tell her, just as someone walks up and stands next to the table.

Ahh, fuck. Here we go.

"Hello, Jaxon, long time no see," Rebecca purrs, resting her long blue nails on my shoulder.

"Rebecca," I say, acknowledging her. I don't believe in being rude or mean to women I've been with. A man doesn't do that. But I also want Scarlett to know that she's my priority. So I have two options here. I can either tell Rebecca it's nice to see her and wait until she walks away, then salvage the situation with Scarlett, or I can introduce the two women and hope for the best.

Olivia used to always say, *Only people with class introduce people to each other.*

So that decides my next move.

"Rebecca, this is Scarlett. Scarlett, Rebecca."

It might be a little awkward, but it allows me to bring Scarlett into the situation, letting both women know which one is more important.

"Is this your new girlfriend?" Rebecca asks, after Scarlett says hello to her. "Or just another *friend*?"

She crossed a line with that comment, so I feel no guilt when I say, "I don't think that's any of your business."

"I guess not anymore," she mutters, flashing Scarlett another look before sauntering away.

Jesus Christ.

"Maybe we should just skip dessert," Scarlett now suggests, looking down at her empty plate. "Unless you really want some?"

She's upset, and I can see why. If I ran into someone who had been with her, I wouldn't like it either. It's not a logical thing. I didn't even know Scarlett existed when I was with Rebecca, and everyone has a past. But I get it.

"I'm fine," I say, asking for the bill. "I can get you something to take home if you like."

"No, thank you," she says, her tone subdued.

Shit.

I pay the bill, leave a tip, and lead her out with my hand on her lower back. I open the car door for her, then close it before walking to the driver's side and sliding in. The second we're on the road, I ask her, "You going to tell me what's going on in that pretty mind of yours?"

She's silent for a few seconds, then says, "It's not the fact that you slept with her. I mean, it's not like you slept with her after you met me. It's just that . . ."

"What?" I ask gently as she trails off, not finishing her sentence.

"You won't even kiss me," she blurts out, looking from the window to me. "She's had you, and fine, whatever, but I haven't even had a kiss from you. Why don't you want to kiss me? Is it because you want to fix me first? Because I don't need fixing, Jaxon, I just need love." She huffs, and then adds, "And you to fucking kiss me."

I don't think I've ever heard her swear before.

Safely, I wait until I'm able to park on the side of the road, then turn and grab her face, and kiss her. Not just a small, quick kiss, no, I *kiss* her. I taste her lips, I let my tongue explore hers; I give her everything in this kiss. She tastes sweet, her lips soft, and the quiet humming sound she makes deep in her throat urges me on even more. My hand moves to the nape of her neck, where I gently hold her.

And when I pull away only because I need to catch my breath, she's wide-eyed, panting, her lips still open.

Then, without saying a word, I drive back onto the road, and back to her house.

She sits there quietly, maybe processing what just happened, but I don't miss the upward curve to her lips.

She's smiling to herself.

I try to keep my face straight, hiding my amusement, and also try to control my dick, which is hard and wanting a little attention from the woman next to me. I wasn't going to kiss her so soon, but I can't have her thinking I don't want her. I had no idea she was waiting for me to kiss her so badly, or I would have done it earlier.

She has a demanding side, and I find myself drawn to it.

The more I get to know her, the more I like her.

Olivia would have liked her.

Yeah, she really would have.

chapter 18

SCARLETT

I BRING MY FINGERS TO my lips, touching them. Wow. I've never been kissed like that in my life. Ever. I want more. I *need* more, right this second. Can he drive faster so we can get home? I shift in the seat, feeling a little . . . needy. I've never been so turned on from a kiss before.

Crap.

The kiss was smoking hot.

The tension rises in the car, and I don't know if I should say something or not. Is he going to kiss me again? Or did he just kiss me because I pushed him? If that's the case, I have no problem pushing more. I don't think I've ever wanted something so much. He can't just tease me like that . . . give me a taste of passion and then take it away. I've always read about chemistry and connection and sexual tension, but until right now, I realize I've never experienced it.

We finally get to my house after what feels like an hour but was probably only fifteen minutes. I open the door and get out, waiting for him before walking to the front door.

Neither of us says anything.

I unlock the door, step inside, and wait for him to enter before shutting and locking it behind me.

"I hope you enjoyed dinner." He pauses, and then adds, "and maybe next time we'll actually make it to the movies."

"I think I know what the highlight of the night was," I say, feeling bold.

Horniness will do that to you.

It trumps all other feelings.

"And what was that," he asks, closing the space between us and gripping my hips with his strong hands. He walks me backward until the back of my legs hit the couch.

"You going to pretend like you don't know?" I croon, licking my bottom lip. "Perhaps you need a reminder."

"Perhaps I do."

I crook my finger at him. "You're going to have to come down a little."

He lowers his head.

"A little bit more," I whisper.

In a quick movement, he lifts me in the air against his hard body so our faces are in line.

And then, *I* kiss *him.*

I take out all my frustration on him—the car ride, and the fact that he took so long to kiss me in the first place, and then only did it because I egged him on. I wrap my arms around his neck, pulling him as close as he can get without being inside of me, and show him that there's passion in me, dying to come out, to be let free. I just needed to give it to the right person this time, and that person is him. I know he's been patient with me in some aspects, and I know he's not a mind reader, so I need to tell him what I want and what I'm ready for, and this is me doing just that.

I'm so ready.

It's me who ends the kiss this time. I look into those gray eyes and smile when he says, "You are the furthest thing from cold, Scarlett. Fuck, you taste so good." He lays me back on the couch, covering me with his body without putting his weight on me. "I need more."

That's what I'm talking about. "Me too."

He starts to kiss down my neck, the sensations indescribable. I arch my neck, giving him more room, silently begging for more. My whole body is tingling, and I've never felt so alive. I squeeze my thighs together and run my hands down the material of his shirt. I want to touch his bare skin. I lift the shirt up and gently run my nails down his back. Jaxon moves the neck of my dress to the side to kiss my collarbone, and I make a soft moaning noise that I can't stop even if I want to. When he slides off the couch onto his knees, I miss him immediately. I want him back on top of me, his mouth all over me, I need more torturous kisses. He does something even better though. He pulls me to sit up, lifts my dress up, and I help him pull it over my head.

"Fuck," he groans, and I grin.

I'm wearing the new lingerie I bought today, a black strappy lace bra and matching panty set. The bra has a thin strap that goes around under the cup part, which gives it an even sexier, almost bondage-like look. When I saw it I knew it was perfect. He cups my breasts over the bra, then pulls the cups down and kisses each nipple, before sucking on them in turn. Pleasure shoots through my body, right to between my legs. I've never experienced passion like this, and now that I know what I've been missing, it almost makes me sad. So much time wasted, but better late than never. The timing is finally right for me, and I'm going to enjoy this more than I can explain.

Jaxon glances up at me and says, "Tell me if you want me to stop."

I know he's worried about me, but I'm fine. The past is staying where it belongs, and I'm in the now, with him. I know he won't hurt me. Nothing he's done has triggered me or set me off, and I think it's because of the simple fact that I trust him. Maybe I trust too easily, but I think it all comes down to making sure it's the right person. It feels right with Jaxon. I will never regret this, or him.

"Okay," I tell him, then kiss his lips, my tongue doing a little exploring while his fingers gently tease my nipples. He breaks the kiss to bury his face in my breasts again, then he undoes my bra and throws it on the floor.

"Shame to take that off, but you look even better without it," he says, looking into my eyes. "You are fucking beautiful, Scarlett. You have no idea what you do to me."

I feel beautiful when he looks at me like that, like the most beautiful woman in the world. He pays a little more attention to my breasts before he starts to kiss a trail down my stomach. When he stops at the top of my panties, our eyes lock. When I give him a slight nod, he pulls them off. Ever so slowly, he spreads my thighs. He can see all of me right now. My sex is right in his face, but he's still looking into my eyes, something passing between us. There's something here, I can feel it and I hope he can too. At the first swipe of his tongue, a shiver runs down my spine and my mouth opens as my breath hitches. And then he lowers his head, finally breaking eye contact, licking me everywhere, sucking on my clit, and driving me absolutely insane. I thread my fingers through his thick head of dark hair and gently tug, needing to do something. I can't sit still. The pleasure is too much, and it's been so long. He's so good with his tongue; I can barely handle it. I'm panting, my thighs are starting to tremble, and I can feel myself on the verge of something amazing. I lift my hips up, squirming, and he pins them back down onto the couch, keeping me in place, then continues to lick me and suck on my clit until I'm whimpering.

When I come, it hits me in one quick shot. My thighs shake as the pleasure spreads outward, all over my body, making me cry out. When I've come down from a euphoric high, I'm breathing heavily, and I'm tired, like he's wrung every last ounce of energy out of me. My body is like jelly, there's no tension left in me.

"Oh my" is all I can think to say. "That was amazing, Jaxon. I don't even know what to say right now."

He wipes his mouth with the back of his hand, kisses my stomach, and then moves to sit next to me.

"Where are you going?" I ask him, wondering if he thinks I'm just going to sit here and do nothing about his erection. I just need a moment to come back to myself.

"Nowhere," he murmurs, watching me with heat in his eyes. "I'm not going anywhere, Scarlett."

"Good," I whisper.

Because I haven't even started with him yet.

Time to put my newfound skills to practice.

chapter 19

JAXON

*M*Y LITTLE TEMPTRESS. I love it when she's confident; nothing turns me on more.

"And what do you plan on doing with me exactly?" I ask, leaning back on the couch and watching her, like a wolf watches its prey. I know I said tonight would be for her, but I'm not going to say no if she wants to please me. It's up to her though; there's no pressure for her to do anything. Naked, she stands in all her beauty, giving me a show of that stunning body. From her tiny waist to her sexy wide hips and perfectly shaped thighs, the woman is a fucking goddess. She brought me to my knees, and apparently she's about to return the favor. She lowers herself in front of me and reaches out, a little timidly, to undo my belt. I lie back and make no movement. This is all on her. If she asks me for something I'll give it to her, but otherwise I'm just going to sit here and see what she's going to do. She gets the belt undone and then lowers my zipper.

"Help me slide these off," she says, so I quickly remove my shoes, then slide the jeans down my ass and thighs. She pulls them off my legs. I'm left in my boxer shorts and my shirt, which is the next thing she demands that I lose. "Take your shirt off. And your boxer shorts."

I oblige, removing the items, then sit on her couch buck naked. She takes me in from head to penis, starting with my eyes, then down to my chest, my pecs, my abs, and then my cock. She lingers on my cock for a few moments, her eyes going wide. "It's even bigger than the guys on the video," she mutters, raising her eyes. "I knew it."

"Babe," I grit out, my cock practically pointing at her, begging for some attention. She's naked in front of me, on her knees, those tits right in front of me, and I'm about to lose my damn mind.

Oh, right. I'm being patient.

I take a deep breath, control my body, and relax.

What's a little blue balls, right?

She licks her lips, then takes my cock in her hands at the base. Then she lowers her head, licking the tip before sliding as much as she can into her mouth and swirling her tongue around it.

Fuck.

I gently run my hands through her hair, making sure I don't push her head down or anything like that. That video she was watching must have been extremely educational, because everything she does feels so good. She starts pumping her hand at the base and using her mouth on the head, a combination that has me on the edge. A few more deep sucks, and yeah, that's me done.

"I'm going to come, Scarlett," I grit out between clenched teeth. I try to gently move her head back because that wasn't a fucking warning. I'm about to explode. "Scarlett."

She doesn't move, or let go of me.

She keeps sucking until she's wrung every drop of my come out of me.

And then she swallows it, and licks her lips afterward.

Fuck.

I think I've died and gone to heaven.

"Wow," I breathe, picking her up and bringing her onto my lap. "You're amazing, you know that?"

"You liked it?" she asks, burying her face in my neck.

"You couldn't tell?" I tease, stroking my hands down her back. "It was perfect. You're perfect. Loving that is not something I can fake, Scarlett."

"That's true," she says, kissing my neck, amusement in her tone.

We just hold each other for a little while, feeling my skin against hers for the first time, peppering soft kisses on whatever part of her I can find. Her skin is so pale, soft, and smooth; I could touch it all day. She has a rare beauty about her, almost an old-school beauty, like she should've been born in an earlier era. I don't know how else to explain it. She just has something about her that is so different from all the women I've been meeting.

"Can we go to my bed now?" she asks after a while, not letting go of me.

"You want me to stay the night?" I ask, thinking how much I'd love to have her in my arms all night long. I can't remember the last time I actually stayed the whole night in a woman's bed without sneaking out in the early hours.

"Yes, of course," she says, sounding sleepy and sated, and I haven't even been inside her. I definitely think we should save that for another day considering the way tonight escalated. I stand with her in my arms and carry her to her room, laying her down on the white sheets, then sliding in next to her. She rests her head on my chest, wrapping her arm around me, and falls straight to sleep. I can't remember the last time I cuddled a woman all night, but I wouldn't want to be anywhere else right now.

The second my eyes close, I fall asleep.

I WAKE UP FEELING warm and content.

Scarlett is still fast asleep next to me, so I gently slide her off me and get out of bed. Luckily for me I woke up early enough to head home and get ready for work, because we didn't set an alarm. Wishing I had time to make her some breakfast, or perhaps pick something up for her, I write her a note and place it on the bedside table, kiss her forehead, then get into my car.

I already can't wait to see her again tonight.

THE NEXT CASE I'M working on is another highly publicized one. A well-known television host by the name of Sharon Beetle has been charged with sexual assault against one of her coworkers. It's going to be a long court matter with a lot of media attention because both involved are public figures.

After Ms. Beetle leaves my office, Hunter walks in, eyes wide. "She's a babe."

"See, you should've done criminal law," I tease, cleaning up my desk.

"You saying all the hot women are criminals? I don't know, I get my quota of hot single moms," he jokes, dropping into the chair in front of me.

"Yeah, ones that are getting a divorce," I remind him, smirking. "Have you ever gone there with any of them?"

"Nah," he says, flashing me a grin. "I don't shit where I eat. It'd be too messy to get involved with any of them, plus I see firsthand how money-hungry most of them are. Want to grab some lunch? I had a date . . . but well, that's not going to happen now."

"Why, what happened?"

"Well, she didn't exactly look like her pictures. She lied. A lot," he says, jaw going tight. "I think we need to go to Riley's to make up for it."

"You got catfished?" I ask, barking out a laugh. "Ahh, fuck. Sorry, bro. Come on, I'll buy you lunch and a beer. Riley's it is."

"That would make me feel a little better," he grumbles, playing with the watch on his wrist. "I don't think online dating is for me."

"Old ways are the best ways," I advise, standing up and closing my briefcase. "What's wrong? Have no game? And how come Kat, Tristan, and Yvonne aren't in here giving you shit about this? Or is it only me who gets that?"

"As if I'm going to tell Kat," he says, rising to his feet and stepping toward the door. "She'll never let me live it down."

"Tell me what?" Kat asks, sticking her head in. "What'd I miss?"

"Nothing," we both say at the same time.

She looks between the two of us. "What happened? Is it women problems? Because I'll have you know that I give excellent advice."

Hunter and I share a look, then exit the room, walking past her.

She actually does give wonderful advice, if I'm being honest, but she'll also give you shit about it later. She follows behind us, an amused expression on her face. "Oh, come on, I'm not that bad."

I wave 'bye to her and exit the building.

Time to try to cheer Hunter up a little.

chapter 20

SCARLETT

"DID YOU MAKE ALL this yourself?" I ask Jaxon as he pulls everything out of the picnic basket. Bread, different cheeses, crackers, olives, sun-dried tomatoes, wine . . . He's thought of everything.

"No," he admits, looking a little sheepish. "There's a place that sells everything just like this, so you just buy it and you're good to go."

"That's a pretty cool idea," I say as I cut a slice of cheese and place it on a cracker. Tonight he's taking me to the concert. Are these things normal men do? I have no idea. I think I need to find some girlfriends so I can talk about these things.

"I'm glad you like it," he murmurs, popping an olive into his mouth.

"Not as much as I liked last night," I mutter under my breath, then grin cheekily and take a bite.

Jaxon stills, then starts laughing, his shoulders shaking. "Plenty more where that came from."

"There'd better be," I say, lip twitching.

He leans over and wipes a little cheese from my lip with his finger. "Feeling bold today, are we?"

"And less tightly wound," I add, laughing when he shakes his head at me in exasperation. "I haven't had an orgasm in quite a while, okay? I forgot how good they are. And that one . . . well, it was indescribable."

"Is this your usual picnic conversation?" he asks, kissing me on the temple, his tone laced with enjoyment. "Or maybe you just feel more comfortable around me now."

"I think this is the first official picnic I've ever been on," I tell him. "How about you? Been on many picnics?"

"Only one," he admits, pouring some wine into two glasses. "I think it was with my first serious girlfriend. I was trying to be romantic, but it didn't exactly work out."

"What happened?" I ask, wishing it was me who he'd met back then. How different my life would have been. Then again, we probably wouldn't be together right now. Timing is everything, after all.

"I put some candles all around the blanket, except one of them fell over and the blanket caught on fire," he explains, cringing. "I didn't get laid that night."

I cover my mouth with my hands, then start laughing, unable to control my reaction.

"Glad you're amused," he grumbles, trying to sound put out, but I don't miss the twitch of his lip.

He's secretly amused too.

"So you weren't always smooth, huh?" I tease, lying back on the blanket and turning to face him. "And how come I don't get any candles?"

"Because I learned my lesson the first time," he says, leaning over me and giving me a lingering kiss. "I liked spending the night with you last night."

"All we did was sleep," I point out. I thought maybe he would've reached for me in the middle of the night, but he didn't. I have the feeling he's letting me call the shots, letting me decide how fast or slow we go, and I like that about him. I can't lie though, sometimes it makes me question whether he wants me as much as I want him.

"I know. It was a good sleep, and I loved having you in my arms," he says, kissing me again. "Why, what did you want to happen?"

I purse my lips as I think how to word this. "I don't know. I thought you'd maybe make love to me. I know you're waiting for me to be ready, but I am." I sigh and add, "I guess I'm just going to have to keep making the first move, aren't I?"

"Babe, you slept like a log last night. You didn't wake up once, so I don't think you could have made the first move even if you'd wanted to."

"Well, tonight is another night, isn't it?" I say, lifting my chin. "And you know what? I still haven't seen your house. What are you hiding there?"

"You can come stay at my place if you like." He grins, kissing my forehead. "You can see what I'm hiding for yourself."

"I think it's going to be super clean and tidy, just like your office."

"The office has a cleaner."

"Maybe your house has a cleaner too, then," I fire back, taking an olive and some feta cheese and putting them into my mouth. I chew slowly as we both watch each other. "Jaxon."

"Scarlett."

"I would've slept with you even if you had almost set me on

fire," I tell him, smirking. I'm in a playful mood today, I just feel so happy. Jaxon is one of the first people I can spend time with without still feeling lonely. I never knew what I was missing out on until now.

He shakes his head, then lies back on the blanket next to me.

We look up into the sky, my arm touching his, and just enjoy being in each other's presence.

It's comfortable between us, whether we're talking or being silent. It's intimate, whether we're kissing or not, and I feel safe.

Safe.

A notion I thought impossible.

But here we are.

And I'm going to enjoy every second, and live it like it's my last.

AFTER THE CONCERT, WE go back to Jaxon's house. It's everything I thought it would be—a modern spacious house decorated in neutral tones, and the biggest TV and couch I've ever seen.

"It's stunning," I say, looking around. "It's the classiest bachelor pad I've ever seen." I then add, "Okay, I think it's the only bachelor pad I've been in, but still."

He laughs at that and grabs me a bottle of water from his fridge while I look at the photos on his shelf. "Who is this? She's beautiful."

She has dark hair and an olive skin tone and stunning green eyes. In the picture, she's looking at the camera, but he's looking at her. And the way he's looking at her, I can tell that he adores her. Is this an ex-girlfriend?

"Olivia," he says, handing me the water and then pulling

me away from the shelf. I take it he doesn't want to talk about it. What happened to this Olivia? How come he's never mentioned her? I decide not to press it, because he can talk about it in his own time, if he ever chooses to open up to me. The thought that he might not hurts. But if he needs time, I can give him that. He's been so patient with me, so I can be patient with him. He gives me a tour of his house. When we stop in his bedroom my jaw drops at the size of his bed.

"That's the biggest bed I've ever seen. It looks bigger than a king!" I sit down on it and stare up at him. "What do you need such a big bed for? Been having many orgies lately?"

He throws his head back and laughs, then decides to give me some shit back. "Have you been watching more videos? This time with orgies in them?"

I stick my tongue out at him, then lie back on the bed. "It's so comfortable."

"I had it custom-made for my room," he explains, sitting down next to me and resting his hand on my bare stomach as my top rides up. "Do you want to have a shower?"

"With you?" I ask, brows rising. "Do you think I'm going to say no to that?"

"I should hope not," he says as he starts to undress me. I lay there, holding my breath as he removes my jeans first, then my panties, then my top and bra. I watch him, as he takes in my body, from head to toe, nothing hidden. It's quite a vulnerable thing, to have a man with a perfect body look at mine. I'm a little on the curvy side, but I'm not overweight or anything like that. Still, I'm far from perfect. Darren would tell me I needed to lose weight, but the look in Jaxon's eyes tells me that he likes what he sees. He likes me just the way I am.

Acceptance.

Another new thing for me.

He starts to strip down, and now it's my turn to watch. He gives me a bit of a show, removing his T-shirt and flexing for me, which makes me laugh and get hot at the same time. My eyes are still glued on those abs of his when he takes off his jeans and boxer shorts.

He's hard.

Why do I feel like he's always hard?

"Come on," he commands in a husky tone, offering me his hand. I take it, and he walks me into his bathroom, which might just be my new favorite room in his house. It's lavish, with a wide two-headed shower and a spa.

"Wow," I murmur, while he turns on the water. "Remind me to get the details of your interior designer."

I feel him freeze up next to me, and I know something is wrong. "What is it?"

"Nothing," he says, brushing it off. "Don't worry about it."

He goes cold, and for a second I feel a little awkward. Why won't he just tell me whatever it is that gets to him? Does it have something to do with Olivia? I don't know. I know I shouldn't push, but I don't want to have to watch what I say to not have him go cold on me and ruin the moment between us.

"You can't do that, Jaxon," I decide to say, in a soft tone. I don't want to start our first argument, but I want him to know that it doesn't exactly feel good when he shuts me out.

Gray eyes soften. He takes me in his arms, and places me under the warm water. My hair gets wet, and even though I washed it this morning, I don't mind.

"It's not something I like to talk about," he explains, water dripping down his body. "I just need a little time before I can talk about it. Can you give me that?"

"Okay."

I can leave it alone for now and hope that, when he's ready, he will talk about it. I lift up on my tiptoes and kiss him. The perfect distraction. The mood shifts and everything else is forgotten for now. He pushes me back against the cold tiles, kissing me deeply, his hands wandering down the sides of my stomach and landing on my butt. He grips it, and lifts me up, pinning me against the tiles. I wrap my legs around his waist and my arms around his shoulders. He's strong, and it's so sexy. Everything about him is sexy.

Including his mind. Especially his mind.

His dick is hard against my skin, so hard. "I want you," I say against his lips, droplets of water trying to escape into my mouth. "Please, Jaxon."

"Let's go to the bedroom," he says, about to put me down, but I want him here, like this, and right now. We can make love in the bedroom afterward; right now I want him to take me against the wall. I've never been fucked in this position, never been held up like this before, and it's exciting and new and I want to experience it with him.

"No, here. Please."

I think it's the begging that gets to him, because one moment he looks like he's not sure, and the next he's slowly sliding himself inside of me.

I dig my nails into his back and hold on for dear life.

chapter 21

JAXON

WHY DO I ALWAYS lose control when I'm with her? No, better yet, why can't I say no to her and those hazel eyes? With all the restraint I muster, I slowly push myself into her, not wanting to hurt her. She's so fucking tight, and I'm not a small man. I take my time, groaning when I'm finally all in and resting my forehead against hers. This would have been much easier on my bed, which is why I wanted to take her there, but the little minx didn't want to. She never wants the easy option.

"You feel so good," I tell her as I start to move, thrusting in and out in a gentle pace, holding her weight up by her thighs with my hands. "Are you okay?"

She nods, her eyes heavy-lidded, and starts kissing me hungrily.

Yeah, she's more than okay.

I push away the satisfaction I feel at that and continue to . . .

I can't even say fuck. It's more than fucking. So much more. Her breasts press up against my chest, her pebbled nipples begging for attention. With one hand, I turn the shower off, and carry her into my room and onto my bed. I don't bother grabbing a towel, there's no time for that shit. I lift her off my dick and lay her down on the bed, spreading her thighs so I can have a taste. I don't think I'll ever get tired of eating her pussy. Actually, changing my mind, I decide to roll with her onto my back, so she's straddling me.

"Climb up on me and put your pussy on my face," I tell her.

Her eyes widen. "You want me to . . . what?"

"Sit on my face," I clarify, running my hands over the globes of her ass. I give her a light slap. "I want my mouth on you, but I want to try it this way this time."

"Okay," she agrees, looking a bit skeptical, going by how wide her eyes still are. She climbs up, a little shyly, and spreads her thighs on each side of my face. I flash her a grin that's all teeth, then lift her down onto my face, my tongue ready and waiting for a taste of her sweet flesh. She makes a moaning sound at first contact, and I can tell the second she gives in, as her body relaxes and she grabs hold of my headboard. I love it when she loses her inhibitions like this, when she forgets all her worries and insecurities and just enjoys the moment and the pleasure. There's nothing like it. I put my tongue to work until she comes, her thighs squeezing the shit out of my head. Once she's done, I grip her hips and gently lift her off me, laying her onto her back.

"Are you on the pill?" I ask. I don't want to use a condom, but I will if I have to. The feel of her on my dick raw is the best thing I've ever felt, but I can't let that cloud my senses.

She nods. "Yeah, I am."

That's good enough for me. I slide back into her, muttering a curse, and start to move. My lips find her breasts and I take my time playing with them, licking, sucking, and running my teeth along them. I look up at her from between them, our eyes connect in an intense moment. I want her to come again before I do, and I hope I can hold out until then. I reach down and play with her clit, using her wetness on my finger, which does the trick.

Only then do I allow myself to finish, looking her in the eyes and letting her see every emotion that crosses my face, all the pleasure that she's giving me.

"Fuck," I grit out, my chest heaving. I pull out of her slowly, and then lie next to her on the bed, reaching my arm out so she can rest her head on it. She does, and kisses my rough cheek before settling.

She's quiet for a moment before she says, "I could get used to that."

I let out a deep chuckle, then turn to face her and give her a quick kiss. "So could I."

"Jaxon?"

"Yes, babe?"

"How soon can we do that again?" she asks, her teeth sinking into her lower lip.

Apparently I've created a monster.

A beautiful monster.

I REACH FOR HER during the night—three times. She's so giving, so uninhibited in bed, I don't know how anyone could ever call her cold and frigid. I guess we all know Darren was a fucking idiot, but still, I can't get over the fact he tried to blame their problems in the bedroom on her. She's fire, not ice. She's everything a woman should be. And fuck him for not noticing that, or for noticing and deciding to destroy her anyway.

"Good morning," she croons, her voice husky with sleep. She stretches her arms above her head. "You have the best bed. I think we should stay here from now on."

I smile and kiss the top of her head. "What do you want for breakfast?"

"I can make it for us," she says, yawning. "Do you have stuff to make pancakes? And some bacon maybe?"

"No, I'm making it," I tell her. "You're going to lie in bed and relax."

"You're the one who has to go to work," she argues, trying to sit up. I pull her back down, and pin her with my weight.

"Will you do what you're told for once?" I ask, getting turned on again at the feeling of being on top of her.

"I did everything you asked last night," she reminds me, lifting her stubborn little chin. "I even sat on your face. I'd never done that before."

"If you're trying to distract me, Scarlett, it's working," I groan, feeling myself getting hard. I haven't fucked this much since I was a lot younger, yet apparently she brings it out of me.

"I just want to make us breakfast is all," she huffs, trying to push me off her. "And it's not because I'm a woman, blah blah. It's because you have a long day of work ahead, so let me make myself a little useful! You don't let me pay for anything, and you're always doing nice things for me, so can't you let me have this little thing?"

Well, fuck. All I wanted to do was make the woman breakfast, since she's already cooked me a meal I don't want her to think I expect that from her. I love and appreciate it, yes, but I don't expect it. I've been looking after myself for a long time; I don't need a woman to do those things for me, but it is nice.

I sigh and roll off her. "Fine, you win. But for the record, you've cooked for me before. You do nice things for me, so this isn't a one-way street."

"I never said it was." She greets me with a smug look, jumping off the bed, her boobs bouncing enticingly. "It's just this is one of the things I like doing for you, and it's one of the only ways I know how to show you that I care."

She shakes her ass at me a little, then runs into the kitchen. Naked.

Where did this woman come from? She's come so far from the woman I first met in my office that day. She's come out of her shell, and I like that she's being who she was meant to be the entire time. It's amazing what can happen to someone when they feel safe, when they know that nothing they do will be too much to handle. A sense of pride fills me at how things have turned around in such a short time. Not for me, but for her. She might not think it, but she's strong.

Resilient.

And whether she knows it yet or not—mine.

chapter 22

SCARLETT

AFTER BREAKFAST JAXON DROPS me off at home and heads to work while I get ready for a day at the shelter. When I arrive there, I smile as I run into one of the other volunteers, Becky, walking two of the dogs.

"Good morning, Scarlett," she says, smiling warmly at me. Her smile soon drops as she tells me that three more dogs have been brought in today.

"I'll go give them some love," I tell her, heading inside. I step inside the gate and sit down on the floor next to the first dog. She's scared, I can tell, her tail between her legs. I wonder if her owners brought her here to abandon her, or if she was found on the street.

"Hello, sweetie," I tell her, reaching my arm out. I make a gentle noise and slowly she comes next to me, letting me touch her. Sometimes your life only gets better with a second chance, and I hope that that's the case for all the dogs here.

I stay at the shelter for a few hours, then go home to take a shower. Once I'm dressed, I decide to go shopping for a few things. After buying some plants and loading them into my car, I walk through the mall, having a look at all the clothes and variety stores. I come to a stop when I see Valentina in one of the jewelry stores, browsing through some bracelets. I smile when she sees me.

"Hey," she says, coming over to me straightaway. "How are you?"

"Not bad, how are you?" I ask in return, knowing she's probably not doing too well considering the man she loves is behind bars.

"I've been better," she admits, pushing away an errant red curl. "But I'm trying to be positive and keep busy. It's one of the girls' birthdays, so I'm trying to find something for her, except it's hard to buy something for a woman who has everything."

"Want some help?" I ask, not knowing why I offered. Even though we should probably hate each other, I find I feel a connection with her instead.

"I'd like that," she says, a little sadness to her smile. We browse multiple pieces until we find a bracelet that's really different and unusual. I think Valentina likes it because of the dragon pendant it has on it too.

"Faye will love this," she beams, glancing at the now-wrapped gift. "I'm going to go grab something for lunch, want to join me?"

"Sure," I say, happy to have some company. "What do you feel like eating?"

"There's a food court here, so we can just grab whatever we feel like," she says, looking at me like she wants to say something.

"What is it?" I ask her, letting her know with my tone that it's okay, she can say whatever she likes.

"I was reading some information about the case; Faye gave it to me . . .," she says, looking down. "He stole from you, his wife. I don't know why, but I would never have suspected that."

"It's okay," I say, forcing a smile. "I honestly think he only married me for my money and the property I owned."

It hurts to say that, not because of anything to do with Darren exactly, but because it's an ego hit no matter who we're talking about and it hurts my pride to admit it.

"I'm so glad he's dead," she admits, cringing as the words leave her lips. "I know that sounds bad, but with what he did to you . . . It hurts me to know I wasn't the only woman whose life he made a living hell. I'm sorry you had to go through whatever he put you through."

"Me too," I say, linking my arm through hers. "I wouldn't wish that on anyone, and I'm sorry Irish had to pay the price, but both of us are free now, and I think we need to make the most of that."

"You're right," she nods, curls bouncing. "I'm trying to. It's hard without Ardan—Irish—here, you know? I know it doesn't seem that bad, especially after everything you and I have been through, but the man is my soul mate and I feel like I'm just wandering around aimlessly without him."

"I'm sorry," I say, meaning it. "I would never wish any more pain on you."

"It's not your fault, Scarlett," she says gently, stopping and looking me in the eye. "No one blames you for anything. You're innocent in all of this. It sucks that Irish has to do prison time, it really does, but he killed Darren, so it is what it is. Two years will fly by, right?"

"Right," I agree with her.

"I know that people will probably look at us and wonder how we both got caught with a man like Darren, but I think only you will understand when I say he wasn't always like that," she says to me, shrugging. "Before the drugs, I mean. He was good to me. Loving."

"I know," I whisper. "But the person he became was a monster."

"He was," Valentina agrees. "And I don't feel bad for how things have ended up. He was a weak man. Did you know his father was abusive to his mother? Instead of breaking the cycle, he ended up turning out just like him."

I actually didn't know that about Darren, so I stay silent. He never spoke about his now-deceased father much, and his mother is in a senior-care facility. Despite the pain he caused me, it does make me feel better to understand where that side of him came from.

We stop at the food court for pizza and soda and sit down opposite each other. We talk about Darren, about what we went through, the mental abuse. The physical. The threats. His using his cop buddies to make it look like he was doing nothing wrong. Feeling like there was no way out. And then we talk about now. About being free. About how life goes on, and that our past doesn't define us, all it's done is make us stronger. I used to see myself as weak, a doormat, someone who was lost and too scared to get out of the situation I was in. But now I'm out, and I'm ready to take on the world.

"So are you seeing anyone?" she asks me, making me almost choke on my bite of pizza. "That's a yes." She smirks, arching her brow. "Come on, give me the goss. Your secrets are safe with me."

"Well," I say, swallowing the rest of my bite.

"Who is it? I'm sure the men of the city will all be in mourning," she says, and I smile as I remember my conversation with Preston and his friend in the diner.

"It's actually my lawyer," I blurt out, bracing myself for her reaction.

"Jaxon Bentley?" she asks, eyes going wide. "Fucking hell, when you upgrade, you *upgrade*. He's so hot! And badass! Even Faye admitted so, and trust me, that's no small feat."

"He's . . . amazing," I say with a sigh. "He saved me, and he keeps saving me every day."

"Sounds like you have it bad," she says, taking a sip of her soda. "I'm glad you've found someone worthy of you."

"I'm glad you did too."

We share a smile.

It's nice to have another woman to talk to, because I think Aunt Leona is sick of hearing me rave on about Jaxon and how wonderful he is.

"I'll give you my number," she says once the meal is done. "Call me and we can hang out or chat. Whatever you want."

"I'd like that, Valentina," I reply, feeling really good about the chat we had, and about us being friends. Who would have thought? But it makes sense when you think about it. I think only we can know what the other has been through, what we've overcome in our lives. Like I said, we're connected by our pasts, by pain, by the same man who tried to break both of our spirits and failed.

He failed.

"There's my ride," she says, nodding toward the big black motorcycle that pulls into the parking lot. "Ever since Irish got locked up, they aren't letting me out of their sight."

"So who is that one?" I ask, as the huge man parks the bike and gets off, patiently waiting for Valentina.

"That's Vinnie," she says, waving at him. "Where's your car parked?"

"Just over there," I tell her as I point to the left. "It's not far, I can see it from here."

"Okay. I'll wait until I see you drive off safely—you never know these days."

She's sweet.

"You know what? With all his faults and evil ways, Darren did have good taste in women."

She throws her head back and laughs, and it's a glorious sight. "You're right on that one. Always look for the positive, right?"

"You have to," I say, shaking my head at her as we share this moment of amusement.

We hug as we say 'bye and head our separate ways, but I know it's not the last time I'll see her.

And that makes me happy.

HE THRUSTS INTO ME from behind, while I bite down on the pillow, moaning. I feel like I've been missing out on good sex and now I need to make up for it. So when Jaxon walked through my door this evening, he didn't stand a chance. He stops moving his hips and cups both of my breasts with his hands, sliding them underneath me.

"Oh my god," I utter as he pinches the nipples, then continues a slow, delicious grind that has me so wet, I can feel it all down my inner thighs.

"Beautiful," he murmurs, placing a kiss on my spine, and letting my breasts free. His hands go back to my hips, gripping then firmly as he pushes back and forth. "Play with your clit for me, Scarlett."

I instantly do as I'm told. Wanting to wet my finger, I dip it inside of me, stopping when my finger touches his cock.

Fuck.

Moving my finger up, I start to rub my clit, just the way Jaxon normally does, knowing it'll soon make me come, even though it doesn't feel as good as when he does it. He pulls out of me, rolls me over, and slides back inside. Kissing me, he continues to absolutely destroy my past sex life, touching my mind and my body. Having a connection like this, a mental one—I can't explain how it makes the sex so much better.

We come together this time, and it's something I will never forget.

Gray and hazel clash, our bodies bringing each other pleasure in sync, both of us completely vulnerable and open to each other in this moment.

No boundaries, no walls, just us.

A gentle kiss, and then he's off me, but right beside me.

"A man could get used to coming home to that every day," he says in a raspy tone. As soon as he'd opened the door, I'd run up to him, jumped into his arms, and started kissing him. It probably is the best way to be greeted after a long day at work. That, and I cooked him a delicious dinner, which we now get to eat as soon as we can make our bodies move again.

I'd say it's the small things in life, but with Jaxon, nothing about him is small.

I grin and roll over into him.

chapter 23

JAXON

I'M NOT A MAN who has a big ego or anything like that, but I'm a man who is aware.

And I know when a woman is hitting on me.

Normally I'd be the first to smile and charm said woman, but this situation is a little different. One, she's not Scarlett, and two, she's my new client. It's obviously not a line I haven't crossed, but I don't consider myself single anymore, and it's making for a very awkward meeting. There's also the issue that I'm defending her from a sexual assault charge while she's hitting on me. Oh, the irony. If I've ever questioned a client's innocence, it's definitely hers.

How do I get into shit like this?

"Are you free for a drink, Mr. Bentley?" Sharon Beetle asks, cocking her hip to the side. She's an attractive woman, like Hunter pointed out, but I'm not interested.

"I actually have to get home, Ms. Beetle," I tell her, closing up my briefcase. "Let me walk you to your car."

The sun has just gone down, and I'll walk her to her car like I would any woman who leaves my office at this time. Sharon is a well-known television host, so she's famous in town. I think she's used to getting her way, but she needs to realize I'm here to help her win her case, and that's it. Scarlett is the only woman I crossed the line for with the whole client thing, and she's the only woman I will *ever* cross that line for. She's an exception.

"I just thought we could discuss my case further," she pouts, which is ridiculous because we just spent the last two hours debriefing everything. "Besides, I'm getting a ride home, and he isn't here yet."

I grit my teeth. "I will wait with you then. And anything else you have to discuss we can do it at our next meeting, Ms. Beetle."

I keep my tone even and pleasant, but the truth is, I just want to get home to Scarlett. I walk to the door, and wait for her to follow. She does, rubbing her body against mine as she passes. I grit my teeth, not liking the fact that she thinks anything she wants is hers. Life doesn't work that way, and there's no way I'm dumb enough to go for a woman like her. Harsh, but true. I like them sweet, gentle, and real. Sharon sways her hips exaggeratedly as she walks in front of me, but I pay her no mind. There's nothing she can do to tempt me. I'm not that man, and I've never been that man. Olivia used to tell me that if she ever found out I'd cheated on a woman, she'd kill me. I'd never betray any woman like that, especially Scarlett. She turns around to face me. "Are you sure there's nothing I can do to persuade you to change your mind?"

"Sorry, no," I say, jaw tight.

It's not long until her ride pulls up, and I raise my brow when I see it's a cop I recognize.

"Good-bye," she says to me, winking, and then opens the passenger door.

"I'll see you next week," I call behind her.

She climbs into the car, slamming the door harder than necessary, and the older gentleman drives off.

I'm about do the same.

Finally.

When I get to Scarlett's, dinner is on the table and she's dressed in red lingerie.

Holy fuck.

"Wow," I mouth, walking over to her and giving her a kiss. "You look fucking sexy."

"How hungry are you?" she asks me, pushing my jacket off my shoulders and letting it fall to the floor.

"Hungrier for you than for food," I reply, lifting her into my arms and pushing her back against the closest wall. "These look amazing in this," I tell her, cupping her breasts and pulling the bodice down so I can see a peak of her pink, pebbled nipples. "Fuck, look at them. They're just begging for my mouth, aren't they?"

"I've been waiting for you," she says, biting her bottom lip. "I missed you."

"I missed you too," I tell her before slamming my lips onto hers. I carry her to her bedroom, throw her on the bed, and undress myself.

Then I show her just how much I missed her.

"HOW MANY WOMEN HAVE you told that you love them?" she asks me. She's lying on her stomach, the sheet covering only half of her deliciously curved ass.

"Well there's my mom," I start, chuckling when she rolls her eyes and mutters, "That's not what I meant."

"The only woman I ever said I love you to was my high school girlfriend. The one I almost set on fire. And to be honest, I don't think I did. I cared about her, wanted her, and definitely lusted after her, but I don't think I even knew what love was back then. I was too young," I tell her, running my fingers down her back. I always like touching her in some way or another, even if it's just a light caress. "Why do you ask?"

"Just curious," she murmurs, resting her head on the pillow, tilting it toward me slightly. "I want to know everything about you. I'm learning things, slowly, bit by bit."

"And what does my answer tell you?" I ask, knowing that women generally don't ask questions for no reason.

"That you're careful with your heart."

It's a true statement; I can be guarded. When I love, I love with my whole heart, and I'm not just going to give someone the power to hurt me, especially if they turn out to be something else. "That's a valid observation. Isn't everyone these days though?"

"Some people love like they've never been hurt before," she says, closing her eyes. "They're either really brave or really stupid."

"Maybe they're both," I say, pulling the sheet from her body, taking a slow peruse.

"What are you doing?" she asks, and I can hear the smile in her tone.

"Having a look," I say, rolling her over and moving closer so our bodies are pressed together. "Are you hungry?"

"A little," she says, opening her eyes and stretching her arms above her head. She has no tattoos or piercings, just smooth skin, yet her body is still a piece of art.

"We should eat something; it's getting late."

"We should," she agrees, but neither of us moves. "I've been thinking. I need to find something to do. I'm getting bored. My garden is almost done, and when it is, I'm all out of projects. I just need to buy the outdoor furniture and plant a few more roses."

"You should figure out what will make you happy, and then do it," I tell her, liking that she can never sit idle. I'm the same. I also like that she has the choice of doing nothing because of her financial security but doesn't want to. She likes to be useful, needed. Sitting around and being pretty isn't an aspiration for her like it is for some other women I've met. They just wanted a man to look after them so they didn't have to work. They wanted to use their looks to get by, as some kind of currency. A thought like that would never even cross Scarlett's mind.

"I will," she says, lifting her chin, as if I'd ever doubt her.

Her comment about furniture does give me an idea though.

"HOW HAVE YOU BEEN, Jax?" Demon asks me from my spot on the couch. Bastard always steals it.

"Fine," I tell him. I'm pissed with him and how he handled the whole MC debacle. It felt like he chose them over me, and not just because of his undercover work, but I felt like that's where his loyalty now lies. This man I consider my best friend, so when I need something he should be able to be there for me. Instead, he chose the club and didn't share the information he knew with me. I don't really know what to say to him about it. Something has shifted between us, and I don't think anything can fix it. Will we always be cool? Of course. But do we have that same level of undeniable trust and loyalty? I don't know.

He's an undercover cop, but right now he just feels like a

biker, not the guy I grew up with, the one I met in fucking kindergarten. Demon and I have been through everything together. I remember the first time Olivia cried over a boy. She was in the ninth grade, and I was furious. I'd gone to find the boy, only to see that Demon had gotten to him first. He's family.

"I'm sorry about what happened, Jax," he says, running his hand through his hair. "Irish is a good man, and that dirty cop deserved to go, all right? I couldn't give you the information you needed, and I'm sorry. But tapping the MC lines? That wasn't cool either."

"I did what I had to do, D," I say, sitting down on the end of the couch. "You were doing your job, and I was doing mine. I had to save Scarlett. Irish might be a good man, but he's a guilty one. Your liking him and Darren's being a dick doesn't absolve him from the crime. An innocent woman shouldn't have to pay for that. You're a police officer, D, not a biker. Maybe you're forgetting that if you're siding with them over justice."

Whenever I'm feeling lost or unsure, Demon is the person I want to be around.

He *knows* me.

But I feel like this undercover stint with the MC is changing him, and I'm not sure how to handle that. I don't think he's sure either. I don't know if he even knows how much this has affected him.

He's silent for a few moments, but I know him, and that's when he's at his most dangerous. "I know who I am, Jax," he says, standing up and walking over to the window. "We're not going to see eye to eye on this, and I know we're living completely different lives right now, but you're still my family. So be angry at me, that's fine; we'll fight it out like we always do. I need to go now. I shouldn't be here in the first place, but I just wanted to see you."

Fuck, he's right. At the end of the day he is my family, no matter what.

I stand up and hug him as he passes. And just like every time he leaves my house, he stops to look at the picture of Olivia.

Then he leaves without another word.

chapter 24

SCARLETT

IT TAKES ME A few weeks to find a job, but when I do I know it's the right one for me. The library was looking for someone to do everything, from checking in books to reading to a group of children, and I thought it'd be something I'd really enjoy. It's only a part-time job, which is good because I don't want to stop volunteering at the shelter. I think by also getting a job I've kind of decided that I'm staying put for the time being, and I've told my aunt as much. I don't want to leave Jaxon, and as long as the two of us are good I'm not going anywhere he's not. After coming home from my first day, I'm over the moon. The day went really well, and I can't wait to tell Jaxon all about it. When I walk past the sliding door to the backyard of my house, I stop and do a double take. Unlocking the door, I slide it open.

"Oh my god," I mutter as I walk through my beautiful garden. There's furniture here. Beautiful wooden pieces that look hand-crafted. Unique pieces, not ones you'd find in just any old furniture store. My garden is now complete, and it looks epic. I pick up the note left on my new bench and open it.

Hope you had a wonderful first day at work.
Hope you like what I made for you.

Jaxon

He *made* these? I had no idea he was so talented—in the carpentry department anyway—I know he's talented in other areas.

Wow.

I'm absolutely blown away by this gift. He knows how much I love my garden, and how hard I've been working in it to make it my little slice of paradise. And now it's complete. I've never known such a thoughtful man in my life. I sit down on the bench, running my fingers over the smooth wood, wondering how long it took him to create this. Is there anything he can't do? I send him a picture of his card and type:

Thank you. You are absolutely amazing. I can't stop smiling.
What other hidden talents are you hiding? Love, Scarlett

I focus on the word *love*.

Should I put that in? Is he going to read it and get freaked out? I take a deep breath and contemplate just taking a risk and sending, but then decide to be safe instead.

So I delete the love Scarlett part and hit SEND. Is it too soon to tell him that I've fallen in love with him? Because I have. So deeply, I don't know how I'm going to take it if he doesn't feel the same. I spend some time admiring the five different wooden pieces, then head to the bathroom to have a hot shower before getting started on dinner. We've been staying at each other's houses several nights a week. With his work schedule, it's pretty much the only way we get to see each other, which is how I don't know when he found the time to create that stunning furniture for me. Sometimes he'll hit the gym before coming here, but usually I'm his first stop. It's weird seeing him on the news next to his famous client because of her high-profile case. Jaxon just has me in awe with everything he does. He's smart, funny, good-looking, and I'm sure he's one of the sweetest men to exist.

How can I not love him?

Once dinner is finished I make myself a hot cup of tea and sit in my garden, admiring how everything has come together. The garden is like my life. Once barren and a complete mess, it's now beautiful, well taken care of, and flourishing. I can't wait to sit here and read a book during the day, rays of sun hitting my face.

"I thought I'd find you out here," comes his voice. I jump a little, luckily not spilling any of the tea. I place my hand on my chest, calming myself.

"I don't think I'll ever be leaving here again," I say, lowering my hand and standing to greet him. "Thank you so much for this. You have no idea how much I love it. And I had no idea you could do something like this!"

His lip twitches. "Just a small hobby to pass the time. Happy you like everything, babe." He kisses my forehead, and then my lips. "Now tell me about your first day as a sexy librarian."

"Only if you join me on my one-of-a-kind, absolutely beautiful bench," I say, sitting back down and patting the spot next to me.

He sits and mutters, "It'd be awkward if it broke under my weight."

"It won't," I say with confidence. "And work was so good! They showed me how to use the computer and the filing system, and there were these supercute kids who came in for a group reading session. I had a lot of fun."

"I can tell by the way your eyes are lighting up as you talk about it," he says, shaking his head when I offer him some of my tea. "I'm happy you found something you love."

I did.

Him.

"Me too," I answer, resting my head on his shoulder. "Today has been the best day ever." I pause, just enjoying the moment. "Dinner is in the oven if you're hungry."

"What'd you make?" he asks, kissing the top of my head.

"Lasagna." I run my hand over his knee and then rest it on his thigh. He lifts it to his mouth and kisses my knuckles.

"You spoil me," he says, standing and offering me his hand.

I take it. "Says you who made me this," I say, pointing at the bench, and then at the table and chairs. "I feel extremely spoiled today."

And loved. He hasn't said it, but I feel loved. No one has ever been so caring and thoughtful with me before. I can't stop smiling, and I just feel so happy all the time. Is this what a healthy, loving relationship feels like?

"Just wait until I get you into the bedroom then," he says, wiggling his eyebrows.

"Are we the old couple who only have sex in the bedroom now?" I tease, greeting him with a smug look.

"Oh, you're going to pay for that one." He grins, shaking his head at me. "Nothing old about us."

I laugh and walk past him. He gives my butt a little slap as I head back inside to get the food out on the table. I've just opened the fridge when he closes it, spins me around, and lifts me up against it. "How about this? Different enough for you?"

My breath taken from me, all I can do is look at his mouth, those lips that keep talking when all I want them to do is kiss me.

"Nothing to say now?" he asks, smirking. We kiss, and then he slowly lowers me back to my feet. I want to be up against the fridge again. "Shame we're a boring old couple, right?"

"That's just mean," I say, huffing. "You're going to turn me on and then leave me hanging?"

"You going to take back what you said?" he asks, trying to keep a straight face. He then grabs me and throws me over his shoulder. "So if I took you to the room now and fucked you, you wouldn't find that any good?"

"I would," I say, slapping his butt, which is now right in front of my face. "I was just joking! I take it back!"

I can practically feel the satisfaction coming off him. He doesn't like to lose, even when we're playing around like this. Lawyer complex much? He starts walking toward my room, but then stops in my office, where I keep my computer and bookshelves. "How about here?" he asks, sitting me on the desk and lifting up my top.

Here?

Here is good.

He gets me naked and makes love to me right on my damn table, and he teaches me important lessons.

1. It's easy to get him worked up. All it takes is a few carefully chosen words.
2. If it's even possible, working him up makes the sex better. And it's already amazing.
3. I wouldn't care if we never left the bedroom. I just like being with him.

I've never had this playful side to me before, it's him who brings it out of me.

He makes me a better person, and I can only hope that I do the same to him.

Jaxon Bentley is everything I never thought I'd find.

And now that I have him, I just have to hope that he wants to be kept.

chapter 25

JAXON

"YOU ARE *NOT* GOING to hang out with the Wind Dragons," I tell her, groaning when her face drops. I don't want to tell her what to do—she's had enough of that in her life. But how do I let her walk into a place filled with biker thugs who have no problem engaging in illegal shit? What if something happens to her and I'm not there to protect her? I didn't get invited to this fucking MC expedition. I think I'm about to lose my shit. Men will be all over Scarlett, because, well, look at her, and I don't know how she'd handle that.

Okay, maybe I don't know how *I'd* handle that. "I'm not going to the clubhouse. I'm just meeting Valentina for a drink at a bar," she says, sounding confident. Only Scarlett would make friends with her former husband's mistress. Don't get me wrong, Valentina seems like a nice woman, and I appreciate the kind things she's said to Scarlett, but why can't they just meet for a lunch or something? If they go to a bar, all the Wind Dragons are going to be there too—I know they don't let their women wander around alone; there's always someone making sure they're safe and protected.

"Can you try to see this from my point of view though?" I ask her, trying to keep my tone even. I don't want to get angry and raise my voice. I need to stay calm. "You're going out partying with bikers. I don't know what that entails exactly, but I don't think it's just cake and soda, Scarlett."

"I was thinking of taking her to Riley's, Jaxon. I'll be fine. You talk about that place all the time, so I thought I'd check it out. And you don't have to worry about me so much." She pauses, looking down at her feet, and then right in my eye. "I'm stronger now. I can handle myself. It's *just* Valentina, not the whole club."

"I know you are," I say, softening. Fuck, what do I say to that? "It's not that, babe. You're beautiful and you're going to a bar with a biker chick who knows all the biker men in town. Do you get what I'm saying? They will be all over you, and I'll be sitting here stressing out, wondering if you're okay."

She lifts her chin. "I'm going. I want to see Valentina. She wants to catch up, and you know I don't have any friends. I'll be fine, Jaxon. I promise."

I grit my teeth. She's looking at me like I'm the enemy all of a sudden, like I'm telling her what to do and being unreasonable about it when I don't think that's the case at all. Her defiant hazel eyes are watching me, waiting for me to say something to her declaration. I don't know what she wants from me. I shouldn't have to back down and not say what I want because of her past; at the same time it does play a big role in her actions and reactions. I get that she doesn't have any female friends, and this is her opportunity to make some and be a little social, but fuck. I should introduce her to Kat and Yvonne, so she doesn't have to hang around fiery-haired biker chicks and their friends.

"Okay, if that's what you've decided," I say, watching my words very carefully. I don't want her to think that she can't be open with me about things. Maybe she'll be fine with Valentina, who maybe won't bring the Wind Dragons to this little bar date. Maybe Valentina will take care of any situation that arises. But if she doesn't? Maybe Scarlett just needs to learn the hard way; I don't know.

"Really?" she says, eyes widening.

What, did she think I was going to argue? Put my foot down or some other shit like that? I'm not a controlling man at all. I'm protective though, so no, I don't like this. And yes, I'm going to think of a way that I can protect her from this situation she's put herself in. Right now though, I'm just going to let it go. There's no other way without her getting defensive. I don't want to become her enemy, or her keeper. She needs to be a woman who can take care of herself when I'm not around, and maybe these biker chicks will teach her a few things.

"You're a grown woman, your decisions are your own," I say, shrugging. "I hope you have a good time. If you want me to drop you off and pick you up, let me know." I decide to change the subject until I figure out a way to handle the situation. All I know is that Scarlett and a bunch of big men, mixed with alcohol and drugs, isn't my version of a good time. The thought alone makes me want to kill someone. Maybe I'll be seeing Irish very soon after all. "Do you want to come for a jog along the beach with me? I don't feel like going to the gym today."

"Okay," she says, sounding a little wary of me. "When do you want to go?"

"Whenever you're ready," I tell her, needing to work off my frustration.

"I'll go get changed and put my sneakers on," she says, disappearing from the living room. I sit there, wondering why Darren had to choose a future MC old lady. Couldn't he have chosen a teacher or a yoga instructor or something? I'm being ridiculous, I know, but so is Scarlett. I don't think she'd like me going to hang out with a bunch of strippers, and, yes, it would be the same. I've heard Kat going on about how hot the men in the MC are, and now they might be around Scarlett.

Wait, am I jealous?

No.

No, I'm just concerned for her safety. They're a fucking outlaw motorcycle gang, not some Cub Scouts or something.

Okay, maybe I'm a little jealous. I trust Scarlett, and I know she won't do anything, but if I'm being honest with myself . . . I don't fucking like it. I know she needs to do her own thing though, and I'd never stop her from doing what she wants. She is her own woman. Still, that caveman part of me seems to be raising its head. What if something happens to her, and she's put in an unsafe situation? An idea pops into my head, and I wonder why I haven't thought of it up until now. Demon. Demon can keep an eye on her, protect her, and make sure she's safe. I've never been more thankful that my friend is undercover in a motorcycle gang.

Scarlett walks out in yoga pants and a tight top that shows a little of her stomach, and it's hard to stay angry. The shape of her ass and thighs in those pants are making me want to work out my frustrations in another way. When she bends over to retie a shoelace, I grit my teeth and adjust my cock, which is growing harder by the second.

"I'm ready. I'll just grab us two bottles of water," she says, opening the fridge.

I'd like her to grab something else right now.

She closes the fridge door with a cock of her hip and faces me. "Why are you looking at me like that?"

"You just look really sexy right now," I say, standing and wincing as my hard-on doesn't make it easy for me.

She closes the space between us and smiles. "Does that mean you're not angry at me?"

"No," I say, reaching around her to grab her ass. "It means I think you're sexy."

"Jaxon."

"Scarlett."

She rolls her eyes, takes me by the hand, and leads me outside to my car. I open her door for her, which she smiles at. Did she think I wouldn't because we had a small argument? Our first one, might I add. I'd open her door for her even if we weren't together, never mind if I was a little angry at her. Did Darren punish her like that when she did something he didn't like? The thought makes me mutter a curse under my breath before I slide into the driver's side.

"Can I drive your car one day?" she asks, eyeing the steering wheel.

"You can drive it any time you like," I reply as I put my seat belt on.

"Really?" she asks, sounding surprised. "It's so expensive though. Don't most men not want anyone else driving their cars? Their most prized item."

"A car is a car, babe," I say, pulling out onto the road. "It's just a thing, and it can be replaced. You can drive any of my cars whenever you want."

I can feel her eyes on me. She reaches her hand over and rests it on my thigh. "There are much more important things, aren't there?"

"Yes," I agree, with her. "Does this mean you aren't going to hang out with the biker chick?"

"No," she says, smirking. "Nice try though."

I sigh and drive us to the beach.

Nice try indeed.

WHEN I GET HOME, I give Demon a call.

"Jaxon?" he says into the line. "Everything okay?"

"Yeah," I tell him. "Everything is fine. Scarlett is going out with Valentina—does that mean all the Wind Dragons are going to be there too?"

He's quiet for a second, and then he starts laughing like he finds this hilarious. "Are you jealous, brother? I assure you that your woman is safe around the Wind Dragons, you don't need to worry about it if any of them show up."

"That's not what I asked," I grumble.

He chuckles, then puts me out of my misery. "If Tina's going, then yeah, one of the men will probably tag along to make sure she's okay. Irish has been adamant on her protection while he's not here."

"And what if that one man tagging along was you?" I suggest in a casual tone.

"You want me to tag along with your woman and Tina and make sure they don't get into any shit?" he asks, unable to hide the amusement in his tone.

"Yes," I reply.

No point lying.

"You don't think I have anything better to do on a Friday night?" he asks, and I can picture the bastard smirking.

"You owe me" is all I say.

"Oh fuck, here we go," he groans. "What old shit are you going to bring up now?"

I smirk. "I don't know, there are so many times I've taken

one for you. Let me think. How about when you were in the academy, and you wanted to impress a girl, so you made me go on a date with her friend"—I pause—"who ended up being a man."

"Fine," he replies, then starts laughing to himself. "Fuck, that was a funny night."

I'm glad he thinks so.

chapter 26

SCARLETT

GLANCING AROUND RILEY'S, I tug on my black crop top, pulling it lower even though it only exposes maybe an inch or two of my stomach. I decided to wear it with a long, flowy maxi skirt and black strappy sandals, red lips, and my hair down and wavy. An edgier look for me, but I'm trying new things, right? I remember the look on Jaxon's face as I left, knowing that he didn't like what I was doing, but I did it anyway, even though it probably isn't worth it. To be honest though, I just like knowing that if I want to do something, I can. He won't stop me or threaten me. I won't come home to a slap in the face or complete emotional manipulation. He won't treat me badly because I did something he didn't want me to do. It's freeing for someone like me. Someone who would've never dared do something like this before, something her man openly didn't want her to do.

"Do you want another drink?" Valentina asks me, dancing to the beat of the song.

"Sure, I'll get one for us," I tell her, leaving the small dance floor to head to the bar. The owner, Riley, is one of the most beautiful women I've seen. She has that whole pinup-girl vibe, with her dark hair, red lips, and winged liner.

"Could I get two more beers, please," I ask her.

"Sure," she says, smiling.

I lean over the bar and tell her. "My boyfriend comes in here all the time. He loves the place."

"Which one is yours?" she asks, grinning.

"Jaxon," I tell her.

"Ahh, one of the lawyers," she says. "He seems nice. I'm glad they've made this place their regular. Being such a new bar, I really need the business."

"The place is great," I tell her, glancing around. "I can see why he likes it so much."

She places the beers on the bar, and I hand her the money.

"Hey, I know you," a man says, coming to stand next to Riley. "You're the chick on bail."

I shake my head in surprise as I see Preston, the man from the diner. "Actually, those charges were dropped, but thanks for saying that superloud."

Riley barks out a laugh. "He's not one for subtlety."

"Where's your partner in crime?" I ask, referring to Parker.

"Parker has a real job," he says with a straight face. "He's a doctor, actually. I'm a mixologist."

"Is that a thing?" I ask him, bringing the beer to my lips.

I actually have heard of mixology before, but I just want to annoy him. It's funny that he works here, in a place that I've heard Jaxon talk about so often.

He nods, looking offended. "I'm the best cocktail maker this town has ever seen."

"That's quite the proclamation. I'll have to order a cocktail next," I tell him, grinning. I take Valentina's beer and return to the dance floor and hand it to her.

"Thanks," she says, taking a big sip.

We dance together for the next few songs, then head back to the bar to sit down for a little while. It feels good to dance again without feeling self-conscious. I don't even hear Darren in my head anymore, telling me that I can't do things.

"What are you doing here?" I hear her ask a man.

"Just came out to grab a drink," he tells her, a smirk on his face. "What a coincidence."

Valentina sighs, pursing her lips. "What trouble could I possibly cause in a random bar with Scarlett?" she asks him. "The worse thing we'd probably do is start a Darren Hate Club."

I smirk at that. It'd probably be the best thing we could do. I wonder if she'd let me be president.

"Can I get you another drink?" The man turns and asks me, studying me from beneath his thick dark lashes. I'd actually noticed him in the bar before, watching me. I don't get any bad vibes from him though. I had no idea he was one of the Wind Dragons. I shake my head. "No, thank you. I think I'm fine for now."

"She's taken, Demon," Valentina says, wrapping her arm around me. "No matter how hot you are." She lowers her voice and mutters, "Which is pretty damn hot."

I have to agree with her, the man is extremely good-looking, with his baby-blue eyes and dark hair, but I don't feel anything when I look at him, not even that spark of attraction. Everything in me is for Jaxon only, but I can appreciate when a man is very, very handsome.

"Just being a gentleman," Demon responds, not fazed by Valentina's comments one bit.

"How considerate of you." Valentina smirks, tucking a curl behind her ear. "I had no idea you were such a gentleman, Demon."

"Don't let the name fool you," he replies, flashing straight, white teeth. "My mama raised me right."

"Thank you, Demon," I say, meaning it, the unusual name sounding foreign on my tongue.

"That's what I'm here for," he says cheerfully. "To ply you both with alcohol, let you have a good night, and then safely take you home."

"Sounds like a good time," Valentina replies, downing her drink. "What about you? You going to have one too many?"

"Nope," he replies, scanning the bar. "I'm going to be an adult and pace myself."

Valentina points. "Oh, look. A beautiful woman."

"Nice try," he replies, barking out a laugh. "I'm surrounded by beautiful women every day. Going to need more than that to catch my eye."

"If you're here, you might as well do shots with us," she says, calling Preston over. "Can we get three shots of whatever you suggest?"

Preston looks to me. "I know just the shot."

Demon flashes me a curious look, probably wondering why Preston gave me a friendly look, but I just shrug. Preston makes the shots, then slides them over to each of us. I notice mine has a little love heart on the top. Demon notices it too, and brings his narrowed eyes to Preston.

"To new friends," I say, lifting my shot up. We clink, then down them.

"That was actually really delicious," I tell Preston.

"Thank you," he beams, then moves on to serve another customer.

"Someone has a crush." Valentina grins at me. "Maybe he'll give us free drinks from now on."

"Doubtful," Demon mutters, nodding his head in time with the music. "This place is pretty cool, isn't it?"

"Yeah, I like it. Something different," Valentina tells him, then pulls his arm. "Come on, let's dance."

The three of us stand in our own circle and dance with our drinks in hand. I smile, laugh, and just enjoy the night and the company, feeling free and wild. I see Demon pulling his phone out and sending a text, tilting his phone so no one can read what he's typing. Maybe he's sending out a booty call, who knows.

"Do you want to dance?" Preston asks me, coming up behind me.

"No, she doesn't," Demon tells him, coming to stand next to me. I throw him a dirty look and pull Preston aside. "I'm taken, Preston. But hey, if you want to be friends, I'd like that. I don't have many of those."

"Why are all the hot chicks taken?" he asks, frowning. But then he offers me his hand. "Friends sounds good though."

We share a grin.

"Is that guy your boyfriend?" he asks, nodding to Demon.

"No," I say, laughing. "He's just someone I met tonight, actually."

"Mmmm," he hums. "Come to the bar if you want some free drinks."

He walks away, and Demon and Valentina close in on me.

"Told you," she says, while Demon just silently broods. "You're a babe."

"Look who's talking," I tell her, nodding to the bar. "Want some free drinks?"

She throws her curls back and laughs. "Fuck yes, I do."

We twine our arms together and head to the bar, Demon scowling and following behind us.

"YOU COULD TOTALLY BE a biker chick. You have the strength of all the women in the MC, Scarlett. Don't let anyone tell you otherwise."

We're drunk, really drunk, and having deep and meaningful chats.

I study her for a moment, wondering if she knows how much that comment means to me. Most of my life I was weak. But I'm not that person anymore. I saved myself. And Jaxon gave me my freedom back. With those two things, I'm now unstoppable. I can do anything I want and be anyone I want to be.

"I'm so glad I met you, Valentina," I say, resting my shoulder against hers. "I wish I had known you before, but now . . ."

"Now works too," she finishes for me, taking a sip of her drink. "If you need someone, I'll be here for you, you hear me? You will never be stuck in any situation like that again. Ever."

I smile into my drink and nod. "No, I won't be. But I don't have to even consider something like that again with Jaxon in my life. He's the most amazing man I could have ever imagined."

Demon makes a sound of amusement, but there's something else in his blue eyes, almost like he agrees with me.

"What? He is," I tell Demon. "He treats me like a princess, except in the bedroom. Does a man get any more perfect than that?"

Demon starts to choke on his drink, and Valentina starts slapping him on the back. "Nope, doesn't get any better than that. I always say, respect me out of bed, but disrespect me in it."

We both start laughing, like she said the funniest joke in the world.

"I'm so happy I came out tonight," I tell her. "Jaxon was worried all the biker men would come." I lower my voice to a whisper. "I think he was jealous."

Demon starts chuckling, and I look at him and nod. "I know. Like he has anything to worry about."

Riley comes up to us and jumps on the bar counter. "We're about to close, you three."

I see her eyeing Demon, and I don't blame her. He's a very attractive man. I wiggle my eyebrows at her, and she just starts laughing.

"I like you, Scarlett," she says, then leans closer to me. "Do you have any inside gossip on Hunter?"

"The family-law guy?" I ask raising my brows. "He's nice, but I don't really know him. Although I can tell you he's an excellent attorney. He was able to get all my accounts and property transferred back into my name after my dead husband stole it. Why? Do you like him?"

"Just curious," she murmurs, then pours herself a glass of whiskey.

I make a drunk mental note to ask Jaxon about Hunter and Riley.

"I think I'm going to get Jaxon to come pick me up now. I haven't been out this late in . . ." I try to rack my brain to think of the last time I had a night out. "Jeez, I can't even remember. So I think I've done well under the circumstances. Thanks again for inviting me out; I had a really good time."

"We have to do this again," Valentina says, leaning her body against Demon's. "I had a good night with you both. I need the distraction sometimes, you know?"

"I do. Trust me I know how you feel," I tell her. "I know

Jaxon was worried about me coming here, but I'm in one piece with no horror stories to tell." I hiccup. "And I'm not that drunk. My words aren't slurring or anything. And any time you need a distraction, or to get away, you can always come to my house. We'll have a great time."

I pull out my phone and send Jaxon a quick message telling him that I'm done, and I can take a cab if he's asleep or too tired to come get me. "I'll have to have you over for dinner or something soon."

"I'd like that."

Jaxon responds not even a few seconds later.

I'm on my way.

I'm unable to hide my smile.

I hope he's not too tired for what I have in mind next.

chapter 27

JAXON

I PARK THE CAR OUT in front of the bar, and just get out to go find her when I see her walking toward me with Demon and Valentina. She looks hot in her outfit, and as she gets closer I can tell she's a little drunk by the flush in her cheeks and her lopsided smile.

"You got here quickly," she says, wrapping her arms around my torso and squeezing me tightly. I hug her back, thankful for her being back in my arms. I see Demon's amusement at her comment, and choose to ignore it.

"Well, I had nothing else to do at"—I glance at my watch—"three in the morning."

Scarlett giggles a little and glances up at me. "Thank you for coming to get me. I think I'm ready to be tucked into bed now." She turns and hugs Valentina, whispering something into her ear, then Demon. I raise my brows at him as she hugs him tightly and thanks him for a fun night. He shrugs slightly at me, but then grins.

Asshole.

I say 'bye to her new friends, one of them my oldest friend in the world, and open the car door for her, patiently waiting for her to get in.

"You're a lucky man," Demon says to me, before wrapping his arm around Valentina.

"You don't need to tell me that," I say, tapping the roof of my car before sliding in. I turn to Scarlett, who already has her eyes on me. "Good night?"

She nods twice. "I wasn't so sure at the start—I felt really out of place, and it was a little intimidating—but I'm glad I stuck it out. It ended up being a really good night. I'm glad I went. I need to be pushed out of my comfort zone sometimes, you know?"

I start the car as I say, "I'm glad you had a good time in the end."

"I did," she assures me, placing her hand on my thigh. I pull out of the parking lot and start taking us back to my place. I can feel her gaze still on me, so I glance at her. From the look in her eyes, I know she's in a bit of a mood, and the way she bites her lower lip only validates that. She wants some dick. Mine, to be exact. And she wants it now. I pretend I don't notice all of this, flash her a smile, and return my attention to the road, both hands on the steering wheel. From the corner of my eye I see her shift in the seat a few times, suddenly uncomfortable, and I know exactly why. I turn on some music, the sounds filling the car but not easing the building tension. I know she's decided to take matters into her own hands when she moves closer to me, as much as she can with her seat belt still on, and presses a kiss onto my neck. I grit my teeth, wishing we were already home so I can have my way with her. She's not the only one feeling this way, especially after waiting up for her ass all night, hating the fact she was surrounded by fucking bikers.

"Jaxon," she murmurs, breathing onto my skin.

"Yes?" I reply, keeping my eyes on the road. There's no way I'd allow myself to lose concentration and put us in danger by crashing this car.

Another kiss to my neck.

She turns my head slightly toward her so she has access to my lips, kissing me softly at first, then deeper, her tongue peeking out to taste me. I want to take control, grab her face in my hands and devour her lips, but I can't, so I allow her to kiss me how she wants while I continue to drive. I stifle a moan as her fingers move to my zipper, undoing the button of my jeans, then sliding the zipper down. I'm not wearing anything underneath because I was lying in bed naked when she called and just threw something on quickly to come get her, so it's easy access for her to take my cock out. She glances at me before stroking it a few times, then lowers her head.

Fuck.

I don't move my eyes from the road as she takes my hard length into her mouth, deeper, deeper, all the way to the back of her throat, then makes a humming noise, a noise of pleasure, like she likes what she's doing.

There is nothing sexier than that to me.

"Fuck," I grit out between clenched teeth, the pleasure hitting me with each swipe of her tongue, each suck, as the woman drives me crazy. A moment later, I mutter "Fuck" again, but this time for a different reason. As I see the lights on, I quickly tell her, "Baby, stop. A cop is behind us."

She lifts her head and wipes her mouth. "What?"

"Don't look," I tell her, amusement in my tone. She sits back in her seat and stares forward, her body straight and stiff like we're both about to get arrested. I quickly do up my jeans, wincing as my still-hard cock is shoved away under the denim, and pull over. I roll down my window and wait patiently for the officer. When I see him walking toward the car, I realize I know the man. He was the first officer called in for a case I was working on, and I had to write down his testimony to use in court. He can probably guess what was going on in here, whether he actually says anything about it is another situation though. Scarlett looks like she's about to have a panic attack, so I reach over and give her my hand. She has nothing to worry about. Has she forgotten already what I do for a living? This is nothing. I can talk my way out of anything. It's late and the officer is probably bored and making sure I'm not drinking and driving. That, and he probably noticed Scarlett bobbing on my lap, but it's really his word against mine. For fuck's sake, I'll say she lost her earring or some shit.

Officer Carlton's eyes widen when he sees me. "Jaxon Bentley. How the hell are you?"

"Good, thanks," I reply, smiling. "How are you? How're the wife and kids?"

"All good," he glances into my passenger seat, flashing a tiny flashlight at Scarlett. "You two on your way home from a night out?"

"She is," I say, nodding toward her. "I just went to pick her up."

"You haven't had anything to drink?" he asks, and I shake my head. I can tell that he considers giving me a Breathalyzer test, but decides not to. I appreciate that.

He nods once and steps back. "All right; get home safely you two."

"Thank you," I say, waiting until he walks away before continuing on.

I look to Scarlett, whose hand is now on her chest, which is heaving up and down. "Holy crap."

I bring her hand to me and kiss her fingers. The car is still filled with tension, although it's different now because it's mixed with her shock. After a few seconds, I see her shoulders relax.

"We're almost home," I tell her, turning onto my street.

"A cop nearly caught me with your dick in my mouth," she whispers, eyes going wide.

I grin and park in my driveway, turning the car off and getting out. I move to walk around and open her door, but she's already out and coming over to me. When she jumps into my arms and kisses me, I catch her and press her against the car. I never know how she's going to react sometimes, and I'm not going to lie, I like seeing what she'll do next. There was a chance she wouldn't want to start where we left off after that, but here she is, tongue in my mouth and nails running down my back over my thin cotton T-shirt.

"I missed you tonight," she says against my lips, and I can taste the alcohol on her, mixed with mint.

"I can see that," I mutter, moving my lips down her neck. The moaning noise that leaves her pouty lips makes me rock-hard again, and I find myself lifting her in one arm and heading for the front door. With my other hand I unlock the door and push it open, closing and locking it before dropping her on the first place I come across, which happens to be the couch. I get down on my knees and lift her long skirt up, sliding the silky material over her skin. I slide down her white lace panties and spread her legs apart. I lift my head to make sure she's watching me before I pull her ass toward me and bury my face in her pussy, my tongue diving into her, licking, sucking, and devouring.

"Jaxon," she moans, and I love hearing my name come out of her pretty mouth, I love her knowing who she belongs to.

I belong to her too.

chapter 28

SCARLETT

I WAKE UP EARLY, MY head hurting a little bit, but nothing too bad. I slide out of bed, brush my teeth, and drink some water, all while replaying the night's events in my head. I decide to thank Jaxon by waking him up in the best way possible. I slowly lift up the sheet and crawl under it, then kiss down his stomach, his hip, and then his inner thighs before taking him into my hands and gently stroking. Even asleep he gets hard, and I know the second he wakes because his hands tangle in my hair, and he says, "Good morning, beautiful," in a husky tone filled with sleep. I smile against his dick, then take it into my mouth, twirling my tongue around and over it, teasing him a little more. I love the taste of him, the feel of him. Taking him deep into my mouth just like I did last night in the car, I hollow my cheeks and suck as hard as I can, rising and lowering my lips on him. When he comes in my mouth, I swallow every drop without even thinking about it, and then lift my head and smile at him.

"Good morning," I say, then climb up and lay on top of him. His arms come around me straightaway.

"And what a good morning it is," he murmurs, kissing the top of my head. "That was amazing, baby."

I smile to myself and close my eyes. "Glad you enjoyed it. I was going to go make us some breakfast, but I don't see myself moving from this spot for a long time."

His arms tighten around me. "I don't see you moving from this spot either." He sighs, and rubs his fingers down my bare back. "So since you had a good time last night, does that mean you're going to be traipsing voluntarily back into an outlaw motorcycle clubhouse?" he asks in a dry tone.

My lip twitches as I reply. "I like them, Jaxon. And you saw, I was safe. No one made me feel uncomfortable in any way, no one tried to hit on me."

Except maybe Preston, but I can't even take him seriously.

"Someone stayed with me for the whole night, mainly Valentina. I played some beer pong with Demon on my team, and he even drank some of the beer for me because I knew I wouldn't be able to drink so much of it without throwing up."

"He did, did he?" he murmurs, sounding a little curious.

"Yes," I tell him. "I like Demon. And Valentina said next time I can bring you along if I like. She said you're welcome, as long as you aren't trying to put any more of them behind bars."

He makes a sound of amusement. "You had to go and make friends with a bunch of criminals on wheels, didn't you?"

"They aren't all criminals," I say, yawning.

"Just some of them," he says in a dry tone, then changes the subject. "I have to drop into work later, I have a few things I need to finish up for this case."

"The Sharon Beetle case?" I ask, and he makes a sound of agreement.

"Yeah. I'll be so happy once it's done. But for now," he says, and I can hear the smile in his voice. He rolls me off him gently, and then pins my arms up with him on top of me. "I have some business to take care of."

He kisses me and I forget everything except his name on my lips and his taste in my mouth.

"HEY, AREN'T YOU THE chick who was on the news for killing her cop husband?" the woman asks me, not sounding angry or judgmental, just curious.

I stop stacking books and turn to her. "I suppose so. I guess now though, I'm just a librarian."

"Cool," she murmurs, chewing on some gum. "I thought you looked familiar, and the news is the only TV I really watch anymore, so I knew it had to be from that."

"Okaaay," I reply, not sure what to make of this woman. She's dressed in all black, with a choker around her neck, and red lipstick. She has a chest tattoo that peaks up her neck toward her throat. She's beautiful, but not in the traditional meaning of the word. She clearly has quite a perky personality too. "Is there anything I can help you with?"

"Yeah, I'm looking for these books," she says, handing me a list. I take it from her and scan it, then approach the closest computer to do a quick search.

"I'm Gwen, by the way," she says, standing next to me. "And

I'm sorry I had to ask you. I forgot to bring my glasses and I can't see the screen."

"It's no problem," I say, smiling. "That's what I'm here for, Gwen. I'm Scarlett."

Or the chick who *didn't* kill her cop husband, but that's okay. I go and get all the books for her, and hand them to her in a pile. "There's only one missing; someone has borrowed it, but it'll be back on Wednesday."

"That's okay, thank you," she says, smiling, then walks with the books to a table. She pulls out a notebook and starts to take some notes. I wonder if she's in college, even though she looks to be in her late twenties. It's never too late to pursue a dream. I smile to myself and continue stacking books, then go back to the counter to finish up the office work I have there. With fifteen minutes left until close, I'm full of pleasure and surprise when Jaxon walks into the library. He's dressed to kill in his business attire, like he always is, today in a black suit with a white shirt.

"What are you doing here?" I ask, smiling ear to ear. I move away from the counter and step toward him with my arms open.

"I finished work early so I thought I'd take you to dinner," he says, pulling me into him and wrapping me in his warmth. "Unless you're feeling too tired?"

I shake my head. "No, I'd love to go to dinner. Just let me finish closing up. I have to wait about ten more minutes before I can shut the doors."

"No problem, take your time," he murmurs, glancing around. When he brings his eyes back to me, there's a glint in there that I recognize instantly.

"Oh no you don't," I chastise, arching my brow. "I'm at work."

He licks his bottom lip and lowers his gaze over my body, which is dressed in a long, floral dress and a cardigan. "You look beautiful."

"You say that every day," I backtrack, smirking as I get back behind the computer and shut it down.

"I can't help that you look beautiful every day," he states, stalking toward me, intent in his gaze. He leans over my desk with his knuckles planted on the table. "Perhaps you shouldn't have sent me that picture this morning so I'd know what you're wearing underneath that dress."

My lip twitches at that. I was at my house getting ready this morning when I sent him a saucy picture of me in my red silk bra and panties. "Hey, if you can't control yourself, that's on you. I sent you a sexy picture, so you think you can stalk your way over to my workplace? Who do you think you are, Jaxon Bentley?"

He smirks, his eyes turning heavy, and reaches over to cup my chin. When he brings his lips to mine, I don't stop him, instead I lean forward, falling into the kiss. Apparently I can't even pretend to put up much of a fight. The kiss soon turns heated, and I pull away and hold my finger up to tell him to stop for a second. Rushing to the door, I lock it and turn the sign to CLOSED, then return to him, this time walking over to his side of the desk.

"You're trouble, you know that?" I croon, shaking my head at him. "Only you would do something like this."

"Only you would let me," he replies, lifting me up and walking with me in his arms to the back corner of the library. When he rests my back against a shelf, I moan and press my breasts against him, wanting more friction. "Be patient," he whispers, kissing the sensitive part where my neck meets my shoulder.

I narrow my eyes at him, but they shutter close as he starts to kiss me again and slides his hand up under my dress, his finger into my panties. As he starts to stroke me, rubbing my clit just how I like it, I start making sounds I hope no one else ever gets to hear, desperate for the release he's about to give me. We didn't see each other last night, and apparently one night without him has made me act like I haven't had sex in months. He's spoiling me. I'm getting used to this, and now when it's taken away, I need it. I crave his touch, his body, everything that he is.

If this isn't love, I don't know what is.

chapter 29

JAXON

I NEEDED TO SEE HER.

After dealing with Sharon all evening, who seems to care more about trying to fuck me than her actual case, I couldn't wait to see Scarlett. I left the office and drove straight to the library. I didn't plan for what happened there to happen, but now I'm sitting at dinner feeling happy, sated, and much more relaxed.

"Can you stop smiling?" Scarlett asks, laughing. "You should see your face."

"Can't help it if I'm happy," I say, picking up my chopsticks. "And less stressed."

"Always happy to help you de-stress," she says, licking a drop of sauce off her lips. "Is the case not going well then?"

I haven't told Scarlett about Sharon and how unprincipled she is because I don't want her to worry, but maybe now might

SEDUCING THE DEFENDANT ◊ 191

be the time to open up a little and let her know what's been going on.

"Sharon is a diva. She thinks because she's a television personality and she's famous that no rules apply to her," I start, sighing, feeling a migraine coming on at just the mere thought of the woman.

"So she's difficult? You think she wouldn't be when it's her case, and her money and life that you're dealing with?"

"She's . . . unprofessional," I say slowly, then clear my throat. "It's making my life harder, especially when I'm not . . . interested."

Scarlett places her glass of ginger beer down and studies me. "Are you trying to tell me gently that your client is hitting on you?"

I cringe as the words leave her lips. "To put it mildly. And she's been accused of sexual assault. You'd think the woman would learn."

She purses her lips, then does something I never thought she'd do in this moment.

She laughs.

"So you have to go to work, try to win the case, but in the meantime you also have to fight her off?" she asks, smirking now. "I must say, I can't blame the woman. You in those suits . . . Mmmmm."

My jaw tightens. "Seriously? That's how you're going to react to another woman making it her mission to bed me? By objectifying me?"

"Women get objectified every day; it's only fair," she returns, sticking her tongue out at me. "Come on, Jaxon. You're a good-looking man. You should be used to such attention by now."

"I'd expect a little . . . I don't know . . . jealousy?" I admit, lifting my chin. "She runs her hands over me whenever she gets the chance, you know? My shoulder, my hand. Nothing is off-limits."

"Is that right?" she says, laughing even harder now. "Nothing is off-limits? So has she touched . . . anything farther down south?"

"No," I say, dragging the word out. "Why? Would that get a reaction out of you?"

I sound grumpy, and I don't even bother trying to hide it. Inside though, I love how secure Scarlett feels. Knowing her past, I'd have thought that she might be a little insecure, which is why I didn't tell her about it. Apparently, I was wrong. In fact she's finding the whole thing entertaining, at my expense might I add.

Scarlett tries to school her expression but fails because there's still amusement written there. "Well, it's not like you're tempted in any way, are you? I trust you, Jaxon. I know you'd never do anything to hurt me."

I soften instantly at her words. "Of course I wouldn't, and hell no, I'm not even tempted, but that's not the point. It's like no one has ever told the woman no, and now I have to deal with it. She's unbelievable. Rejection doesn't do anything to her ego, no matter how many times I say no, it's like she thinks I'm playing hard to get."

"Want me to take her down?" she asks with a straight face.

"Yes, actually I do," I grumble, taking a bite out of a dumpling.

"Seriously though," Scarlett says, clearing her throat. "All jokes aside. Is there anything you can do about this? Maybe have telephone or video-call meetings? She can't touch you if all communication is via technology."

"That's actually a good idea," I say, nodding. "I don't know how long I could claim to be too busy to meet with her in person though. She's my main case right now and my priority client."

"Might lessen the personal meetings though," she says, sitting back in her chair and tucking her hair behind her ear. "I don't know. I'll try to think of other ideas for you without having to file a sexual harassment claim and getting shit from Hunter and Tristan for the rest of your life."

They really would give me a heap of shit too. I wonder if I could get Kat in on a plan, maybe get her to say something to Sharon from a legal perspective. I'm this close to telling her to find a new lawyer. I've never given up on a case though, and I'd hate to have to do that. I'm sure I'd be given shit for that in the office too.

"Maybe you should be a lawyer," I tell her, smiling at how she tries to fix the problem for me with a level head.

"I'm happy being a librarian for now," she says, winking. "Especially when my man decides to drop in unannounced and have his way with me against a stack of books." She pauses, cringing. "Yeah, let's hope I don't get fired over that one."

"Are there cameras in there?" I ask, really hoping there aren't. I'd feel like shit if Scarlett lost her new job that she already loves.

"Just around the building," she explains. "Not inside. I wouldn't have even kissed you if there were. Making a porno is not on my bucket list."

"What if it's on mine?" I tease, laughing when she rolls her eyes at me.

"Then it's something you won't be ticking off, buddy."

"We'll see," I mutter, watching her closely. She just arches her brow, like *Yes, we will.* She's so different from when I first met her, now that she feels comfortable and free to be herself. It's been such an amazing thing watching her grow.

"Have you ever played beer pong?" she randomly asks. She must be thinking of her night with Valentina and Demon.

"A few times in college," I reply, playing it down. I partied a lot in college. I was one of those typical frat boys, and when I wasn't studying my ass off, I was drinking my ass off. I never even cared about getting into any shit because I'd just call Demon and he'd have my back. What nobody probably knows, even the Wind Dragons MC, is that I'm the one who gave him the nickname Demon back when we were in high school. He broke so many girls' hearts, I used to tell him he was like the devil. He replied by saying he wasn't that bad, he didn't even mean to hurt any of them. Which was true. He's a good-looking man, and women have always swarmed to him. My reply to him was *Fine, maybe you're not the devil, more like a demon*, and the name stuck.

"I want to practice so next time I can beat everyone," she says, a scheming look passing over her face.

"Okay, we can play," I tell her. "Why don't we mix things up a little and play strip beer pong?"

"You have a one-track mind, Jaxon," she chastises, her tone giving away her lack of annoyance. "Are you going to eat that?" she asks, pointing to the last dumpling.

"No, baby. You eat it," I tell her gently, then watch as she does so. It hits me then, as I consider her, just how crazy I am about the woman sitting opposite me.

How crazy in love I am with her.

Fuck.

I don't know when it happened, but I fell in love with her.

She swallows her bite, then glances up at me through her long lashes and smiles. "Do you want dessert?"

I shake my head, mind still blown by the revelation.

"Me either," she says, rubbing her stomach. "I'm paying."

That snaps me out of it. "No, you are not."

"Don't be ridiculous. What's my money meant for then?" she asks, scowling at me. "To sit in the bank and collect dust? I like to spoil you sometimes too, you know."

"Buy something for yourself," I suggest. "I don't know. Buy another house, a car, a vacation. Do whatever you want, but when you're with me I'm not letting you pay for anything. I don't know why you bother to continue to fight me on this."

"Because it's not fair. Gender equality, Jaxon; get with the program. Everything should be fifty-fifty in this relationship. We both hustle, we both spoil each other, we both clean."

"Did you see that on a meme? Because I'm pretty sure I did," I reply, brow furrowing. "And you don't let me cook or clean. So you're being a little hypocritical right now."

"Fine," she says, lifting her chin. "I'll pay for dinner, and tomorrow night you can cook."

I cringe inwardly, both because I don't want her to pay and I don't want to cook, but I can't back down now. "Fine."

Fuck.

I make decent money, and if it's not to spoil and take care of the people I . . . love, then what the hell is it for? When she reaches for her purse, I can't take it.

"Nope, I can't do it. I'm paying. And I'll cook dinner tomorrow night. I'll make a scene."

She slides her wallet back in and expels a deep sigh. "You are something else, Jaxon Bentley."

"I'm yours," I state simply.

That's the bottom line.

She has to deal with me, and I have to deal with her.

And I'm more than okay with that.

chapter 30

SCARLETT

I'M DRIVING TO JAXON'S when I see a policeman on a motorbike coming up in my rearview mirror. He signals for me to stop, so I turn onto the side of the road and wait for him to approach. I don't think I've done anything wrong: I was driving the speed limit and I can't think of any other reason he'd have to pull me over. He climbs off his motorcycle and approaches my window, which I quickly wind down.

"License and registration, please," he demands, glancing at me and then over the car.

I grab my purse and take out my driver's license and the papers from the glove box and hand them to him.

"Scarlett Reyes," he murmurs, and I pick up a hint of distaste in his tone. Instantly, I'm on alert. I don't always trust police, because I'm more than aware that there are good ones and bad ones. If this man has it out for me for no reason, there could be a chance he was friends with Darren. Did he recognize my license plate? Maybe he ran it and saw who the car belonged to. Either way, I start to feel uneasy about the situation. It's dark outside. I'm driving straight from work to Jaxon's house, and although the road isn't completely deserted there aren't that many cars driving up and down.

"Yes," I reply, keeping my tone soft and even. "Is something wrong, Officer?"

"Many things are wrong," he replies, handing me back my license and papers. "Sometimes justice doesn't always prevail, does it, Ms. Reyes?"

I don't know what he expects me to say to that, because justice did prevail. Darren got what he deserved, and I'm now free to live a happy life without him. I decide to stay silent, because no matter what I reply, there'll be no right words. Who knows what Darren said about me to his fellow officers? If this man was friends with Darren though, he's probably just as dirty as Darren was. Filth sticks together. I make sure to remember the officer's name.

Gilmore.

He taps on my hood and tells me I'm free to go.

I continue on my way feeling confused, scared, and angry.

This whole thing was meant to be over for me, and sure, he didn't actually do anything, but I still shouldn't have to deal with this type of behavior from an officer of the law. I've done no wrong, I'm guilty of nothing, and I should be treated like any other civilian. I shouldn't have to deal with some passive-aggressive shit from a cop because of who my late husband was. I don't want to be dealing with the past anymore. Darren crosses my mind less and less these days, and everything in my life is finally at a place I never thought it would be. I wake up and go to bed happy, and I have a love that I never thought I'd find. I never knew men like Jaxon even existed outside of movies and books, but here I am.

My own heroine.

In a story I finally like.

I tell myself this is a one-off thing, and I should forget it. I won't run into this man again, and who cares if Darren's friends are sour. I won; they lost. Not only did I win, justice won. If they can't see that then . . .

They don't deserve that badge they wield around.

I push what happened out of my mind and lift my chin.

I'm not going to let anyone ruin my day.

When I walk into Jaxon's house using the key he gave me last night after we had dinner, I come to a standstill as I take in the scene before me.

Candles.

Dinner.

Red roses on the center of the table.

And a handsome Jaxon standing there with a single rose in his hand.

"Wow," I say, smiling wide. "What's the occasion?"

He grins and closes the space between us, handing me the rose and kissing my lips softly.

"I love you," he tells me. "I wanted to find the right moment to tell you. So I decided to create the right moment instead."

I take the rose, shaking my head in disbelief, pure happiness spreading throughout my body. I jump into his arms, wrapping my legs around him.

He loves me.

I've known that I'm in love with him for some time now, but I didn't say the words. I didn't want to jinx what we have, or scare him off, but deep inside I knew.

And he loves me back.

"I love you too, Jaxon," I say, kissing him deeply, then looking into his eyes. "You have no idea how much."

His hands, holding me up by the curve of my ass, tighten on me. "I think I do know how much," he says, nuzzling my neck. "I can tell by the way you take care of me. I will never take that, or you, for granted, Scarlett."

Another kiss, one I smile through. In fact I don't think I'll stop smiling for the remainder of the night. He lowers me to the floor, and I slide down his body, give him another tight hug, then move to the table to see what he's cooked tonight.

"Steak, mashed potatoes, asparagus, and garlic bread," I say, my mouth watering. "You did well, Jaxon. Maybe I should let you into the kitchen a little more, especially when you do all this."

I lift the rose that's still in my hand to my nose, breathing in the sweet scent. Jaxon pulls a chair out for me and gestures for me to sit. I take my seat and lay the rose down next to my plate. I was going to tell Jaxon about the cop, but I'm not going to ruin this moment. I'll tell him about it another time. Tomorrow, maybe, or the day after.

Right now though, I don't want this moment to end.

Jaxon Bentley is in love with me.

Me.

The same woman who once stayed with an abusive man because she didn't feel she was strong enough to leave. Didn't feel like she was worthy. A victim. A woman who never smiled, and one who didn't think she was beautiful enough to ever attract the attention of another man. It feels like a lifetime ago, and a whole different person.

I lift up my glass of red wine and make a toast. "To love."

"To my love," Jaxon clarifies, raising his glass, then bringing it to his lips.

His love.

I'll never tire of hearing those words.

I'll never stop loving this man.

IN NOTHING BUT A silk white nightdress, I open the fridge and scan the contents inside of it. Grabbing the milk carton, I close the door with my hip, then scream, the milk dropping to the floor. Jaxon runs into the kitchen, switching the light on, looking like he's ready to kill someone, his body tense and braced for some kind of altercation.

"What the fuck?" he grits out, looking at the third person in the room.

"What are you doing here?" I yell. "You scared the crap out of me! Did you have to come and stand so close to me in the dark? What the hell is wrong with you? And . . ." I pause, and study him. "Are you bleeding?"

"Yeah," he replies, looking down at his arm, which he's got covered with a ball of what looks like a flannel top, to stop the bleeding. "I got into a fight. And got stabbed."

Worry fills me. "I'll grab the first-aid kit."

I rush into the bathroom and grab it. When I walk back into the room, I see Jaxon examining Demon's wound. Why is Jaxon not angry that there's a Wind Dragon who apparently broke into his house? And how did Demon even know where we live?

"What's going on here?" I ask, and Jaxon immediately straightens and steps back from Demon. I'm missing something here, I know it. Do these two know each other? And if so, how? This makes absolutely no sense.

"Just seeing how deep the cut is," Jaxon says, holding his

hand out for me to pass him the kit. "I think he's going to need stitches. We might need to go to the hospital."

"If I could go to the hospital I wouldn't have come here," Demon points out, shaking his head. "I can't go there. The cops are up the MC's ass right now, and I don't need them asking questions as to how this injury came about."

"And how did it come about?" Jaxon asks, cleaning the wound and not being too gentle about it.

"I'm a biker. We get into the occasional fight," Demon replies, not bothering to elaborate or give an actual reason. "I know I shouldn't have come here, but your house was close by, and like I said, I can't go to the hospital, okay?"

"Jaxon, why are you not surprised that Demon is in your house?" I ask, needing answers.

Demon glances at me, then at Jaxon. "I didn't know she'd be here. Her car wasn't out front."

"It's in the garage," I say, pursing my lips together. "Explain. *Now.*"

"I'm about to pass out from blood loss, Scar. Give a man a break," Demon says, wincing as Jaxon pokes around his wound. I step closer, trying to see what he's doing to the poor man. The cut looks nasty, quite deep and painful-looking. I don't know how he's standing there acting like everything is fine. I decide to grab a glass and pour him some Scotch. When I hand it to him, he flashes me a grateful look. "You're a keeper, Scar."

He downs it, so I pour him another.

He downs that too.

"I'm going to have to stitch it myself," Jaxon says, sighing. "Let's just fucking hope it doesn't get infected, Demon. Or else you will have to go to the hospital or lose your fucking arm."

Demon sends me a pleading look, so I quickly pour him

another drink. Jaxon heads into his room and comes back with a needle.

I pour myself a drink this time.

Jaxon stitches, and Demon doesn't make a noise, not even a whimper. Once Jaxon's done, he examines his work and mutters, "A doctor needs to look at this. I can drive you out of town so no one knows who you are. This isn't something to fuck around with."

"Fine," Demon mutters, but he can't hide the relief in his tone.

I wait until they're finished before I start the interrogation, because they have some damn explaining to do.

chapter 31

JAXON

I CAN'T BELIEVE HE CAME here when Scarlett was here.

Fuck.

How are we going to explain this one? She's friends with the MC, and I don't know how she's going to handle this tidbit of information. Demon and I exchange a glance, having a silent conversation that only people who have known each other for years can have.

"Don't even think about lying to get out of this," Scarlett says, her cute face turning all mean. "I know you two know each other. What I want to know is why you pretend that you don't."

I don't lie to Scarlett. Ever. But the fact that Demon is undercover is a life-and-death situation, and it's not my secret to tell. He stays quiet, so I know he's trusting me, leaving it up to me to explain, but I kind of wish he'd step in with some bullshit lie and save me from having to come up with something.

"We do know each other," I say slowly, trying to explain this the best way I can. "We knew each other as kids. Now he's a dickhead biker, and I'm a criminal lawyer, end of story."

Not exactly a lie, right?

"He obviously trusted you enough to break into your house in the middle of the night for help," she points out, not looking impressed with my answer. She can know anything, except that Demon is actually an undercover cop. That's the bit I need to steer her away from. It's not that I don't trust her with the information, but it's something that can put her into danger. I also don't need her getting drunk with the Wind Dragons women and accidentally letting something slip. I won't gamble with Demon's life, no matter how much I trust and love Scarlett. She doesn't need to know this. I don't want her to feel guilty about having known this. And if it ever comes out, her friends won't like the fact that she knew. They'll see it as a betrayal. I also don't mention that he didn't break in, the bastard has an emergency key.

"He's one of my closest friends," I admit to her, throwing him a dirty look. "But as you can see, we lead very different lives. I don't get to see him much anymore. But that doesn't mean that when he needs me, I'm not there for him, and he knows that. I'll always have his back, and vice versa."

She contemplates that for a few moments, and then says, "So that's why Demon was at Riley's? You told him to keep an eye on me!"

Demon tries to stifle his laugh, fails, then winces because it must hurt his arm. "Ahh, fuck. Don't make me laugh, Scar."

"I asked him to keep an eye on you, not watch you get piss-poor drunk," I grumble, but nod. "But yeah, he said he'd make sure you were safe. Oh come on, don't look at me like that! Any man would have done the same. And it's not because I don't trust you; it's because I don't trust men. I don't even like the thought of them looking at you, so I thought I handled it pretty well."

She sighs deeply and eyes the two of us. "The two of you, I swear. So the Wind Dragons don't know about this little friendship you have going on here?"

"I'm a private person," Demon speaks up, and I'm grateful for it. "I keep my life before the MC to myself, and I'd like to keep it that way."

"Secret is safe with me," Scarlett promises, looking to Demon. "Can I get you anything? Water? Something to eat? A blanket?"

"I'm fine, thanks, Scar," he says, smiling at my woman. "Are you going to come for a drive to the hospital out of town? It might be an adventure."

A smile spreads on her beautiful face. "I wouldn't miss it for the world. I'll pack some snacks."

She stands and walks out of the room, and our eyes follow her until she disappears.

"I'm sorry, brother," he says, puffing out a breath. "I didn't see her car. I should have been more careful. I don't want to get you into any shit with your woman."

"Don't worry about all that," I say, scowling at him. "I'm just worried about you. This can't be good for your case. Fuck, Demon. If anyone finds out the truth . . ."

"They won't," he says, sounding sure. "It's not a crime to be childhood friends with a lawyer, all right? It's fucking fine."

"The same lawyer who put one of your fellow MC members in prison? It doesn't look good, Demon. They might think you gave me information for the case, or even worse, that it was you who tapped the lines for me! Then what?" I ask, standing and starting to pace.

Fuck.

This is not good.

And he didn't even help me do anything, he was loyal to the MC. I had to do everything on my own. I don't want him getting into shit, and messing up his undercover work because of this. I don't even know who Demon is loyal to anymore, if I'm being honest—the police force or the MC—but either way I'm going to be by his side.

"She won't say anything," Demon tells me. "Have you seen how she looks at you? She isn't going to tell anyone anything about this. She's loyal to you."

"I know she is," I tell him, glancing to make sure she's not there. "It's not that, Demon."

It's just safer when no one knew about this.

Scarlett walks back into the room with a picnic basket filled with God knows what and a smile on her face. "Should we get going? If Demon's wound gets infected we're going to be in for a rough time."

We.

She's in this with us, no matter what.

Fuck, I'm so lucky to have this woman by my side.

She has a body to die for, the most intense fuck-me eyes, an amazing smile that can be mischievous when she's up to no good, and she's a good, loyal woman.

Gold mine.

"Yeah, we should," I tell her. "Are you sure you want to come? You can go back to bed and get some rest if you like, Scarlett."

I look down at her and realize she's been wearing nothing but a nightdress for this entire time, and I can see the outline of her nipples. "And maybe put on some clothes."

She looks down, and like me, only just remembering what

she's wearing. "Yeah, I should probably do that." She puts the basket down on the couch and disappears again.

I turn to Demon, who is now wearing a smirk. "I liked what she was wearing."

"Keep going if you want your other arm broken," I tell him, jaw going tight. "Are you ready to go?"

Demon nods, then glances down at his arm. "Yeah. And, Jaxon?"

"Yeah?"

"Thank you. I mean it," he says, blue eyes showing me his gratitude. "Can always count on you, brother."

I offer him my hand to help him up, and he takes it. "What are friends for, right? If not to take you to the hospital in the middle of the night after a knife fight. How does the other guy look?"

"You don't want to know," he murmurs, wincing. "In fact, the less you know the better."

Jesus.

I thought the Wind Dragons had gone boring, but apparently I was wrong. Who the hell would he be getting into a knife fight with? At least it wasn't with guns, but still. I don't know what shit Demon is getting into, and I don't like that I don't know because I can't help him. I may wear a suit every day, but that doesn't mean I can't fight and take care of shit that needs to be taken of. It's not who I am, but a fighter is buried inside of me. If anyone hurts the people I care about, there is nothing I wouldn't do to protect them.

"Noted," I say, sighing. "What have you got yourself into, Demon?"

"Just a little bar brawl, Jaxon. Don't you worry your pretty head about it," he defends, brushing off my worry.

Scarlett returns in jeans and a black top, white sneakers, and her hair tied up. "Okay, let's go."

We all get into my car.

Scarlett moves to sit in the back, but Demon opens the passenger seat door and tells her to sit in the front.

He gets in the back.

It looks like Scarlett has won the respect of one of the biggest badasses in town.

I'm not surprised one bit.

chapter 32

SCARLETT

"AND HOW DID THIS wound happen?" The nurse asks Demon. "I need to file a report, sir. I can't just turn a blind eye to the fact that you have what looks like a hand-stitched knife wound in your arm."

Demon simply turns to Jaxon. "As my lawyer, Mr. Bentley, what do you recommend I do here?"

Jaxon looks to the nurse and says something to her that I can't quite hear. She shifts on her feet, then starts to tend to Demon's wound. I don't know what Jaxon said, but I'm not surprised he got her to do her work without any further questions. The man can talk his way out of anything. After Demon is all mended, and given antibiotics, we head back home.

The trip took a few hours altogether, and I'm pretty exhausted now. I'm glad Demon is okay, and even though I don't know what to make of their friendship, their secret is safe with me. I'm surprised that they are friends, to be honest. Demon is a biker, and Jaxon seems to have an issue with them. But I trust Jaxon no matter what, and I'm not going to pry. I like Demon too—I did from the first moment I met him, even though he was being so friendly to me only because of Jaxon. I still can't believe Jaxon did that. I don't know whether to be grumpy over it or smile at his sneaky protection.

"Do you want to crash here?" Jaxon asks Demon as we walk inside. "Get some rest before you head back to the clubhouse?"

"Yeah, I might do that," he replies. "If you don't mind."

"Make yourself at home, like you always do," Jaxon says in a dry tone, but I can see how much he enjoys being around his friend. Demon heads to the guest room like he's been here a million times before, and I slide back into Jaxon's bed.

"Well, that was an eventful night," I tell Jaxon, yawning. "And you have to get to work, don't you?"

Lucky for me, I have the day off.

"Yeah, I'm going to jump in the shower and head there now," he says, but sits down on the bed and kisses me instead. "Although you're making the bed look like the best place to be right now."

"It is the best place to be." I grin.

"Can you keep an eye on Demon?" he asks, kissing my forehead and standing up. "He should be fine, but just in case."

"Of course," I tell him. "I'll make him some breakfast when he wakes up too."

"Thanks," he says, amusement lacing his tone. "He'll love that. In fact he'll probably randomly drop by even more after that."

"And you'd love that, wouldn't you?" I ask, already knowing the answer. Jaxon is just a big softy when it comes to his friend. I'm glad he has someone, even if it's some weird, secret friendship, because his parents don't live here and he doesn't seem to have anyone else outside of his work colleagues.

"Perhaps," he replies, flashing me a knowing smile. "I'd better hurry."

"Okay," I mumble, burying myself into the sheets.

What an eventful morning this has been.

I WAKE UP BEFORE Demon, who must have been tired after all the excitement of a bar brawl, breaking in, dealing with us, and then having to go to the hospital to get stitched up. I'm not sure what he likes to eat for breakfast, but I assume pancakes and bacon are a safe bet. I also scramble some eggs and bake some fresh bread to cover all bases.

"Good morning. How are you feeling?" I ask him, gaze going straight to his arm when he walks into the kitchen an hour later.

"Yeah, I feel okay," he says, eyeing the spread I've laid out on the table. "Fuck, Scar, you cooking for an army, or what?"

"I didn't know what you'd want, and I had heaps of spare time," I say, shrugging. "Have a seat. Do you want some coffee?"

"Love some," he murmurs, sitting down and starting to pile food on his plate. "Is this how you trapped Jaxon? With your cooking?"

"I didn't trap him with anything." I smirk, bringing a mug of coffee to him. "But I'm sure the food helped. You know what they say . . . the way to a man's heart is through his stomach."

He takes a bite of his pancake and moans. "I can vouch for that statement being very true."

I roll my eyes and sit down opposite him, grabbing a piece of bacon and taking a bite. "Are the men going to ask you where you went last night?"

"I'm not a prisoner there, Scar. I don't have to explain my every move. We all have our own shit going on," he says, glancing up at me after trying the bread. "Did you bake fresh bread this morning?"

I nod.

"You woke up and baked bread, from scratch, just for my breakfast?" he clarifies, a bewildered look on his face.

"Well, for both of us, yes," I reply, wondering where he's going with this.

"If he doesn't marry you soon, I will," he mutters under his breath, then takes another giant bite of the bread. "You'd make a good old lady, Scar."

"After having met Valentina, I'll definitely take that as a compliment," I tell him, feeling happy as he demolishes the meal.

"You should. And I haven't seen Jaxon open up to anyone like he has to you, especially after losing his sister. That really hit him hard. I didn't think he'd recover from it, if I'm being honest."

I stay quiet, and try to control my expression.

Because I didn't know Jaxon had lost a sister.

Isn't that something you tell someone you love? It sucks that I didn't know about such a big part of who he is, and something that obviously affected him a great deal. Pain changes people. I wish he'd have shared this with me, opened up to me. I want him to be able to feel like he can tell me anything. I want him to tell me everything. At the same time, I don't want to bring this up to him—shouldn't he be the one to come to me with it? I don't want to push him to talk about something he's not ready to, but at the same time what if he never says anything? I don't want to ask Demon about it, because this is something that has to come from Jaxon himself.

"Were you close with her?" I ask, not wanting him to know that I didn't even know Jaxon had a sister. It makes sense now though. The picture on the bookshelf, the one I assumed was an ex-girlfriend.

It was his sister.

Demon's baby-blue eyes turn melancholy. "Yeah, we were close." He smiles sadly, and takes a deep breath. "Jaxon adored Olivia, and so did I."

I study him for a moment, and then ask, "Did you two . . . ummm . . . have a thing?"

"No," he says, making a sound of pain. "I loved her, Scar. She was the one. The timing never seemed right, you know? So I waited. But I waited too long, because she found someone else. I thought she was happy, so I let her be so she could live her life. I should have been selfish and gone after her, because deep down inside I knew that no one could ever love her like I do."

Do, not *did*.

"I'm sorry," I tell him, not knowing what else to say. "You didn't know, Demon."

"We never know," he mumbles.

"You did what you thought was right to make her happy. I understand that. All I want is to make Jaxon happy," I tell Demon. "Like he does to me."

"Have you seen the way he looks at you, Scar?" He chuckles and adds, "Trust me, the man is happy. And when he's happy, so am I. And so are you, apparently." He chews slowly while watching me, then swallows before he speaks. "Irish is one of my brothers, but I'm glad it's him in there and not you. And I'm glad Jaxon fought for you to win your case. I'm sorry I didn't help him. It's something I regret, but my loyalty is also to the club, so my hands were tied."

I didn't know anything about this, but I guess it makes sense. "You don't have to apologize, Demon," I say, my eyes gentle on him. "I understand. And after spending time with Valentina, I understand even more. You would never betray your family."

He nods once. "Yeah, but Jaxon was my family first," he says, then goes a little quiet.

After a few moments of silence, I decide to change the subject. "Do you want me to check your arm?"

"It's fine," he says, shrugging me off. "The nurse said I was lucky because it didn't hit an artery, just the fleshy part. I just have to take the antibiotics and pain meds."

I don't think he has a fleshy part on his arm, or anywhere else on his body, but anyway. "Did you take them?"

"No."

I purse my lips, stand up, and grab some water from the fridge, sliding the bottle over to him. "You might want to do that."

"You trying to boss me around, Scar?" he asks, amusement etched all over his expression.

"Just trying to take care of you, Demon," I reply, not taking the bait. "If you want me to drop you anywhere let me know, otherwise I'm going to be hanging out on the couch all day watching movies, so you're welcome to join me."

"That actually sounds good," he admits, wincing as he lifts his arm up. "I don't think I'll be able to do much else today anyway. Don't ask me how I rode here on my bike, because I have no idea."

"Adrenaline, maybe?" I suggest. "I don't think you should ride home though. Let me know what you want to do; I'm free all day, so I'm flexible."

"Can I choose the first movie?" he asks, apparently having made his decision.

"If you take your pills first," I counter.

"Deal."

chapter 33

JAXON

WHEN SCARLETT DOESN'T ANSWER her phone, I rush home as fast as I can.

"Scarlett?" I call out as I open the door and all but run inside. I stop as I enter the living room to see both her and Demon fast asleep, the TV on. Scarlett is lying on the couch, and Demon is on the floor, a pillow behind his head and a thick blanket covers his body. Is this what the two of them did all day? I can't stop the grin on my face if I tried, as I pull out my phone and take a picture of the two of them. Not wanting to wake them up, I jump in the shower, trying to wash away the day. It was a long one.

The good news is, I won't have to deal with Sharon for much longer. I've been thinking of taking another break—maybe I'll take Scarlett on a vacation somewhere. It's always work with me, and for once I'd like to be able to relax and enjoy more time with her. By the time I'm dressed and resurface from my room,

Scarlett is still asleep, but I see Demon at the fridge grabbing some juice.

"Good morning," I say to him in a dry tone. "Looks like you had a productive day."

He chuckles and replies with "Your woman keeps cooking, so it's hard not to spend the day in a food coma. Jesus Christ, how are you not triple your size?"

"Gym and sex," I reply in a dry tone. "How's the arm?"

"Not bad. Scar made me take painkillers," he tells me, closing the fridge. "She can be a real pain in the ass when she needs to be."

I grin at that. "Considering you fell asleep around her, that tells me everything I need to know."

Demon has trust issues. He will never, ever fall asleep around someone he doesn't trust. He rarely gives his back to people. He can be very paranoid, although I guess he does have reason to be that way. Especially with his job, he knows better than most that people aren't always what and who they seem to be.

"Yeah, yeah," he mutters under his breath, but I see through him. He likes Scarlett. And I'm glad that he does—what's not to like? "She won't let me ride home either. In the morning my arm was hurting like a bitch, so I agreed, but I'm feeling fine now. I might head home while she's asleep so she doesn't have a panic attack."

I softly chuckle and touch his unharmed arm. "It's up to you. I can drive you, or ride your bike back for you if you want to take my car, but then they'll see me."

"Yeah." He sighs. "Better I just ride alone; it'll be fine." He pauses and smirks. "I've done worse. Hell, we've done worse."

I can't deny that one. "I know."

I walk him outside, hug him, and then watch as he rides away.

I don't know what he's doing, or what he's going to do when his case is over, but I'm worried about the man. When Scarlett rushes outside when she hears the rumble of his motorcycle, I know she's worried too.

"You let him ride? His arm!"

I wrap my arm around her and kiss the top of her head. "He's fine, baby. Don't worry about him."

"I can't help but worry about him," she admits, shifting on her feet. "Even if it was just a flesh wound."

"Is that what he told you?" I ask, not sure whether to laugh or cringe.

"Wait, what?" she growls, turning to face me, her eyes narrowing. "He told me he cut the fleshy part of his arm so it wasn't a big deal."

Yeah, that was not what happened at all.

The knife hit an artery, and he'd lost a lot of blood.

"It's fine, Scarlett," I say, hiding my amusement at her reaction. You'd think Demon was her grown kid or something. "He'll be fine. Come on; let's go inside. Is there any food left over? I'm hungry."

She nods. "There's some in the oven."

Demon sends me a message a little later saying he's back at the clubhouse and that he's fine. I show it to Scarlett, hoping she can stop worrying about him.

"Any other friends going to drop by in the middle of the night at any point?" she asks as she lays in bed, kissing my rough cheek.

"Nope, I have no other friends," I tell her. "Unless Tristan or Hunter get into a bar fight at some point."

"Are they fighters?" she asks, arching her brow. "I imagine them fighting in the courts instead of with their fists."

"Hey, don't underestimate us lawyers," I say, rolling her onto her back and pinning her arms above her head. "We're sneaky, and we don't like to lose."

"I think some of them are a little rough around the edges too," she murmurs, licking her bottom lip. "No matter how much they disguise it in expensive suits and good vocabularies."

I throw my head back and laugh. "You're only saying that because you met Demon, and you now know that we grew up together."

She grins and lifts her head to kiss me. "You're adaptable, Jaxon. I think you'd fit in anywhere, be king anywhere."

"Are you going to be my queen anywhere?" I ask, kissing down her neck. "Because that's the only way I'd want it."

She sighs in pleasure as I suck on her smooth skin, just enough so I don't leave a mark, then lift my face up and move my lips to her breasts, which are covered in a black push-up bra. I pull the cups down and latch on to one of her pretty pink nipples, sucking and biting enticingly, knowing how much it turns her on because her nipples are so sensitive.

"Jaxon," she whispers, her mouth dropping open, her eyes turning heavy. I love when she gets like this, so submissive, just waiting for me to please her and take care of everything. Trusting that I will take care of everything. I slide the straps of her bra down so I have easier access and continue to tease her until she pleads to give her more. Only then do I let my fingers roam farther down, inside her panties, feeling how wet and ready she is for me. I'm hard as a fucking rock, but I want her to be so damn turned on before I slide into her. I want her to be begging for my dick, and then I'm going to give it to her and make her come more times than she thinks is possible. I pull her panties all the way down and remove her dress. Her bra is still clasped at the back, so she sits forward and takes it off for me.

I appreciate that.

I move down the bed, spread her milky thighs, and start to lick her from bottom to top. She squirms, and I pin her thighs down and continue to taste her until she comes.

Only then do I let go of her thighs, lift her into my arms, and carry her into the shower. She stands there on shaky legs while I turn the water on, testing the temperature before placing her under the warm water. I take off my clothes, then join her, pressing her against the tiles and kissing her until neither of us knows who is who.

Then I get down on my knees, lift one of her legs up and over my shoulder, and go down on her again.

And I'm only just getting started.

"YOU NEVER TAKE TIME off work," Tristan says, surprise written all over his face. "I don't think you've ever taken time off since I've known you. Except when Olivia . . ." He trails off, then clears his throat. I tried to take time off after Olivia died, but that didn't last long. "Who are you and what have you done with Jaxon?"

"Leave the man alone," Kat pipes in, winking at me. "He never had anyone to go on vacation with before. Now he does. I think it's cute."

Not amused, I sigh at the two of them, and shake my head. "Thank you to the peanut gallery. I was actually thinking of surprising Scarlett with a trip somewhere. And you're right, Tristan, I haven't taken any vacation time, so I hope you can hold down the fort while I go away for as long as I want."

I haven't taken on any new cases, and I won't until I know what I'm doing. A break is needed, and spoiling my woman is necessary. I just hope the library will let her take some time off too, or this will all be for nothing.

"Hawaii?" Kat suggests, her eyes sparkling with excitement. "Or how about Greece? Croatia is meant to be absolutely beautiful."

"I'll have a look," I tell her, offering her a smile. "Thanks for the ideas."

Hunter sticks his head in and glances around. "We having a meeting without inviting me?"

"Just all making comments on Jaxon's latest life decisions," Tristan says, smirking at me.

"What? Did he finally sleep with Sharon?" Hunter teases, earning a dirty look from me. "Because otherwise, I can take one for the team."

"You're a pig," Kat says to him, but without any heat. If anything, she sounds amused by it. "And by the looks of things, she only has eyes for one criminal lawyer, the unattainable Mr. Jaxon Bentley."

Oh how I'm not going to miss these daily unwelcome meetings in my office.

"That's because she hasn't seen how ripped I am under this shirt," Hunter says with confidence. He starts flexing, and Kat starts laughing, which makes Tristan scowl and mutter, "Okay, that's enough. Show-off."

Callum walks into my office next and glances around at everyone. "Are we having a secret meeting that I'm not invited to? Not cool, guys. It's because I'm the youngest here, isn't it?"

"Yes, that's exactly why," Kat tells him. "Have you told Jaxon your plans?"

"What plans?" I ask him with curiosity.

"I've decided to apply to be a law clerk for a judge," he says to me. "It won't start until after I graduate law school, but I thought it might be a good career path."

"Hopefully you get Judge Williams," Hunter says, then blurts out laughing. He's referring to the one judge every lawyer in the county tries to avoid.

"That's cold, Hunter," Tristan says, looking to Callum. "Judge Greer is a nice guy. Maybe you will get him, instead of the Dragon."

That's actually what people call her behind her back.

Callum looks between all of us. "I'm sure I can handle whoever it is," he says, confidence in his tone. "If I can survive you lot, pretty sure I can survive some old-ass boring judge."

"You'll have to let us know who you end up with," Kat tells him, eyes sparkling. "We're going to miss you, but how exciting."

"Doesn't anyone have any work to do?" I ask, to which they all answer with a collective "Not really."

"How are we one of the top firms in town?" I wonder out loud.

"The other ones really suck," Kat suggests, shrugging. She pulls on the red material of her blouse and adds, "And we are pros at winging things. Oh, and we all have pretty great minds."

"And we're all good-looking," Hunter adds, a smirk playing on his lips. "I heard one of my clients discussing it on the phone, actually."

I scrub my hand down my face. "I feel like I'm losing some of my IQ listening to this."

"Why are you grumpy? You're going on vacation soon," Tristan points out. He turns to Kat and smiles at her. "Maybe we should christen his office when he's gone."

I point at him. "I'm locking my office up, thank you very much. Jesus, where else have you christened? And when do you find the time? Someone is always here. Poor Yvonne."

"Yes, poor Yvonne," Hunter says, clearing his throat. "Not like she gets any sex here at all. Nope. Not. At. All."

We all turn to stare at him, my eyes going wide at that admission. So I'm the only person not getting laid in the office? I need to call Scarlett in for a visit.

"You and Yvonne?" Kat asks, mouth forming the shape of an *O*. "Well, I didn't see that one coming." She looks to Tristan, and then me. "And I'm telling the cleaner to disinfect everything, and I mean everything."

"Really appreciate that," I tell her, meaning every word. "I didn't realize the firm moonlighted as a brothel. And, Hunter, never say the sentence 'I don't shit where I eat,' ever again."

"I never said it was me she was having sex with in here," Hunter throws out, looking amused. "But thanks for the faith you all have in me, guys."

"Don't act so innocent," Kat tells him, laughing. "So who is she having sex with?"

"Why don't you ask her?" he returns with a stubborn lift to his chin. "That's her business."

"Her business that you just told everyone in here," Kat points out, arching her brow.

I didn't realize just how badly I need this time away from this place. I love these guys, I do, but I could really do with having to miss them just a little bit. My phone rings, and everyone clears out so I can take it. Maybe there's a little professionalism left in them after all. I smile at the thought.

My circus, my monkeys.

"Jaxon Bentley," I say into the phone.

Croatia is sounding great right now.

chapter 34

SCARLETT

"SO ARE YOU STUDYING something in college?" I ask Gwen, smiling as she walks over with piles of books in her hand.

"I am, yes," she beams. "I'm one of the oldest students in the class, but I love it. I also love books, feeling them, smelling them. I could do all my research on the internet, but I don't know, I like doing it this way."

"Well, happy to have you here," I tell her. "Sometimes there's no one in here, so it's nice to have some company. What are you studying?"

"English literature," she says, a dreamy look appearing on her face. Today she's wearing all black, as usual, fishnets with black shorts, and an oversize off-the-shoulder top. She's a charac- ter, that's for sure, and after having a few conversations with her

I've found her to be a really nice person. She's clearly a dreamer, and I like that about her.

"That sounds amazing," I tell her, nodding to the books. "Although I should have guessed from all the classics I've seen under your arms."

She laughs at that. "Everyone is telling me I won't have many job opportunities, but you know what? At least I'm trying to make a career out of something I love. I'm twenty-eight years old, and right now I work as a waitress in a strip club." She looks me in the eye and adds, "A fully clothed waitress."

"No judgment here, Gwen," I tell her, offering her a small smile. "And it's good to have dreams. If you can't follow them, and whatever you're passionate about, what's left, right?"

"Love," she replies, ducking her head. "I suppose. I wouldn't know much about that either."

"It's out there and will find you when you least suspect it," I tell her. "Hey, what are you doing this weekend? Do you want to hang out?"

"SO NOW IN CONJUNCTION with being friends with an old lady in the Wind Dragons, you've made friends with a stripper?" Jaxon summarizes after listening to the story about my day at work.

"She's not a stripper," I tell him, rolling my eyes. "She works at Toxic as a waitress. There's a difference."

"Have you even been to Toxic before?" he asks, tone laced with amusement. I haven't, and he knows I haven't. I've hardly been to any clubs, never mind a strip club. I can picture it in my head though, and I imagine women dancing topless on poles, while Gwen walks around serving drinks.

"I think the better question is, have you?" I fire back at him, tightening my lips. I flick my hair over to the other side so I can see him clearly, tilting my head toward him. He's driving, so all I get is his profile and a quirk of his lips.

"I have," he admits, checking my reaction before looking back at the road. "A few times actually. Why, do you want to go?"

"Why did you go there so much?" I ask, curious, not angry. What he did before he met me is his business, and although I like to annoy him and play around, I don't actually get angry or hurt about his past.

"I don't know, I remember taking Demon there once when he got caught up on some chick. He was moping," he explains, trying to remember his times there. "Once was for a guys' night out. I don't really remember; it was so long ago."

I wonder if that *chick* was actually Olivia. I think it most likely was.

"Fair enough," I reply. "Gwen is actually just a waitress though, and she's in college. She's supersmart. I think you'd like her."

"I think you make friends with anyone who is unique," he tells me. "If you like her, then I'm sure I'll like her too. As long as she's good to you."

I smile at him. "You haven't told me where we're going yet."

"Just out to grab something to eat," he says, reaching his hand over to my upper thigh. "Today was a long-ass day, I'm exhausted."

"I'll give you a massage when we get home," I tell him, reaching over to massage the back of his neck. "Anything else I can do to help you relax, let me know."

He works so damn hard, every single day. And he's still always in a good mood when he comes home to me. He's just a genuinely good, hardworking man. I'm such a lucky woman, and I'm never going to take that for granted, ever.

"You're doing it right now," he says, hand tightening on my thigh.

When we arrive at the restaurant, Jaxon pulls out my chair and waits for me to sit down before taking his own. He waits until we both order before he slides me an envelope.

"What's this?" I ask, curiosity and excitement filling me.

He doesn't say anything, just smiles.

"What have you done now, Jaxon?" I ask, shaking my head at him. I rip open the envelope and pull out its contents. I read over the piece of paper that says Jaxon and I are going on a trip around Europe.

Holy crap.

"You didn't," I mutter, eyes going wide as saucers. "Are you serious? We're going on a vacation together?" I glance down at the paper. "For a month?"

"Yeah," he says, looking a little unsure. "I mean, if you want to, and if you can get off work."

"If I want to, are you kidding me? And I can work out something at the library. There's no way I'm going to miss this," I get out of my seat to hug him, wrapping my arms around him, not caring if people are looking or not. "Thank you so much. You have no idea how excited I am, and how much I love you."

"You have no idea how badly I want to take you away and have you all to myself, all while we travel and see part of the world together," he says, giving me a soft kiss. "New experiences with you. I can't wait."

I sit back down and beam at him. I did not expect something like this, and I know he's a workaholic and hardly takes any time off, so this is a huge deal.

"I've always wanted to go to Italy," I tell him, unable to stop smiling.

"I know," he says, grinning. "I remember you telling me that."

Our eyes hold.

He remembers everything I say.

I don't know how this happened, how I found Jaxon and how he became mine, or how I was the lucky one he picked, but I am.

And damn, it feels good.

"I don't even know what to say right now," I admit, my cheeks starting to hurt from smiling. "I'm so happy."

"You don't have to say anything. The look on your face tells me everything I need to know," he says, thanking the waitress as she brings us our drinks.

"Thank you," I also tell her, then give my attention back to Jaxon. "You know I don't care where you take me. It could have been the next town over and I would have been happy. I'm just really excited to get away with you."

"The next town over," he repeats, chuckling to himself. "You may need to raise your standards, Scarlett."

I roll my eyes at him. "What, should I become more demanding? Only be happy when you do something extravagant like this? I'm just happy to spend time with you, Jaxon, and if that's a crime, then sue me."

He smirks at my choice of words. "You going to say sue me to a lawyer?"

"I believe I just did," I reply with an arched brow. "What are you going to do about it?"

"Tie you up and punish you," he replies instantly, gray eyes sparkling.

"Doesn't sound like much punishment to me," I say, lifting the glass of water to my lips. "I think you're going to have to come up with something better, Jaxon. Or are you losing your touch? Maybe love has made you soft."

He glances down at his crotch. "Love has definitely not made me soft, Scarlett."

I cover my mouth with my hand as I laugh, trying to stifle it. "You are not hard right now."

"Actually, I am," he says in a low growl. "Lift your leg up and see for yourself."

"No," I say instantly, but then consider it. I bring my leg up and gently rub my foot along his dick, which is indeed hard. I smirk. "What made you hard? Was it the tying-up part?"

I would've never thought I could talk so openly about things like this, yet here I am, in the middle of a restaurant, asking him what exactly turned him on enough to make him rock-hard in a public place where we can't do anything about said hard-on.

"I'm always hard when I'm around you—you know this," he says, then scowls. "And that's not helping. Stop flicking your hair, and being cute and shit."

I lower my hand. "I'm not doing it as foreplay; my hair keeps falling on my face!"

"Looks like foreplay to me," he mutters grumpily, but I don't miss the twitch of his lips. "I really hope I ordered the better meal this time."

"You didn't," I say, leaning back in my chair and studying him. "You went for your safe option, which is steak, but I took a gamble on something different, so it's going to be something exciting."

"When you gamble, it's a hit or miss. So either I'll be eyeing your plate, or you'll be wishing you opted for the safe option," he says, reaching over and taking my hand. "Don't worry, baby, I'll share my food with you when your salmon fettuccine doesn't work out as planned."

"Well, there you go. Either way I win then," I tell him, smiling widely. "I can't believe we're going to Europe together." I shake my head in disbelief. He smiles and squeezes my hand. "I'm glad you're happy, baby."

He's right—I shouldn't have gambled on the salmon, but lucky for me he shares his steak, and he doesn't even throw it back in my face.

Now that's love.

"YOU LOOK STUNNING," HE tells me, eyeing the flash of leg through the slit of my maxi dress.

"Thank you," I reply, glancing down at the paisley floral print. I wasn't sure what to wear tonight, and I really want to make a good impression. We're having dinner with all of Jaxon's colleagues—Hunter, Kat, Tristan, Yvonne, and Callum—and if I'm being honest, I'm a little nervous. He walks me through the restaurant with his palm on my lower back, which relaxes me slightly. He stops at a table where two people are seated. The woman sees us first and smiles. She's beautiful, with dark hair and eyes. She has a petite build and is wearing a pretty red dress.

"Scarlett, this is Kat and Tristan," Jaxon introduces. "I thought we were late, but I guess the others are even later."

"They're all coming together," Kat tells Jaxon, standing and offering me her hand. "It's so nice to officially meet you, Scarlett."

"You too," I tell her, smiling warmly. "And I just wanted to say thank you for all the work you all did on my case. I know it was a team effort."

"You're welcome. I'm glad it all worked out," Kat replies, then glances up at Tristan. "Just another day in the office with these guys."

Tristan shakes my hand next, his blue eyes searching mine. "It's good to see you again." I remember Tristan from my bail hearing and while he also is a great lawyer, I'm glad Jaxon took my case. "By the way, you're way too good for him," Tristan continues, pointing to Jaxon.

Kat laughs, nodding. "I agree."

"Who needs enemies when you have friends like these," Jaxon mutters, pulling out my chair for me in between himself and Kat.

I sit down with a grin on my face.

"I love your dress," Kat says to me, smiling. "Have you been to this restaurant before?"

"Thank you," I tell her. "And no, I haven't, but Jaxon tells me every time you have a work dinner you end up here."

Kat smirks and fiddles with the cutlery by her empty plate. "It's true. I don't think I even need to look at the menu anymore."

"The food is good though, right?" I ask, wondering why they keep coming back otherwise."

"The food is great," Tristan tells me as Jaxon passes me a menu. "I love this place."

"He doesn't like change," Kat whispers to me.

"If it ain't broke, don't fix it," he says, just as the others arrive. I'm introduced to them all, and they all seem really nice. It's a little awkward seeing Yvonne, considering she's the receptionist, so I've had to interact with her every time I came into the office to see Jaxon. She doesn't make anything of it though, and treats me like a friend.

"Do you want some wine?" Jaxon asks me, then turns to the others. "I don't have to ask you, maybe we should order several bottles of it."

Yvonne raises her hand. "I'll have some red, thank you. And by some, I mean a lot."

"Scarlett's here," Kat tells her. "Can we at least try to act normal?"

"Oh, don't act normal on my behalf," I tell them, smiling, feeling amused. They all continue with their banter, including me when they can. I can feel Jaxon watching me, so I turn my head to my left and arch my brow at him. I suddenly feel my hand on his thigh, and I look back at Kat, who asks me a question.

"Sorry, what did you say?" I ask her.

She pours me a glass of wine and slides it to me. "I said that we should do something this week. A little female bonding, what do you think?"

"I think that sounds perfect," I beam.

I'm slowly becoming a part of Jaxon's world, and I couldn't be happier.

Our world.

chapter 35

JAXON

I OPEN MY FRONT DOOR and cringe, knowing that I'm not meant to be here right now. Scarlett is having a movie night with her friends—the biker chick, the stripper, and now Kat and Yvonne—and I was going to have a few after-work drinks with Tristan and Hunter. But I forgot my wallet today, so now I need to sneak inside and grab it before I head back to the bar. Acting like a special ops agent, I tiptoe into my bedroom undetected, then glance around frantically for my damn wallet. I look under the bed but it's not there, so I try the pants I wore to work yesterday, which are still in the hamper.

Bingo.

I slide my wallet into my pocket and prepare to make a quick departure without being undetected. "Goosebumps" by

Travis Scott plays through the house, and I have to wonder what kind of party these women are having. I just step out of my bedroom when I walk into Valentina Sullivan.

"Jaxon Bentley," she says slowly, narrowing her eyes on me.

"Valentina," I say, glancing down the hallway. "I need to make a quick exit, so let's pretend you never saw me."

"Why?" she asks, arching a brow. "Don't you like your woman's friends? We're a great bunch. You should spend some time with us."

"I'm good, thanks," I say quickly. Too quickly.

"Scarlett!" she yells, smirking at me. Fuck, the woman is pure evil.

"Shhhh," I tell her, trying to hush her. "I just came to grab my wallet. Wouldn't want to ruin your girls' night. I'll just be on my way."

Scarlett comes down the hallway and smiles when she sees me. "Jaxon! What are you doing here?" She runs to me and jumps up into my arms. "I thought you'd be at the bar."

"Forgot my wallet," I say, kissing her quickly. "I'm just on my way there now." I look into her eyes, which are glassy. "Are you drunk?"

"Nope," she says, then starts laughing.

Fuck me.

I need out, now.

"Jaxon wants to meet everyone," Valentina tells her with a straight face. "But he doesn't want to ruin our night."

In this moment, I feel no guilt for sending her boyfriend to prison.

"You could never ruin anything, Jaxon," Scarlett says, threading her hand in mine. "Come on. I know Gwen's been waiting to see you."

I grit my teeth and head out into the living room where everyone is lingering about. The women are either dancing, chatting, or eating, and all of them are in their pajamas.

I feel like I've crossed enemy lines.

Scarlett even turns the music down. Jesus.

"Everyone this is Jaxon. Jaxon you know Valentina already, and this is Gwen and her friend Nina," Scarlett introduces. "And you know Kat and Yvonne already, obviously."

"Hello," I say, smiling at them. "Nice to officially meet you all." I look at Kat, who smirks at me.

When Scarlett had come to the office to bring me lunch this week, Kat and Yvonne cornered her. While I normally like to keep my professional life and personal life separate, I'm glad Scarlett has made friends.

"Do you want something to eat or drink?" Scarlett asks.

"No, baby, I'm good. I have to go meet the guys, they're waiting for me," I say, leaning over and giving her another quick kiss. "You guys have fun. Let me know if you want me to bring some food or anything back for everyone."

I rush out of there like my ass is on fire.

RILEY'S IS PACKED TO the brim, but the atmosphere and the company are good so I can see why.

"Kat looked like she was having a good time," I tell Tristan after Preston hands me my next beer.

"Good. She hardly goes out anymore," he says, scanning the bar. "She deserves a night out. Woman is a workaholic."

"We should all do dinner sometime this week," I suggest to him.

"What about me?" Hunter interrupts, crossing his arms over his chest. "Do I need to find a woman to be invited to this?" He points to Riley. "How about her?"

Riley comes over to me, and I don't like the smirk on her face. She slides me a beer. "For you, from the woman in red over there."

I share a look with Tristan, who starts laughing. I'm almost too scared to look over to see who it is, but I do.

It's Sharon.

Of course it is.

"Fuck," I mutter under my breath, then ask the men, "What exactly does one do in this situation? Sending it back seems rude, but I also don't want to give her any fucking ideas right now."

"I know what to do," Hunter says, grabbing the beer, drinking half of it in one gulp, then blowing Sharon a kiss.

"If you want to take one for the team, now is your chance," I tell him, trying not to laugh. But seriously? The woman is everywhere. I didn't take her for a Riley's kind of woman, but what do I know?

The doors open, and in walk Scarlett and her crew.

"Here comes trouble," Tristan mutters, and I can hear the smile in his voice. Kat runs up to him and he pulls her into his arms. Scarlett approaches me with a smile playing on her pink lips, wrapping her arms around my neck.

"Hello, handsome," she says, letting go of me and turning to her girls. "I'm going to order us some drinks."

"Who is this?" Sharon asks as she approaches, acting like a jealous girlfriend.

"Scarlett, this is my client, Sharon Beetle. Sharon this is my girlfriend, Scarlett," I introduce, inwardly cringing.

"I see," Sharon coos, taking Scarlett in from head to toe.

Scarlett steps closer to me and takes my hand into hers. "Nice to meet you, Sharon. However I need to steal Jaxon now."

She pulls me away to the other side of the bar, as Sharon goes back to where she was sitting. Scarlett gets on her toes and kisses me, then asks. "What the hell is she doing here?"

"Maybe she has a tracker on me," I grumble, kissing her lips. "You look amazing tonight."

"Thank you," she says, smiling. "I need to go get my drink."

She walks back to the bar, where her group's drinks are being made. When she greets Preston with a hug, I scowl. How the hell does she know this guy?

The women all head to the dance floor while I turn to Preston and eye him skeptically. "How do you know Scarlett?"

"Scarlett?" he asks, eyes going wide. "Fuck, you're her man? You lucky bastard."

I narrow my gaze on him. "Just remember that next time you touch her."

"We're friends," he says, hands up. "Plus now that I know you're her man"—he trails off—"and not that biker guy . . ."

He heads off to serve other customers, and a few minutes later, Riley comes over and sits next to me. "Having a good night?"

"Yeah," I tell her, smiling as I watch Scarlett dance. She looks so free, a big smile on her lips.

"She's beautiful," Riley says to me. "And not just on the outside."

"I know," I say, then look to her. "What about you? Single?"

"No," she shakes her head. "I'm married."

She doesn't say it like it's a good thing. She says it in a sad, almost wistful way. I'm about to ask her more when I'm dragged to the dance floor by Scarlett, where we stay for the rest of the night.

She loves to dance, and I love seeing her do something she loves.

Even if I have to hang around her crew for the rest of the night.

chapter 36

SCARLETT

I WAKE UP TO A bottle of water, a banana, and two painkillers on the side table next to the bed. "What a legend," I say to myself as I pop the pills and swallow a large gulp of water, hoping it'll cure my current predicament. I allow my head to fall back to the pillow but smile when I remember everything we got up to last night. I've never had a girls' night out like that before, but the big surprise of the night was Jaxon singing. I wish I could have recorded that so I could replay it on more than just my mind.

"Good morning," Jaxon says as he walks into the room, looking like he wasn't out until all hours of the night.

"Did you go for a run?" I ask him, wondering how he does it. "How do you find the energy?"

He lifts his shirt up to flash me his six-pack abs. "These

don't come easy, babe. If you want me to look good while eating your cooking, I need to run and spend time in the gym."

"Can you bring those abs over here?" I ask him, my fingers itching to trace them. My tongue wants in too.

He steps forward, chuckling at my request. "Why? Feel the need to get reacquainted?"

"Indeed," I murmur, placing my fingers under his T-shirt and letting them roam. "Oh yeah, that is nice. Are you going to come back to bed? I might need a closer inspection."

"Do you now?" he asks, lifting his shirt over his head and letting it fall to the floor. "This might help."

He slides onto the bed in nothing but a pair of low-riding basketball shorts, and climbs in next to me. "Is this close enough?"

"I don't know," I say slowly, feeling playful. "Let me have a look and I'll let you know."

I lift the blanket and run my fingers down to the V of his hips, and then back up through the center of his muscular stomach.

"That feels nice actually," he says, sighing in content.

Just nice?

I need to up my game.

I start kissing him down his stomach, from in between his pecks down to his navel, and then lower. He doesn't stop me, just watches my every move with intent. When I pull down his shorts, he makes a sound deep in his throat, a guttural moan of pleasure, which turns me on so much that I take his cock into my mouth without any teasing. And he loves it. I move down to his balls and lick in between them, before sucking on each in turn. I make sure to be gentle, and look up at him in the eye so he can see who is pleasuring him.

Me.

Only I can give him this.

He's mine.

"You look so beautiful right now," he tells me, pushing my hair off my face. "You're a temptress, Scarlett. Fuck. A seductress. One look into those deep, soulful eyes, and all I want to do is be inside of you."

Well, he's going to have to wait until I finish playing.

"Come here, Scarlett," he murmurs, and I lift my head to look at him to see what he wants. He touches my ass and adds, "Want you to sit on my face."

I move into position, lowering myself onto him, facing his cock and then lower my own mouth onto him.

I gasp on his dick.

Couldn't think of a better way to wake up in the morning.

THE REST OF THE week passes by in a blur. Jaxon is busy with court, and I keep myself busy at the library. I do a little more gardening and catch up with my new friends whenever I can. This morning though, I can tell something is weighing on Jaxon's mind. He's been quiet since he woke up and seems to want his space. Every time I come into the same room as him, he doesn't say anything, lost in his own thoughts. I have no idea what's wrong or why he won't say anything, but something is obviously upsetting him. Is it something I did? I know I shouldn't think that way, but old habits die hard. It's like he's gone cold, and I don't know why. I don't know how to fix it, and I know I should just give him some space, but I don't like being pushed out of his bubble.

"Is everything okay, Jaxon?" I ask him, brow furrowing in concern. "Do you want me to make you something to eat?"

Why do I always think food will fix everything?

"Not hungry, but thanks, babe," he says, trying to force a smile, but it comes out as more of a grimace. "I'm going to head to the gym before work."

He kisses the top of my head, and then walks out of the house.

I have no idea what is wrong.

And I don't like it.

HE COMES HOME FROM work late, and he didn't reply to any of my messages or calls all day. I'm sitting on the couch, feet curled up, a mug of coffee in my hands as he walks in. He doesn't even say anything to me, just gets in the shower. I don't know what to do or what to say. I don't want to push him, but this is our relationship, and he can't just do this to me without giving me some kind of explanation. He needs to tell me what's wrong. I can't help fix it if I don't know. I put down my coffee and go sit on his bed, wanting to talk to him when he comes out of the shower. He appears a few minutes later, towel wrapped low on his hips.

"Jaxon," I start.

He lifts his head and looks me in the eye. He looks sad. I wish he would tell me why.

"Will you tell me what's wrong? I don't want you to shut me out, and something is clearly wrong." I keep my tone soft and even. I don't want him to think I'm attacking him, and I don't want him to get defensive or push me away even further. I think when you speak to someone, tone and body posture is everything. I want to let him know that there is no judgment here, this is a safe place, and he can trust me. It's just me and him.

He *can* trust me.

And he needs to, if he wants this to work.

chapter 37

JAXON

"WILL YOU TELL ME what's wrong? I don't want you to shut me out, and something is clearly wrong," Scarlett says to me, her eyes filled with confusion and sadness. I've been a zombie today, and although I tried to hide it, mainly by escaping, apparently I've failed. I don't want to hurt Scarlett, and she looks like she's upset by me being so closed off, but today is just a really hard day for me.

Really hard.

I'm used to spending this day alone, lost in my thoughts, either working out in the gym until I stop from sheer exhaustion or opening a bottle of whiskey and drinking alone. However this year I have her, and I'm clearly not handling it very well.

Today is Olivia's birthday.

I went to her gravestone on my lunch break, and then I didn't even end up going back to work.

I sat there.

For hours.

Talking to her, asking her questions, like *Why didn't you just come to me?*

I would have saved her.

I would have given anything to save her, anything.

I don't understand why she didn't come to me; I'm her brother. Her protector. And I fucking failed. I scrub my hand down my face, realizing that Scarlett is waiting for my answer, and once again I'm just lost in my own thoughts, not paying attention to anything outside of those. She's probably wondering what the fuck is going on right now, and as my woman, she deserves an honest answer. I wrap the towel around me tighter and sit on the bed.

"My sister died," I blurt out, not knowing how else to say this. "And today was her birthday. I'm sorry if I've been acting off all day, but yeah, I'm just not good at dealing with today."

She reaches over and takes my hand, stroking my knuckles with her thumb. Silent support. "I'm sorry about your sister," she finally says. "Why didn't you tell me? Do you not like to talk about her?"

I shake my head. "No, it's not that. I kind of pretend . . . I pretend that it never happened. It's easier that way. She was my sister, Scarlett, my only sibling. I don't know what happened, or why she didn't come to me, but I wasn't there for her and now she's gone. I don't know how I'm meant to get over that."

"I don't think you are," she says softly. "I think you just miss her and deal as best as you can. Maybe you try to remember good memories, and how she would want you to be living your life if she were here. Maybe you hope that time will help heal, help make it easier, but also accept that there will always be a place missing in your heart because of her, and that's okay. It's okay to feel like this, Jaxon. I just wish you wouldn't shut me out, and maybe one day you'll feel comfortable talking about her. You keep her photo out there. I've always wanted to ask about it, but I didn't because I knew it was something you didn't want to discuss. I'd hoped you would bring it up when you were ready."

"But I didn't."

"No, you didn't," she repeats, sliding closer to me and resting her head on my shoulder. "Will you tell me about her now?"

I take a deep breath. "She was beautiful. Kind. Gentle. Loving. I used to have to threaten boys in school to stay away from her. She just had something about her, you know? Like people could somehow sense that she was special." I stop and smile, thinking about her. "She used to tell me she was an empath because she felt everything so deeply. I don't believe in any of that stuff, but it was true that she was sensitive."

"She sounds amazing," Scarlett tells me, ducking her head. "I have to admit something. When Demon was here he mentioned her, so I kind of already knew that she'd passed away, but I didn't want to ask you about it."

My lips tighten.

Demon loved my sister; it was obvious. I don't know why they didn't end up together, but I wish that they had. Maybe she'd still be here. I sometimes wonder if Demon has the same thoughts, but I'd never raise them to him. It'd hurt too much to even consider. I know the two of them had feelings for each other, and soon after is when she met her husband. The one who made her hate her life so much that she ended it. A man I will hate until my last breath.

"Demon and she were close," I admit, not going any further into it than that. "I should have told you. I don't know; I've never had a woman I'm in so deep with that I had to explain, if that makes sense?"

She places a kiss on my stubbled cheek and sighs. "Can I ask you how she passed away?"

My body stills at her question, but I know she needs the answer. "She committed suicide."

Her eyes widen. "Shit, Jaxon. I'm sorry."

She jumps onto my lap and brings her arms around me, hugging me tightly, like with nothing but her will and love she can put all my pieces back together. "Did you go to her gravestone?"

I nod. "Yeah, I spent most of the day there. I tried to do some work but couldn't concentrate. Tristan knows, and he shook his head at me when he saw me at work. I don't think anyone expected me to show up at all, but I was trying to stay distracted. Ended up sitting at her stone, bottle in one hand. I brought her the biggest bouquet of red roses I could find because I know they were her favorite. So romantic, she used to say."

Little did I know, she wasn't getting any romance or love. I don't know how anyone can harm something so beautiful. Someone. It's like he knew she was special, and instead of trying to embrace that and protect that, he decided to destroy her. I wonder if she thought she could fix him, or if she could love him into being a good person. I wouldn't be surprised, Olivia thought kindness and love were the cure to all evil.

"If you want to go back, I'll go with you," she says, clearing her throat. "If you want me to, of course. If you prefer to go alone, that's okay too."

"I usually go every month," I tell her. "Next month, I'll take you with me."

I don't know if she knows just how big of a deal this is. I've never taken anyone to Olivia's gravestone. I've never even told anyone I go there once a month. I keep it all to myself. This is me really letting her in. Not just in a little, but all the way. Soul-deep.

"Okay," she whispers, glancing up at me. "Come on, let's get into bed. Maybe you can share some funny stories about you and her growing up. I'd like to hear them."

She gets off my lap and climbs into bed, so I do the same.

And then we talk, bodies pressed together, my mind no longer closed off.

I share memories, stories, and jokes with her.

She laughs or she squeezes me tighter. She gives me whatever I need. She shares my pain, my frustration, my longing. She shares the burden, so that when I'm done, I feel lighter.

Freer.

Safer.

Less guilty.

Like everything will be fine, and it's okay to remember my sister and talk about her. Remember the good times. I don't want those memories to fade. I want to remember her smile and her laugh, that scent she always wore. The look in her eyes as she'd watch me, like she adored me, like I could do no wrong in her eyes.

I would have died to protect her, but instead she died trying to be strong on her own.

I look up at the ceiling and think, *I hope you're happy now, Olivia. You were too good for this world anyway.*

chapter 38

SCARLETT

"WHAT THE HELL ARE you doing here?" I ask Demon when I find him sitting in my library, browsing through a magazine, his feet up on a chair. "Making yourself comfortable, I see."

"Just having a bit of a read. Thought I'd see what all the fuss is about."

I glance down at the magazine and scowl when all I see are pictures of half-naked women. "Seriously? Did you bring your own dirty magazine to the library?"

"Are you calling naked women dirty, Scar? I like to think of it as an art form," he says, keeping his face straight. "I had no idea you were so judgmental."

I roll my eyes, and sit down next to him. "Is everything okay?"

He closes the magazine and nods once, slowly. "Yeah, it's

fine. I called Jaxon, but he didn't answer. Guess I was just wondering how he was yesterday."

"It was a rough day," I admit, exhaling deeply. "He seemed a little better this morning though. How are you holding up?"

"I spent yesterday drunk," he admits, looking down at his hands. "So the reality of everything is only hitting me today, and yeah, it's fucked. I'm glad Jaxon had you to be there for him."

"And who do you have to be there for you?" I ask softly, wondering if the real reason he came here was because he needed someone to talk to.

"She wasn't my sister," he says, playing it off. "But yeah, it's hard to deal with, you know? I grew up with her. Jaxon loved his sister so much. And for her to take her own life because she was being abused at home by her husband, something the two of us could've stopped had we known, yeah, it's a hard pill to swallow."

Olivia was being abused?

Jaxon never mentioned that.

"I can imagine," I say, studying Demon. "I'm about to go on my lunch break; do you want to grab something to eat?"

He nods and stands, leaving his magazine on the table. I pick it up and pass it to him, and he grins and takes it. "You sure you don't want to have a look?"

"I'm sure," I tell him in a dry tone.

Jaxon's sister was being abused. I don't know if it was mentally or physically, but it's similar to my own past. I feel for everything the poor woman must have been put through, especially to be so broken and feel so helpless that she took own life. What did he do to her? Why didn't she turn to Jaxon, or even Demon? Two strong men who could have handled the situation and saved her. Olivia had options, so why did she take the way out that she did? A thought crosses my mind, and I wish it didn't, but once it's there, it stays.

And it grows.

My situation was exactly like Olivia's. Is that why Jaxon went out of his way to help me? Is that why he believed me?

Was he trying to save me because he couldn't save her?

In some twisted way, is that what drew him to me? My weakness?

I walk outside with Demon, my eyes closing as the sunlight hits my face. "Do you think that Jaxon helped me because of what happened with his sister?"

Demon's eyes lock on me. "I don't know, Scar, what do you mean exactly?"

"I mean that the moment I told him what Darren had done to me is the moment he decided to take a chance on me, and only now am I figuring out why," I admit, wrapping my arms around myself.

"Does it matter why he did it though?" he asks, placing his hand on my back and leading me down the road toward the restaurants. "He believed you when the evidence was pointing in the other direction, and made it his mission to save you. He did his job, sure, but he also did it because clearly he was falling in love with you along the way."

"What if he wanted to save me only because he couldn't save Olivia, and that's the reason why he's with me now?"

There. I said it out loud.

It may seem crazy, but it makes sense to me. He feels guilty over what happened with her, and now he's saved me from the messed-up situation I was in. To what? Make amends somehow? "If I didn't tell him about Darren and my past, would we be standing here right now?"

Demon stops and turns me to look at him. "Jaxon loves you.

Fuckin' adores you, Scar. Yes, what happened to Olivia messed him up, I know it did me, but that doesn't mean the outcome wouldn't have been any different with the two of you. You were made to be with each other in my book. Don't overthink shit. And I think you should talk to Jaxon about this."

"I will," I say, sighing and forcing a smile. "I will. Okay what do you feel like eating?"

He studies me for a moment longer, but then lets it slide. "Lady's choice."

I lead him to my usual lunch spot. I don't miss the way women look at him as we pass, all practically panting. "Why are you single, Demon?"

"Like being alone" is his reply, and I don't push it.

I guess everyone has issues—you just need to find someone who makes you want to work through them. Makes you want to be better. I send Jaxon a message and tell him I'm having lunch with Demon, asking him if he wants to join us. He replies straightaway saying he's stuck in meetings, but he'll see me at home.

I love you, I send him.

I love you more, he types back.

Demon and I have a nice meal together. Maybe he just wanted some quiet company, I don't know, but I like hanging out with him.

"Are you going to eat that?" he asks as I stare at my dessert, too full to move.

"Yes," I reply, bringing my plate closer. "You should've chosen a better dessert."

He looks down at his sticky date pudding. "I thought I chose fairly well, but now yours looks appealing."

"Always want what you can't have. Typical man," I tease, taking a bite of my cheesecake and exaggeratedly moaning. "It tastes so good too."

"You're evil," he states, eyes on my plate still. "And I believe it's women who want what they can't have, not men. Trust me, I know. If you want a woman, all you have do is tell her no. They get off on that shit."

"Charming," I say, pursing my lips. "I can't imagine many women say no to you though." I pause, and then add, "Unless you open your mouth and say crap like that, then I can imagine it quite well."

His lips twitch, and he takes a huge bite of his sticky date pudding. "Give me an ego boost, then take it away why don't you? Women are easy, Scar. It's not a big deal to me, you know? They come; they go; they're replaceable. Until I find one who isn't, I don't really have any plans to settle down, or even have a girlfriend, or whatever they're calling it these days."

"Bae?" I snicker, pushing my cheesecake toward him. "Go on, have a bite. See if the grass is greener on the other side."

He slides a huge piece onto his fork, then pops it into his mouth, chewing thoughtfully, before swallowing and flashing me a smirk. "Mine's better."

I reach out with my fork and grab some of his. When it hits my tongue, I know he's right. "Dammit."

"Well there you go," he comments, tone superior. "Not is all as it seems, is it?"

"Can we swap?" I ask, being dead serious.

He just laughs and says, "Let's just order another two."

"Deal."

He signals the waitress, and I silently thank myself not just for Jaxon, but for everyone he's brought into my life.

chapter 39

JAXON

I'M MAKING NOTES IN my daily planner when there's a knock at my door. It's late, and the office is about to close, so I assume it's one of the crew coming to harass me about something or other, and I'm surprised when Sharon, in a red dress with red lipstick, walks into my office.

"I'm just about to head out, Ms. Beetle. You'll need to make an appointment with Yvonne at the front desk if you need to see me for something," I tell her, keeping my voice stern. She needs to stop thinking rules don't apply to her, because this is getting fucking ridiculous.

"I left my phone here this morning," she murmurs, glancing around. "I'll just grab it and be out of your way."

I look on my desk but don't see any phone. Nor did I come across one during the day. "I don't think it's here," I tell her.

Only a few more weeks, and then I'll never have to see her again.

"I definitely left it here," she says, looking on the floor. "It might have fallen down somewhere."

In her dress, gold heels, and face full of makeup, she starts crawling around on the floor. I look up at the ceiling and pray for patience. Is Hunter still here? I feel like he'd really enjoy this situation right now.

"Oh, there it is," she says, sounding excited. "It's near your foot, Mr. Bentley."

I look down and see that there is, indeed, a small black phone under the corner of my desk. I pick it up, happy to be rid of her, and hand it to her.

"Thank you," she says, then takes me by complete surprise, by jumping up on me, wrapping her arms around my neck, and kissing me. She misses my lips properly though, so it's more like her sucking on my lower lip and chin. I'm about to push her off, when in a flash, another unexpected turn of events takes place. Demon walks into my office, sees . . . whatever the fuck Sharon is doing to me, except instead of saving me, he assumes the worst.

And that's how I got punched in the face by my best friend.

"I THOUGHT YOU WERE cheating on Scar!" he growls, pacing up and down my office. "How was I supposed to know a woman would be attacking you and trying to seduce you? Fucking hell, Jaxon! How's your nose?"

"Broken," I reply in a dry tone.

I don't think it's actually broken, but the bastard deserves to feel bad over hitting me in the face. "And even if I was kissing another woman, what the fuck happened to bro code? Whose side are you on here, Demon?" I yell, then point to my bleeding nose. "Pretty sure this answers that for me."

"You're angry at me for being close with your woman and defending her honor?" he throws back at me. "If you were cheating on her, you fucking deserved that hit and you know it. And if you cheated, period, you wouldn't be the man I've known my whole life."

"Yet you still punched me without asking any questions!"

"Trigger reaction to what I walked in on, brother! Can you really blame me?" he asks, rubbing his knuckles.

"What, did my face hurt your hand? Should I be saying sorry?" I ask, voice laced with sarcasm.

"Your face is fucking hard, actually," he says, anger gone. He drops into my client chair and scans the room before bringing his eyes to me.

Then the bastard laughs.

Laughs.

There's blood on my carpet, but he's laughing.

"You're an asshole, Demon," I growl, sighing heavily. "How am I going to explain this to Scarlett?"

"I'll explain it to her if you want," he grins, adding. "I'm going to go up a notch in her book."

My eyes narrow to slits, and I take the cloth from my nose. "Explain what? That instead of saving me from that she-devil you hit me in the face? A face she happens to be quite fond of. What did you come here for anyway?"

"I haven't seen you since the knife fight and . . . Olivia's . . . and you know, I just wanted to see how you're doing is all. I don't think it's safe to keep going to your house, so I thought I'd quickly drop by here. A biker in a lawyer's office is probably a pretty common sight, hey?" he says with his expression blank. Sometimes I'm so self-involved I forget I'm not the only person who loves Olivia. Demon must be struggling too, and trying to seek me out because I'm the only one who would know what he's going through right now.

"I'm doing okay, Demon. Or at least I was," I say, tightening my lips and touching my nose. "How are you doing?"

"Yeah, okay," he says, looking anywhere except me now. "I went to her stone and saw your roses. I added some of my own. She's the most spoiled person there now."

I close my eyes and reopen them. "It'll never get easier, will it?"

"No," he replies instantly, sounding miserable. "But that doesn't mean we don't push through like we always do, right?"

I nod. "Something like that. It's just so hard not to think about the what-ifs. I think that's the part that kills me. It didn't have to be like this."

"I know," he whispers, voice cracking. "Trust me, brother, I know. She could have been here with us right now, yelling at us for fighting, then tending to your face."

"Her touch would have been soft, no matter how angry she was," I add, remembering all the times she helped us tend to cuts, wounds, and bruises after getting into fights or doing some other dumb shit.

"The good die young," he murmurs. "And boy, was she good."

He loved her—I know it; he knows it.

And Olivia loved him too.

We share a look, a moment of vulnerability where we don't hide the truth from ourselves. Where we let our weakness, our pain show.

And then we let it go.

Until next year.

"You all right to drive home?" he asks me, standing up. "Or you going to be a little bitch about the tap I gave you?"

I smirk, silently grateful the intense moment is now over. "I'm good to drive, don't worry about me. I'll just send Scarlett over to sort you out."

"Ha! She's just as soft as Olivia was," he blurts out, trying to be funny, but the words must hit us, because we both go quiet again.

I disagree with this comment though, because Scarlett is much stronger than Olivia was. Yes, she's gentle and soft and kind, but she also has a spine of steel.

"Until next time," Demon says, lifting his chin at me and then disappearing. I get into my car and drive home, ready to face Scarlett and explain why my nose looks like Owen Wilson's.

"SHE DID *WHAT?*" SCARLETT growls, rushing to me and turning my face from left to right. "That bitch put her lips on you?"

I inwardly feel smug that she's finally showing a reaction to this whole scenario, but I hide it. "Well, she tried. She mainly kissed my chin."

"And then Demon punched you?" she asks again, making a *tsk-tsk* sound. "What am I meant to do with the two of you? He shouldn't have hit you, but to be fair he thought you were making out with that hag."

I smirk at her choice of word for Sharon. "He should've given me the benefit of the doubt. Fuck, I'd never cheat, Scarlett. He should've known better."

"Don't take it personally. It was a heat-of-the-moment thing. I probably would've done the same," she admits, brushing it off.

"You would have punched me in the face?" I ask, doubt leaking from my words.

"No," she says slowly, but then explains that she already knew Sharon was after me. Demon didn't have any of the background information, which is true. Still, I'm allowed to complain about being hit square in the nose by my best friend, who is a cop and a trained fighter—not that Scarlett knows about that.

"Well, it doesn't appear to be broken," she says, examining me. "Which is the good news. Bad news is it's swollen and looks extremely painful. Why don't you have a shower and get changed, and then we can put some ice on it and give you some painkillers."

I pull her close and rest my forehead against hers. "As if I'd do anything to jeopardize this, Scarlett."

"I know," she says back, kissing my lips gently. "You aren't that stupid. I trust you, Jaxon. I know you're a good man, and an honorable one. You're loyal."

"Yet I still get punched," I grumble, which only makes her laugh. "I'm glad you're enjoying this."

She kisses my cheek. "Do you want me to run a bath for you, Mr. Grumpy?"

I nod. "Yeah, that actually sounds good."

She smirks, like she finds my sulky mood amusing, and heads to the bathroom. I follow her and strip down along the way. "Are you going to join me?"

She nods and turns the water on, then removes her clothes. I stare at her body from behind, the flare of her hips and the soft curve of her ass. She's so beautiful from every angle. I reach out and trail my finger down her spine, and she stills, then turns her head back to look at me, her hair flipping to the side. "Feeling better, are we?"

"Just admiring the view," I say, gaze roaming. "You're so beautiful, Scarlett. And not just on the outside."

She beams at me, and then bends down to test the water temperature.

Well, fuck.

I glance down at my dick, which is now standing to attention, and wonder which position will be most comfortable in that tub. She straightens and turns back to me, a sultry, playful look on her face. She bites her bottom lip, and then steps into the tub, beckoning me. She doesn't sit down though. She waits until I'm in, before she gets comfortable in between my legs. She ignores my hard-on, and I do the same, feeling so relaxed in the warm water, with my woman's back pressed against my chest. Sometimes the most intimate moments you can have with someone don't involve sex. I cup some water in my hands and pour it onto her shoulders, and she rests her head on my chest.

Not a bad way to end the night, "broken" nose and all.

chapter 40

SCARLETT

I HAVEN'T SAID ANYTHING TO Jaxon, but the conversation I had with Demon still plays in my mind. I know it's not fair, especially since I haven't brought it up with him, but the whole "his wanting to save me because of what happened to his sister" thing makes me wonder what would have happened if I hadn't told him about Darren. Would he have walked away from me, from my case? I don't know. I don't even know why I'm letting it get to me, but I haven't been able to stop thinking about it; it's always on the back of my mind. On an upside, my boss said I can have time off to go away with Jaxon, so I won't have any issues with work. For one month it'll just be us, traveling Europe and exploring together. I'm browsing through a travel book when Gwen walks into the library, and my mood instantly brightens. Her black skirt swirls around her legs with each step.

"I did something bad," she blurts out, before I can even say hello. She glances around to make sure no one else can hear her. "At least I'm about to. Tonight. And I need to talk about it, or I'm going to explode."

"If you haven't done the bad thing yet, can't you just . . . not do it?" I ask her, brow furrowing.

"You'd think so," she murmurs, shifting on her feet. "But you see. I need some extra money this week, so I kind of maybe told my boss I'd get on the pole tonight."

My eyes widen. "Gwen, cancel it. If you need money, I'll give it to you. You don't even have to worry about it."

"No," she says, waving her hand in the air. "I don't want you or anyone else to give me anything. I'm a strong, independent woman, and I can make it on my own." She pauses. "Even if it means flashing a little titty to get by."

"Gwen—"

"No."

"But—"

"No. Money is not what I need from you, Scarlett," she says, taking a deep breath and threading her fingers together in front of her.

"What do you need from me then? Tell me, and it's yours," I tell her.

"I want you to be there while I dance," she says, looking nervous already. "And throw money on the stage if no one else does." She tilts her head to the side, thinking. "Oh, and do you happen to know how to dance on a pole?"

I open my mouth, and then close it again. "Let me get this straight. You needed extra money, so you agreed to strip onstage tonight, except you don't know how to dance on a pole? And you want me to come and throw money at you just in case no one else does so you're not embarrassed?"

She sighs, and nods once. "Yeah, I think that sums it up."

"Okay, I've got this. But for the record, I have no problem giving you the money, Gwen. You don't have to do this," I tell her. I don't want her to feel like she's a charity case or something, because she's not, but I have money in the bank and there's no reason for her to strip.

Apparently she's stubborn though, because all she says is, "I appreciate that. But I'm doing this. Can I count on you to be there?"

I nod. "Of course, Gwen. As for the pole-dancing moves, I don't know any, but we could watch some videos online and see what we can come up with?" I point to one of the computers. "Start researching. We can hide in the back and see what you can pull off."

"I love you," she says, throwing her arms around me.

"I love you too." I laugh, watching as she all but runs to the computer.

I send Jaxon a quick message.

We're going to Toxic tonight. Will explain later.

I think about it, and then send the same message to Demon, Yvonne, Kat, and Tristan. The more the merrier, right? We can all cheer Gwen on and make her feel like the best and hottest stripper in the world.

I don't know how you're going to explain that, but okay is his reply.

I smirk.

He didn't even object. Then again, I don't think many men would object to going to a strip club. He's probably celebrating at the news.

Kat replies with an Okay. What time?

And Yvonne replies with a Sure, why not.

I love my friends.

When I get Demon's message, I can't help but laugh out loud.

I was going to go there anyway. I'll save us a VIP booth.
You're so much more fun than Jaxon. I like a woman who can
appreciate some good boobs.

He's such an idiot.

I head over to see how Gwen's getting on, giggling at the video she's watching of some girl doing fancy pole moves, twerking, and even doing the splits.

"Can you do the splits?" I ask her, wondering how flexible she is.

"Most definitely not," she replies in a dry tone.

"I think we need to lower our standards a little," I say, clicking on a beginner video. We watch her dance for a few minutes. "See, even if you can't actually climb up the pole or anything, you can just use it as a prop to dance and grind against. Can you do any of those moves?"

"Yeah, those I can do," she states, tapping her fingers on the desk. "I just can't lift myself up on the pole or anything, I have no upper-body strength."

I point to the screen. "Then this is definitely your goal."

There's a lot of bending over and ass shaking on it, and I don't know how she's going to do all of that in front of an audience. She won't let me give her any money, but maybe I can make it so tonight she makes enough money that she won't have to do this again, at least for some time. If I have anything to say about it, she's going to make thousands tonight. I try once more for her to let me help her without my having to make up a scheme, but she declines.

Crap.

She's so stubborn.

I'm going to be the best customer Toxic has ever seen.

"SO WE'RE GOING TO a strip club to support your friend, the one who you denied was a stripper?" Jaxon asks, looking a mixture of extremely confused, amused, and resigned.

"Yeah," I say, shrugging. "How was I meant to know she'd decide to actually strip?"

"Because she works in a strip club?" he points out, glancing at his watch. "And you invited Demon and the girls. Jesus, all of this on a work night. I don't remember my weeks ever being this eventful before you came into my life, Scarlett."

"You're welcome," I tell him.

"Hunter wanted to come too, so he's going to meet us there," he says, turning to me. "Are you sure your friend wants everyone you know to come see her naked? Isn't that weird? I don't think I want to see her naked, if I'm being honest. Not because she's not attractive, but because she's your friend and I'm going to have to see her and talk to her like I've never seen her boobs before."

"You're overthinking this," I tell him, pointing to the building in front of us. "Is that it? Whoa, it's pretty big."

"Yeah, that's it," he replies, sounding like he can't believe he's coming here with me.

"Do men not come here with their girlfriends?" I ask, wondering why he's being so weird about it. "Surely people do this all of the time."

"I don't know. Maybe we should ask one of the strippers."

I grin as I get out of the car, and send everyone a quick message saying we're here. Demon quickly comes out front and walks over to us. "I have to say, this is not a place I ever thought I'd be meeting the two of you."

I take Jaxon's hand and smile at him. "Makes it more fun, don't you think?"

Jaxon glances down at me and shakes his head, lips kicking up at the corners. "You are something else, Scarlett. You sure you want to do this?"

"Yeah, of course. It's a group event," I reply, nodding to the entrance. "Lead the way."

When we walk through without having IDs checked or having to pay, I look to Demon in question.

"Didn't you know?" he asks me, raising a brow. "The Wind Dragons own this club."

I look at Jaxon, who shrugs. "I had no idea either, although I'm not surprised."

Demon wasn't joking about the VIP booth.

Tristan, Kat, and Yvonne arrive together.

"Thanks for coming out guys," I tell them, giving them a hug in turn.

"You crazy? I've always wanted to come here," Kat says, glancing up at the empty stage. "I once had a dream that I had booked the place for the night just so I could get up there and give Tristan a private dance."

My eyes widen. "That's . . . hot."

"Really fucking hot," Tristan adds, kissing her quickly.

"I know," she says, sitting down in between Tristan and Yvonne.

Yvonne looks between Demon and Tristan. "Need to make sure I can see your hands at all times, boys."

Kat starts laughing at that. "That's so wrong."

I eye Jaxon. "This is going to be an interesting experience, isn't it?"

He wraps his arm around me and places a soft kiss on the side of my neck. "You brought me here, babe. Otherwise we'd be in bed fucking right now. So this one is on you."

A shiver goes up my spine at his words. "And when we go home after this, all wound up, we can do just that."

He smiles at me with his eyes. "You gonna get turned on by this?"

"Watching my friend? No," I say, brow furrowing. "That's just messed up."

"Lots of other women here, Scarlett, not just Gwen," he says, glancing around at all the different podiums at different elevated heights. "You never know."

He'd like that, I'm sure.

I really didn't think this one out. No wonder Yvonne made that hand comment. A woman is introduced over the microphone as Lemon and comes onstage to dance. We all watch, and I find myself kind of enthralled by her seductive moves. In fact, I can't seem to look away. There are a few more dancers who come on before Gwen does, but when she does, she's introduced as Temptress.

And I can see why.

She looks absolutely amazing. She's wearing a black bodysuit, with glittery diamante fishnet stockings and bright red lips. She has her hair down and curly—bed hair—and she looks phenomenal.

"Wow," I say out loud, then look to Jaxon. "How amazing does she look?"

"Lip Service" by Machel Montano plays, and I absolutely love this song.

I open my purse and pull out all the ten-dollar bills I changed earlier, and hand a heap of them to Jaxon. "Let's do this."

"Let's make it rain," Kat says, throwing money onstage. Random men do the same from other sides of the podium, clearly loving her. When she dances it's hypnotic; she might not be able to do any fancy pole work, but the woman clearly has a sensual quality to her that makes her the perfect candidate to be up there. She sways her hips, then bends over with the pole behind her, and does some ass shaking.

We all cheer.

Everyone throws money onto the stage, more than any of the other women got, and I can't help but feel excited for her. When her time is up, we all applaud when she exits the stage.

"She was so good," Kat says, clapping. "How hot is she?"

"Encore!" Yvonne yells out, laughing when Demon stands up to give Gwen a standing ovation.

Hunter arrives just as Gwen is walking off and curses loudly. "Fuck, I missed her!"

He sits down next to Jaxon and stares up at the stage longingly. "How did she do?"

"She was . . ." I trail off and smile widely. "I had no idea she could move like that. She was amazing. I'm so proud of her."

Never thought I'd be saying that, but I am. She did what she needed and wanted to do, and she nailed it. She was flawless. I'm so impressed by her.

We all get up to leave, and I go to meet Gwen out the back.

"How did I do?" she asks me, shaking with nerves. "Oh my god, I've never been so scared in my life. I couldn't even look anyone in the eye."

"You were incredible, Gwen. Absolutely unbelievable. Do you have any idea how stunning you look? You nailed it," I say, hugging her tightly.

"Thank you for being here," she says, taking a deep breath. "And turning it into something it probably isn't."

"It's whatever we make it," I say, winking at her. "Do you want us to give you a ride home?"

She nods, and pulls out the stack of money she got. "There's at least two thousand here," she says in disbelief. "I know I have you to thank for that."

"Me? The men were loving you," I say, leading her to the door. "You made this, Gwen. You deserve every cent of it."

Jaxon is waiting at the door, and flashes Gwen a smile. "You did great, Gwen."

She smiles and ducks her head. "Yeah, let's just pretend that never happened."

Jaxon nods once, looking relieved. "Deal."

We get into the car and drop Gwen off before heading home ourselves.

What a night.

chapter 41

JAXON

"THERE IS NO CAMERA footage showing my client making inappropriate advances," I tell the judge. "It's Mr. Dyson's word against hers. I don't see why we're wasting any more of the court's time when it's clear the prosecution doesn't have any hard evidence of his claims, Your Honor."

"Ms. Beetle is known for making unwanted advances on her coworkers," the prosecutor argues. "This is not the first time she's been accused, it's just the first time someone has taken such claims to criminal court."

"Again," I say, putting my hands in front of me. "I'd like to see the evidence of these claims."

I hate the fact that Sharon probably did make untoward advances on this poor man. Sometimes my job fucking sucks.

"Your Honor, due to the prosecution's lack of evidence, I'd like to motion the court to dismiss all charges against Ms. Beetle."

I WALK OUT OF the courtroom, thrill filling me as my client walks away with the charges dropped. With no real evidence, it was a he said–she said case. And not only that, now I'll never have to see Ms. Sharon Beetle ever again.

Thank fuck for that.

Tonight is cause for celebration.

I walk Sharon to her car. "Good luck, Ms. Beetle," I tell her, nodding at her, then making a clean exit to my own car.

She's not happy.

The judge agreed to drop the charges, but he mandated that she attend a sexual harassment in the workplace class. And she doesn't want to do it. Still, she should be happy we didn't go to trial. It's clear she has a problem with thinking any man is available to her. If she were a man, she wouldn't be getting off so lightly.

"Mr. Bentley, wait," she calls out, running to me and grabbing my arm. "Are you sure you can't get me out of the classes?"

I gently push her hands off me. "I'm sure. This was the best outcome."

"Well, the best outcome would be that I walk out of here with the issue over and done with, not having to attend some stupid class. You could've tried harder, especially after that kiss we shared," she says, clearly trying to push me to the point of needing my own criminal lawyer when I kill her myself.

"You kissed me," I tell her. "And it was unreciprocated, and very unprofessional on your behalf, Ms. Beetle, especially considering the fact that you needed me to defend you because of a sexual assault claim."

She puts on a sad face. "I'm sorry; it just seems that I've stumbled across some feelings for you. I know it was unprofessional, but I'm not your client anymore. So maybe—"

I cut her off. "I'm taken, Ms. Beetle. And very much in love with my girlfriend. I'm sure there'll be plenty of men interested, but I'm afraid I'm not one of them."

I say good-bye once more and get into my car, grabbing on to the steering wheel in a tight grip, knuckles going white. I don't think I've ever disliked a woman so much in my life. She's nothing but a spoiled woman who has been told she's much more special than she actually is.

When I walk back into my office, Hunter sticks his head in and asks, "Can we make the strip-club trip a weekly event? I had a great time. I stayed after you left, and it was such a good night."

"No," I reply instantly.

"A monthly event?" he barters, looking hopeful.

"You can go as much as you like, Hunter, but I won't be joining you," I tell him, smirking. "It was a one-off event."

Although you never know with Scarlett. I'm sure if Gwen dances again, we'll be back.

"Is Gwen single?" he asks, flashing his teeth as he grins. "I should ask her out."

"You can try," I reply, laughing. "Good luck, man."

"Whatever, women love me," he states with confidence. "Gwen will too."

I laugh harder.

"Fine," he scowls. "Well, I'm off to win the hot mom her husband's money."

I chuckle to myself as he leaves, then close my briefcase. Scarlett is off today, and I'm going to leave early to spend some time with my woman.

I can't think of a better way to celebrate getting rid of the hag.

"WHAT ARE YOU DOING home so early?" Scarlett asks, running and jumping into my arms with a huge smile on her face. She's dressed in all blue and looks ethereal, like an angel running to me.

"Won the case," I tell her in between kisses. "I came home after that, no point hanging around the office."

"Congratulations," she says, placing her hand on my chest. "I knew you would. And now you don't have to deal with her anymore, right?"

"Nope. And if she needs a lawyer again, I'm not going to do it. She can find someone else. No amount of money is worth putting up with that," I say, cringing. "I'm so happy it's over with."

"Me too," she admits. "You worked so hard on that case too. I hope you can take a little break or something; you work too much. Which reminds me," she adds. "I forgot to tell you that my leave was approved," she says, excitement bubbling in her gaze. "So I guess we're officially heading overseas."

We share a grin. "That's perfect. I'll call the travel agent and get everything organized. We need to look at accommodations and everything too. We're going to have such a good time."

"I know," she breathes, "I cannot wait. Is it too early to start packing now?"

"A month early?" I tease, then consider it. "Depends, are you a light packer or a heavy one?"

"I guess you'll have to wait and find out." She smirks, taking my hand and leading me to the couch. I sit down and she straddles me, her hands on my cheeks. "I was just about to head back to my house to do some gardening and bake something, but now that you're here, what do you want to do?"

I kiss her lips, then say against them, "I was kind of hoping we could go out and celebrate."

"Of course we can. What would you like to do? You name it, and we'll do it," she says, always wanting to make me happy. Fuck, I'm so lucky. I've found a truly warm, supportive woman. She never nags me or makes my day more stressful. And I make sure to do the same for her, to be there for her in any way she needs me. A relationship is definitely a two-way street, and one that requires effort on both sides. I know it's not always going to be easy, but she's just so easy to love that everything comes naturally. Nothing about us is forced, and nothing about how I feel for her was rushed. We happened because we're meant to be together. Because no one can love her like I can, and no one can be to me what she is.

"How about a day at the beach?" I suggest. "It's been a while since I've surfed or gone swimming."

"That sounds perfect," she replies, sliding off me. "I'll get ready. Should I pack some food? Like a picnic or something?"

"That sounds nice, but we can get something if you don't want to," I tell her.

She waves her hand in the air. "It's no problem; it'll only take me a few minutes to sort out. I'll make us a fruit platter, cheese, crackers, cold cuts, and wine."

She gives me a smile, then rushes off to get everything done. I shake my head, then head to my room to get changed.

A day in the water is just what the doctor ordered.

My mouth drops open when Scarlett walks out in a rustic

orange triangle bikini. "*That's* what you're wearing?" I ask, completely distracted by the sight before me.

"Yeah, why?" she asks, looking down at herself. She runs her hand down her stomach. "Does it look okay?"

She spins around, and I see that while the bottom isn't a G-string, it also shows a lot of cheek.

"Are you bringing something to wrap around yourself?" I probe, wondering if she's trying to get me into a fight today.

"Yeah, of course," she says, sounding like I'm being silly. I then watch as she slides on a see-through cover-up thing that doesn't actually cover anything, and still shows off the round globes of her ass.

"Ummmm," I murmur, not knowing how to approach this exactly.

"I'm ready," she says, carrying the picnic basket. She slides her feet into a pair of flip-flops and places a wide-brim hat on her head. So everything is covered, except her ass, apparently.

"Scarlett," I say slowly, clearing my throat.

"Yeah?" she asks, distracted, grabbing her towel. I step to her and take the basket and towel from her, so she doesn't have to carry anything. "I can see your ass. I mean, it's a very nice one—don't get me wrong. In fact, it's making me want to skip the beach and drag you into the bedroom, but I'd kind of like to not have to share that ass with the beach's male population."

She points to my bare chest. "So you get to flash your six-pack to all the women but I can't show a little curve of booty?"

"Women aren't going to be looking at me," I try to defend.

Her expression remains unimpressed, like she doesn't believe that one bit. "No one is going to look at me either."

"Fine." I sigh, placing my hand on the small of her back. "You walk in front."

"Why?" she asks, looking suspicious.

"Because I hate to see you go, but I like to watch you leave," I tease, giving her ass a little, playful slap.

"Jaxon." She laughs, stepping in front of me and exaggeratedly swinging her hips.

I grit my teeth as her ass jiggles, kind of wishing we weren't going anywhere now. We could have done a different type of celebrating at home, but I think that's going to have to wait a few hours now.

Lucky her company is just as incredible as the sex.

chapter 42

SCARLETT

J GO BACK TO JAXON'S after work the next day, tired after a ten-hour shift. I place my bag on the kitchen counter and plop down on the couch, lifting my feet up and sighing in content. I send Jaxon a quick message asking what time he will be home and whether he can pick up something for dinner because I'm just too tired to cook right now. His home phone rings, but I don't bother to answer, both because I'm exhausted and because there's no way it's going to be for me anyway. It goes to voice mail.

"Jaxon?" a lady says. "It's Mom. Just calling to see how you're doing. Your father and I haven't spoken to you in a few weeks now. Are you still dating that girl? You know, I saw her case on TV." She sighs deeply, like she feels sorry for Jaxon. He obviously told her about me, but she doesn't seem too impressed. "What she went through was awful, just like Olivia, but I don't want you to think that you have an obligation to help a woman, and be with her just because of what happened with your sister. You can't save everyone, Jaxon, even though I know you try to. You're a good man, son, but you don't need to take on problems that aren't your own. Call me whenever you can."

She hangs up, but enough damage has already been caused.

You don't need to take on problems that aren't your own.

Why does his mom view it this way? Has he said something to her? I sit with my hands in my lap, wondering what to do about this. His mom just voiced all the worries I had about the situation in one extremely damning, heartbreaking voice mail. I never spoke to Jaxon about how I felt after finding out that his sister killed herself because she was a victim of domestic violence, that our stories were so similar but with different endings. I kept it to myself. I started to bury it. And now? It's risen to the surface again. His mom is right; Jaxon is a good man. I don't see myself as a problem though. Yeah, I have a messed-up past, but who doesn't? It doesn't mean I'm not a good woman, or that I have so much baggage that no one should ever want me again.

Obligation.

Wow, that hurts.

And it hurts because it taps into my biggest fear, which is that Jaxon felt as though he had to save me because he couldn't save his sister.

Things that happen in your life shape how you think about things and how you act, and how do I know that his scars from what happened and his guilt aren't the reasons he decided to stay in my life? What if he's with me because he feels he has to be, because I needed saving?

Because I was weak?

Because he sees his sister in me?

I stand up and start to pace, my sore feet no longer the most painful thing on my body. I decide to get some fresh air, maybe go on a drive and get some food, anything to get out of the house and clear my head. I need to talk to one of my girls. The first one who comes to my mind is Valentina, because she too has been through the same thing. She'll understand where I'm coming from, and how I feel. I send her a message:

Are you free? I need to chat to someone about something.
Coffee?

A few seconds later, she replies.

Always free when a friend needs me. Name the place and time and I'll be there.

I type back.

I'm leaving now. Café on the corner of Cedar Road.

Getting in the car now.

God, she's such a good friend.

I'm walking to my car, keys in hand, when I feel a thump, and everything goes black.

I OPEN MY EYES and sit up in a quick rush, wondering where the hell I am. What happened? Horror fills me as I look around the room, not sure what to expect. I rub the back of my head and the lump there, wincing as it starts to pound. I'm scared, but I try not to be.

It will be okay, I tell myself.

Be strong.

What would one of the old ladies do? They'd fight with every ounce of energy they had in them, they'd try to outsmart whoever has brought me here, and then they'd kick their ass. I don't think I'm capable of much ass kicking, but fighting to save myself and not giving up, that I can do. That I've done before. I look around for anything I can use as a weapon, but the room has nothing but a bed. It's not a dingy room—in fact it looks like an expensive hotel minus any furnishings. I have no idea who could have brought me here, or why, but I need to figure this out. I walk around the room, then try to open the door. Of course it's locked, so I try to jam it a bit, then try to kick it down with no luck. Having already made a ruckus, I decide to go all out and start banging on the door and yelling. At this point, I have nothing to lose. They've already planned whatever they want with me, and I doubt that's going to change if I play nice.

"Let me out!" I yell, trying to contain my panic.

Darren once locked me inside our bedroom for two whole days. I had water from the en suite bathroom and some snacks I'd had in my handbag, but he didn't open the door in those two days, and he didn't bother to give me any food. This feels like that, but worse. Better the devil you know. I knew where I stood with Darren, and although he was awful and cruel, I didn't have to worry about being killed. Hurt, yes, killed no. These people may want to kill me. Or rape me. I don't know.

Jaxon is going to be so worried about me.

Valentina too.

I search for my phone but it was obviously taken from me. I've got nothing but the clothes on my back and a bed to make do.

Shit.

I take deep breaths, trying to calm myself down.

I need to think.

I look to the window and realize I haven't tried that yet. When I open the curtains though, I see just how high up I am. This room must be on the top floor of a very large house. There's no way I could jump, or even climb down. I could maybe throw something out, or yell and hope someone hears me. When I try to open the glass though, I find that it's locked. And the window is heavily tinted. No one from the outside will be able to see me. This person clearly thought of everything, and fear fills me as I think of all the possible outcomes for this situation. I run back to the door and return to banging on it.

I don't know what to do, but I'm not just going to sit on that fucking bed and wait to die.

Suddenly, the door opens, and there's a gun in my face, pointed right at me.

Crap.

"Don't move," she tells me, voice low and lethal. "Or I will blow your brains out."

I swallow, hard.

Jaxon, I need you.

chapter 43

JAXON

*M*Y PHONE KEEPS RINGING, but it's an unsaved number, so I ignore it. All I want is to get home to Scarlett because she must be hungry. I had to work late tonight, and I saw her text as I was just getting in the car, so I stopped at the Chinese takeout and got something for the both of us. When my phone rings once more, I sigh and pick it up.

"Jaxon Bentley," I say into the line.

The next words spoken send chills up my spine. "Jaxon, please tell me that Scarlett is with you."

"No, she's not," I say quickly, fear and worry consuming me. "I'm on my way home from work now. Who is this? Where is she?"

"It's Valentina," she says, sounding worried. "Scarlett was meant to meet me for coffee about an hour ago, and she never showed up. I have a feeling something's not right. Can you check if she's at your house, then call me back?"

It's not like Scarlett to not show up anywhere. She's always punctual, and this definitely doesn't sound like her. "I'm almost home. I'll call you back."

I speed the rest of the way home, park, and rush to the front door. Her car is here, so when I spot it, I hope she's only on the couch, waiting for me with a smile. When I enter the house though, she's nowhere to be seen. I start calling her name, and search every room. When I come up empty, I call her phone.

It's off.

I call Valentina back. "She's not here," I say in a panic. "Fuck, where could she be, Valentina? I need to find her, now. It's not like her to go somewhere without letting someone know. Her car is here, so unless she went for a walk somewhere . . . But at this time of night? Fuck, I don't know."

"Fuck," Valentina whispers. "I'm coming there with the men right now. We need to find her and make sure she's okay. Stay there, Jaxon. I'll be there in ten."

She hangs up and I walk out the front of the house, looking down the street, wondering if she'd gone for a spontaneous walk and maybe lost her phone. If she did though, she would've been home in under an hour—no one walks longer than that. And if she lost her phone or dropped it and it broke, she'd come straight home. So this makes no sense. I hear the rumbles of the bikes before I see them. Two bikes. I tell you what, these men work fast, and the gratitude I feel for them showing up to help search for my woman will never be unappreciated. I see Demon get off his bike first, Valentina on the back, and he comes rushing over to me.

"Any sign of her, brother?" he asks me.

"No," I say, shaking my head.

"Tell me everything," he demands, in full cop mode.

"She messaged me asking me to bring dinner. Valentina said she planned to meet up with her for coffee but never showed, and she's nowhere to be found. Her car is here, Demon, so I don't know where she could have gone."

"Fuck," he grits out. The other man climbs off his bike and comes to stand next to Demon. I recognize him as the president of the WDMC, a man known as Arrow. Why is he here? Either way, I'm grateful for the help.

Valentina comes up to stand next to me. "What do we do?" she asks us. "Something's not right, I can feel it."

Demon looks to me. "Do you have cameras in your house?"

He knows I do. "Yeah, but the only view we get is the backyard, the sides of the house, and the front door."

"Let's see what we can do with that," Arrow says, looking at me. "Can you let us in? We'll try to get any clues to see what happened to her."

I nod.

He looks to Demon, and says, "I'll do a ride around the block. Valentina, can you go talk to the neighbors and see if they saw anything? They might be friendlier if a woman shows up instead of Demon or me." He pauses, but then adds, "And, Valentina, you come right back here, you hear me? Anything happens to you, and Irish will fight out of prison with his bare hands and kill the lot of us."

"I will," she says, saluting him.

He nods and leaves without another word. Valentina disappears next door.

"Come on, let's see what we can find on the cameras," Demon says, storming toward the house. I open my laptop and show him the footage. It shows her leaving but as soon as she walks out onto the lawn where her car is, we lose sight of her.

Fuck.

"Demon, fuck!"

"I told you to update your security," he tells me, making me want to punch him. He did tell me that, but now is not the time to rub it in my face.

"Don't," I growl at him, letting him know not to push me any further. "Don't even fucking go there."

Valentina returns about ten minutes later, worry written all over her face.

"She told me she needed to talk about something," she says to me. "Something was weighing on her mind. Why wouldn't she have made it to the café?"

She wanted to talk to Valentina about something? Was there something wrong? It's odd that she didn't mention meeting up with Valentina in the first place, because she always sends me messages telling me what her plans are. None of it makes sense. None of it. Fuck, if something has happened to her, I'm not going to fucking survive it.

"There's a message on your voice mail," Demon notices. "What if it's from her?"

I walk over to the machine and press PLAY. When I hear my mom's voice, I shake my head at him, but then when I hear the content of the message, I cringe.

"Fuck."

I can't believe my mom said all that, and that Scarlett would have heard it. No wonder she wanted to vent to Valentina.

"And that's why she would have wanted to see you," I tell her, cursing under my breath. "Fuck, she must have been upset."

"Well, unless she went to murder your mom, it still doesn't explain where she vanished to," Demon says, moving to search the house.

"We have nothing to go on," I tell him, hoping one of them

has some kind of epic plan, because I don't know what to do. I can't think straight. I'm not at my usual levelheadedness. "Should I call the police?"

"Not just yet," Arrow advises me as he walks back into the house. "This isn't our first rodeo, Jaxon. If we can't find her, I doubt the lazy-ass cops can."

I look to where Demon is, walking around and looking for any sign of a struggle or a clue that can help, like any good cop would. Not all cops are lazy.

We walk out the front.

"Do you know a woman of this description?" Valentina asks me. She hands me a piece of paper with dot points she's jotted down. "Your neighbor across the road saw a woman with this description surveying your house."

I read them and they aren't much to go by: shoulder-length brown hair, tight clothing, short.

I read them all three times, and then it hits me who it could be.

"There's only one woman who I could think would have any vendetta against me and Scarlett, and she fits this description," I tell them.

"Give us her name, now," Arrow demands, looking to Demon, probably ready to bark out orders, which I appreciate.

"Sharon Beetle."

"The TV host?" Valentina asks, brow furrowing. "What does she have against Scarlett? How does she even know who she is?"

I give them a quick rundown on my connection to Sharon, and tell them how I think she's psychotic. I also let them know that it very well might not be her, but that's all we can go on right now, because I can't think of anyone else who would be searching around my house like that.

Demon nods, because he saw her the night he punched me in the face. "Makes sense."

"We're going to the TV bitch to see if she has Scarlett or not," Arrow orders.

"I'm staying here in case she comes back," Valentina announces, and Arrow nods.

"I'll call one of the men and tell them to come here and look after you. Only open the door if it's one of them. We don't know what we're dealing with here yet," Arrow warns.

Arrow makes a phone call, then turns to us. "We have two addresses for her. We're going to have to split up."

"I'll go with Jaxon," Demon says quickly. "You okay on your own, man?"

Arrow flashes him a look that clearly says, *What the fuck do you think?*, then hands us one of the addresses.

"Good luck, Jaxon," Valentina says, running her hand through her hair.

"Thanks, Valentina," I tell her.

I'm going to need it.

chapter 44

"SHOULD I PRETEND I'M selling something?" Demon suggests, looking down at his biker attire and smirking.

"Like what? Drugs?" I ask, staring up at the house. "Because that's the only thing you look like you'd be selling. Fuck it; let's just go in. Worst case, they call the cops. We'll be out of there before then," I say, approaching the door.

"Worse case they have dogs and we die," he says, but follows me anyway. True friendship right there.

"If there's a chance Scarlett is in there, I'm going in. I don't care if they have fucking hellhounds," I tell him.

I try to open the door but it's locked, so we move around to the back. Also locked. I'm about to kick the fucking door down when Demon pulls some sneaky lockpick out of his pocket and proceeds to break into the house.

"Is this what they teach you at cop school?" I whisper, entering in front of him. If anyone is getting hurt in any way, it's going to be me, not him. Scarlett is my woman, and I'm going to do anything to save her. Fuck, if it is Sharon, then this whole thing is my fault. I'm going to be the one to put her behind bars myself. The house is empty, and there's no sign of anyone in there.

No Scarlett. No Sharon, no anyone.

Demon's phone rings.

"Yeah? What kind of issue?" he waits for them to reply, then looks me in the eye and mutters, "Fuck."

"What is it?" I ask, hoping to God that she's okay. Let her be okay, please.

"Okay, I'll be there soon," he tells them, and hangs up. "Let's go. Arrow found her."

"Where?" I ask, leaving the house and running to the car. "Is she okay?"

He gets in the driver's seat of my car and turns to me. "She's in Sharon's other property. He hasn't actually seen her, but the men heard Sharon and a man talking about it. They tapped their line."

"Fuck, they work fast," I say again, so fucking thankful that Scarlett brought these men into my life. "So why hasn't he gone in and gotten her?"

Demon cringes, and sighs. "The man Sharon was talking to is a cop. It's become a little trickier now. But she's alive."

"A cop?" I grit out between clenched teeth. "One of Darren's buddies? Or is it something else?"

"We don't know yet. Arrow is staked out. We'll know if they try to move her. We just need to figure out what to do with the dirty cop. If we kill him, there's going to be a lot of backlash and the other cops won't give up until someone does time for the crime," Demon explains to me.

"Maybe we don't have to kill him," I say, formulating a plan. "Maybe we use a distraction of some kind?"

"What are you thinking?" he asks me, sounding intrigued.

"What if I rang Sharon and asked her something, I don't know. I'll make something up. She'll make any excuse to come see me, and then she's out of the house. Now we just need to get rid of the cop. Can't you just maim him but not kill him?"

"I can." He nods, seemingly liking this idea. "But I feel like he'll come back to bite us in the ass; it won't end here."

"Should we worry about that when it happens?" I ask, brow furrowing. "Or is that just asking for future disaster? I mean if we can't kill him, I don't know what other options there are, really. We just need to move soon. I don't want her there longer than she has to be; who knows what Sharon is fucking doing to her? She must be so scared."

"She'll be fine," Demon promises me. "Concentrate on saving her, not on what she's doing right now. She's strong. She'll be okay, we just need to be able to get her out of there, and you're right, it needs to be now. There's no time to waste."

"Okay," I say more to myself than him.

Okay.

We can do this.

I can do this.

I will have her back in my arms before tonight is over.

WE MEET UP WITH Arrow and my plan backfires because Sharon doesn't pick up her phone. "Too busy kidnapping my woman and being a psychotic, jealous bitch."

"Do we have a plan B?" I ask Demon and Arrow as we sit

in a car in front of the place where Scarlett is. "Please tell me we have a plan B."

Demon flashes me a look, and I have a feeling he has a plan B, he's just not telling me what it is. That worries me a little because of the place he's in right now. He's a cop. But he can't be one right now, so it must be hard for him.

"Someone give me a gun—I'll just storm in there and grab her," I say, holding my hand out.

Arrow looks unamused. "If anyone's storming in there, we *all* are. They can't take us all down."

"That's the plan? Just raid the place? Force and weapon tactics?" Demon asks, sounding like he thinks we should be coming up with something better.

"Anyone have a better idea?" Arrow asks us.

No one says anything.

"Load the guns," he says, then turns to me. "We'll storm in and hold everyone hostage, you get your woman."

I nod. "Thank you, Arrow."

"Don't thank me yet," he murmurs, then gets out of the car with Demon and opens the trunk to take out the weapons.

"Do you even know how to use a gun?" Arrow asks me as he slides back in and hands me one.

"Just because I'm a lawyer doesn't mean I don't know how to use a weapon," I tell him, shaking my head. "I'm more than just a man who knows how to look good in a suit."

"Just checking," he says, smirking. "You never know with you business types."

"I've got this, don't worry. I'm not going to let anything happen to my woman."

I'll take down all of them if I have to, but she's coming home with me.

◊

WE BUST INTO THE house, me in the middle, and Demon and Arrow on each side. They actually have a formation for situations like this. I don't want to know how many times it's been necessary to break into an establishment guns blazing, but I'm thankful they know what they're doing.

I suddenly know why the biker men do what they do. I so easily called them criminals, but now I'd do the same as them in a heartbeat, anything to have Scarlett safe and by my side once more. I will never judge them for their methods again. When you take someone's woman—that means war. If you don't like it, then you shouldn't have touched what wasn't yours in the first place.

Sharon puts her hands up when she sees us and starts screaming. She drops her gun on the floor and yells for a man named Brendan.

"Where is she?" Arrow demands, looking every inch of a scary-ass biker president.

She doesn't reply, so I move to check the rooms on this floor. Finding each one empty, I shake my head at Arrow, who grabs Sharon, her back against his chest, and puts the gun to her temple.

"Tell us where she is or I will blow your fucking brains out, lady," he growls, and Sharon starts to cry. When she points upstairs, I'm about to run up there, but Demon stops me. "We don't know who else is up there."

He leads the way and I follow behind, facing the other way with my gun, our backs together so no one can get at us from any angle. Maybe in another life I would have made a good cop, or a good biker.

"Put your hands up!" Demon yells at the man standing

there in front of a door. He's in uniform, the bastard. His name tag has Gilmore on it. I don't know who this guy thinks he is, but I will kill him if he doesn't let Scarlett go. If she's been hurt, I'll kill him anyway.

"You'll all go to prison for this," he says in a calm tone, reaching for his gun.

Demon takes one shot, hitting him in the leg. Gilmore collapses to the ground, crying out in pain.

"Slide your gun to me, or I'll take out your other leg," I tell him, pointing my gun to his other knee. He slides his weapon over, and Demon grabs it. I move to the door, unlocking it and opening it. What I see has my heart galloping in my fucking chest. Scarlett is lying on the bed, knocked out. I rush over and feel her pulse. She's alive, but when I shake her she doesn't wake up.

"I think they've drugged her," I call out to Demon, picking her up in my arms and carrying her out. "She's alive but she won't wake up."

"Take her downstairs," Demon tells me. "I'll handle this . . . cop."

"Okay," I say, but linger for a moment. What is he going to do? If anyone needs to be committing a crime, it should be me, not him. I don't want Demon getting into any trouble.

Demon growls at me. "I've got this. Go, brother."

I don't miss the slip of him calling me by that name, but I ignore it and head down the stairs, where Arrow still has a gun to Sharon's head.

"What did you give her?" I ask the bitch. "She's out cold."

"It's just a sedative; she'll be fine. It wasn't my idea, Jaxon; it was Brendan's. He wanted her dead, I don't know why, please don't let him kill me," she pleads. "He's a cop, of course I just did what he asked me to. He said he knew Darren; he said that

Darren had his money and that now she owed him! That's all I know. I don't even know who Darren is!"

And there we have it.

This Gilmore guy is a friend of Darren's. It always comes back to money, doesn't it? If Sharon is telling the truth and this wasn't her plan—that must be it. Sharon is just a pawn, probably because she was sleeping with Gilmore. There's no other reason for anyone hating Scarlett. Darren is fucking things up from the grave, that stupid bastard. I ought to move Scarlett away so she never has to deal with one of his crooked cop friends again.

I hold her tight against me, and thank my lucky stars she's back where she belongs.

chapter 45

"IF IT'S MORE THAN a sedative, Sharon, you're going to regret your life choices," Arrow throws at her. The man is the scariest out of the whole MC, according to Demon, and I wouldn't want to be in her place right now.

"It's just a sedative, I promise," she tells us. "She wouldn't stop yelling."

"Being kidnapped might make someone do that," he tells her gruffly, unamused.

I don't know what the rest of the plan is—we never really spoke about what would happen now. We can't just leave them here, right? The cops would be at all our doors within the hour. I'm sure that Gilmore bastard will concoct some kind of story and try to put us all behind bars. With me and Faye on our side though, good luck to him.

Three gunshots are fired upstairs, and Arrow and I share a look.

Fuck.

Did Demon kill the cop? I thought we were trying to avoid that.

"Oh God, Brendan!" Sharon cries, plump tears dripping down her cheeks. "Why did you kill him? I love him!"

Fuck me.

When I hear some scuffling from above, I feel like something isn't quite right.

"Arrow," I say, warning in my tone.

He's got Sharon, and I have Scarlett in my arms, so I'm not sure which one of us can go check, but one of us needs to.

"Sit there," he tells Sharon, pushing her onto the couch, then turns to me. "Watch her. I need to see what the fuck is going on up there."

Sharon decides to get up and tries to run, but Arrow quickly grabs her. "Fuck."

"I'll go," I tell him.

"Give me Scarlett," he tells me.

I reluctantly hand her over and watch as he throws her over his shoulder, then turns the gun back on Sharon. I run up the stairs, pointing my gun in front of me, wondering what the fuck is happening up here.

What I see makes me still.

No.

Fucking no.

No, no, no.

I drop to my knees. I just drop, unable to hold my own weight.

Unable to function.

No.

I throw the gun on the floor and crawl over to my childhood

best friend, the one lying on the floor with blood pouring out of his chest. I try to find his pulse, but there's nothing.

"Demon?" I whisper, shaking him. "Demon, wake up. Come on, man. I need you."

Arrow comes up the stairs, still holding Scarlett, then looks at Demon on the floor. Arrow looks down at Demon with such pain in his eyes, such grief, and I know when he looks into mine he would see the same.

There was another person up here, and we missed it.

We fucking missed it.

Across from Demon's body lay two cops.

Both dead.

Demon must've shot them both but got hit anyway. Fuck. Why wasn't I here with him?

I try to stop the bleeding with my hand, and then I take off my T-shirt and try to use that.

"Jaxon," Arrow says, touching my shoulder. "He's gone. He's gone."

"No," I say, shaking my head.

Demon is dead, he died for me, saving Scarlett. No one knew he was undercover. He can take that with him to the grave. No one will know this, ever. I owe it to him.

"Fuck, Jaxon," Arrow growls. "We need to get out of here. How the fuck are we going to explain the deaths of these two cops?"

I block Arrow out.

I cup Demon's face with my hand.

I can literally feel my heart ripping into pieces. It's like Olivia all over again.

A tear falls down my cheek, and I let it.

I don't care.

I lost my sister, and now I've lost my brother.

I don't know how much this world expects me to take. I don't know what else they can possibly throw at me. I pick Demon up in my arms, and carry him down the stairs. He's heavy, but I don't care. I don't want anyone else to touch him.

My tears are now pouring, and I can't control them. I don't want to live in a world without my best friend.

We walk down the stairs, Demon in my arms, Scarlett in Arrow's.

I see Arrow got creative and tied Sharon to one of the pillars in the house.

He looks to her and yells. "If you were sorry, you would have mentioned the other cop, wouldn't you? Fuck!"

"They're dead now," I tell her.

Arrow studies me, and then the man in my arms. "Go put him in the car. I have an idea."

I look down at Scarlett.

"I won't leave her side, Jaxon. Go."

I head outside in the dark and put Demon's body in the backseat of the car. I kiss his cheek and say, "I'm so sorry. This is all my fault. I'm so sorry, Demon. I love you like my brother. I would have rather died instead of you. It should have been me."

If Olivia is watching from heaven right now, she probably hates me.

I saved the love of my life, but I lost my best friend in the process.

Life is a fucking bitch.

ARROW CARRIES OUT SCARLETT and puts her on my lap. "I'm going to sort this out. A few of my men are on the way."

"You shouldn't have to clean up my mess, Arrow," I tell him.

"Just tell me what needs to be done, and I'll handle it. We should call the cops. There's no other way to handle this."

He touches my shoulder. "I've got this covered. You just need to get Demon and Scarlett out of here. I know about Demon, Jaxon. He was a cop, and we won't get in trouble for this because of that. He came to me a while back, and after everything that happened with Irish and Scarlett, we started working on finding the dirty cops. How do you think he got that knife wound?"

I stare at him in shock. He knew?

"I've got a cop friend. Demon introduced us. I'll call him and get his help."

I don't have time to process this right now.

Someone is going to pay for all of this. The dirty cops in Darren's unit—I'm going to see to it that they each go to prison, one by one.

"Okay," I whisper, looking down at them, sitting in the backseat with me.

This is not how I thought tonight would be ending.

I feel numb, and there's a pain in my chest that won't ebb.

What the fuck have I done?

I bring Scarlett's fingers to my lips and kiss them. I would have done anything to save Scarlett, even given up my own life, but I never expected for Demon to be the one to pay the price.

Never.

I squeeze both of their hands, and pray that this is all just a really bad, fucked-up dream.

Then I get in the front seat and drive the two most important people in the world to me home.

◆

NEVER IN MY LIFE will I forget the sound of Scarlett's shrill scream when she found out Demon was gone.

Never.

"No," she cries, shaking her head, looking down at his body. "No, Jaxon! You should have just left me there!"

The men all stand around, with their heads down, watching and listening to Scarlett cry and wail over the death of one of their men.

My best friend.

"Demon?" she says his name like she's begging for him to wake up. "Demon? Please wake up, please. No, this can't be happening. Jaxon needs you. You have no idea how much he needs you."

Fuck.

I look down at my feet, unable to watch anymore.

"Scarlett," I say, my voice raspy and cracked. I lift my head, and my eyes connect with hers. Hers hold so much pain and suffering, and I think mine hold nothing.

They feel empty.

I don't know which one is worse.

"Jaxon," she says, glancing down at Demon once more, then removing her hand from his shirt. She runs over to me and I hold her, console her. I rock her back and forth, and I tell her everything will be fine.

I lie.

Because I don't know if everything will be fine.

chapter 46

SCARLETT

I SIT IN THE BATHTUB, just staring at nothing.

I can't believe it.

I knew that cop Gilmore was dirty, but I didn't think he'd hate me so much to want to kidnap me. And Sharon? What the hell? I don't even know what to think.

And Demon.

I can't even think about him without sobbing; he didn't deserve to die. I flashback to us eating dessert together, us sharing and then ordering more. His smile. The way he loved Jaxon. The very first time I met him, when he was sent to keep an eye on me but the two of us kind of bonded. I felt comfortable around him. I trusted him, even before I knew how close he was with Jaxon.

Demon was a good man, and now, because of me, he's gone. The person Jaxon loves most in the world is gone, and it's because of me. Because of my insecurities. I never should've left the house. I never should've questioned Jaxon's intentions and reasons for loving me, I just should've accepted them.

Now look what has happened.

That bullet was never meant for him. The grim reaper took the wrong man. Another amazing soul taken from us. Jaxon isn't handling it well. I saw the look in his eye. He struggled losing his sister; it's not fair he has to lose a best friend too. How much is one man meant to take? The water turns cold, but I don't bother to add more warmth to it. There's no warmth in this house tonight, there are only sad memories and ghosts of what could have been. There's only heartbreak and sadness.

Mourning.

I close my eyes and silently start to cry.

"Demon," I whisper his name to myself. "We aren't going to be okay without you."

The irony of his name hits me, because there's no way that man is anything but an angel.

And now he's in heaven.

I force myself out of the bathtub and wrap a towel around me. I'm about to walk to the kitchen in my towel when I hear the men talking.

"I paid someone to take care of it," Arrow says. "A hit man. There's no blood on our hands."

"Just on mine," Jaxon says, but he doesn't sound sad about it, just that he's stating a fact.

Arrow ignores his comment. "On any of our hands. The place has been cleaned up, and it's like we were never there at all. Keep your head down, Jaxon. I know you're hurting, but you need to be smart about this or his life would have been in vain."

I sit down on the bed and let the water droplets drip down my leg without wiping them away. It looks like my body is seeping tears, crying with me.

Feeling my pain.

I don't know how we're going to come back from this.

I don't know how I'm going to make Jaxon happy again.

Why can't we catch a break? I tell myself to stop feeling sorry for myself, because it isn't going to help anything. I throw my towel on the floor and climb into bed. I get under the sheets and I just lie there. I don't want to ever move again. Sleep doesn't come for me, and neither does Jaxon, because he doesn't come to bed all night. I don't know what he's doing out there, and if he wants company or not.

I just do not know how to handle this.

I go to sleep and wake up with a damp pillow.

THE OLD LADIES COME around with flowers and food, and they all try to cheer me up. I appreciate them dropping by, but their hugs make me emotional and I start to cry. When some of them start to cry too, I realize they're hurt too. They knew Demon a lot longer than me, he was more theirs than he was mine, so I try to comfort them in return.

"I'm so sorry," I tell them.

"It's not your fault, Scarlett," Faye tells me, stroking my hair. "Don't blame yourself. You did nothing wrong. It was those fuckers who took you. They did this."

"I can't believe he's gone. You should see Jaxon; he's walking around like a zombie, and I don't know what to do, Faye. How do I fix this?" I ask, breaking down in front of her.

"You can't fix this, honey. He needs to get to a better place, and that'll take some time. This is not an easy thing for anyone, but even more so for him. You just need to be patient. Let him know you're there for him, that you have his back, but don't be overbearing. People grieve in different ways, so find out which way is his and adapt to that," she says, speaking to me in a gentle voice.

"I miss him already."

I don't know if I mean Demon, Jaxon, or both.

I want things to go back to how they were, before our world was turned upside down. I want Jaxon here, smiling. I want Demon popping by at random moments, smile on his face.

"So do we, babe. So do we," she murmurs, glancing around at the other women. "This is going to be a hard time for everyone, and we need to all stick together, okay? That's what a family does. Yeah, we lost one, and what an amazing man he was, but he wouldn't want us to be miserable forever. He's probably looking down on us now and giving us shit for all this crying."

My lip twitches at that. "He never really took anything seriously, did he?"

"No," Faye says, smirking. "I remember when I first met him. We used to check him out because we all thought he was good-looking, even though we'd never admit it to our men."

Jaxon walks in while Valentina is talking about the time Demon and she had a food fight, and he sees us sitting there. His expression softens, and then he comes to join us. He sits down in front of me and pulls my legs onto his lap.

"Will you tell me that story from the start?" he asks her.

Valentina nods, eyes filled with emotion as she starts again.

Sometimes you just have to start again, even when you don't want to.

"DO YOU KNOW WHAT makes me feel a little better?" Jaxon says when we're lying in bed that night. He reaches for me out of nowhere, and I flinch a little, just by reflex. He must feel it, because he stills and waits a moment before continuing to run his hand up my arm. "You okay?"

"Yes," I say, taking a deep breath. "I'm fine, sorry, you just caught me off guard."

"Don't say sorry," he murmurs, bringing my fingers to his lips and placing a kiss there.

"What makes you feel better?" I ask him, wanting him to continue with the story, happy that he's opening up to me.

"The idea that Demon and Olivia are together up there. They were always meant to be together, you know? But it didn't work out for them. And now, they're finally reunited."

"That's a really nice thought, Jaxon," I say, resting my head on his chest. "I just wanted to say that I'm here for you, any way I can be. If you want space, I'll give it to you, or if you want me with you all the time, I'll be there. I'm so sorry this happened, and I don't know how we're going to get to a point where it doesn't physically hurt to think about him, but if anyone can do it, it's us."

"Thank you, baby," he murmurs, kissing the top of my head. "I just need some time. It just . . . it hurts. So bad. Even if we didn't see each other often, I always knew he was there, that if I needed him he'd be here, you know? It's like I've lost a part of myself. I just . . ." He takes a deep breath. "He was my family. He was the person who knew me the best. Without him, I don't know who I am anymore."

"I know who you are, Jaxon," I tell him. "I know. And I will spend the rest of our lives reminding you. Every day, I'll remind you of the man I fell in love with." I place my hand over his heart. "I'd know you anywhere. I'd recognize you in the dark. And I will love you forever."

He buries his face in the crook of my neck. "I love you so

much, Scarlett. Don't ever think that I don't. How I'm feeling right now has nothing to do with how much I love you."

"I know," I whisper. "You don't have to worry about that. I know how much you love me. And I know what your mom said on the voice mail isn't true at all. You didn't save me because you felt obligated to—you saved me because my soul called to yours, because you felt the connection between us. Because we were meant to be. And Jaxon? Now I'll save you."

In this moment, I know we're going to be okay.

I kiss his forehead and hold him.

I'll be his strength.

I'll be anything he needs me to be.

"**I** THINK THAT'S ALL THE recent news," I tell the stone. "Everyone is doing well. We all miss you, of course, and that's never going to change, but at least I'm not crying myself to sleep every night anymore." I sigh and admit, "I do cry sometimes, still. Like the other day I found that stupid dirty magazine that I know you left in my library. I brought it home. Anyone who sees it is going to think I'm a creep, but I'm not, I'm just sentimental for a creep, if that makes sense." I smile and imagine him laughing at me right now. "Anyway, I bought you some of that sticky date pudding you like. I don't know if you'd like flowers or not, but I know you loved that dessert. It looks pretty good actually, maybe I should just eat it. Does this make me a shit person? Because I'm really considering eating it. It's not like you can eat it, right? I'm sure you would have wanted me to."

"Scarlett." Jaxon sighs, but I see the amusement on his expression. "I think Demon has had enough of your pudding talk."

"Doubtful. The man loved pudding," I huff, reaching out and touching his stone. "I love you, Demon. And if you had a less psychotic name, I'd name any future sons after you."

"His real name is Arlo," Jaxon decides to point out.

Arlo?

I kind of like that. Why didn't they put his real name on the headstone.

"If we have a son can we name him that?" I ask Jaxon, who nods in return.

"I'd love that," he admits, putting his hand on the stone. "And I know he would too."

"Arlo Demon Bentley," I say out loud, and Jaxon chuckles.

"It has a certain ring to it, doesn't it?"

I nod. "It does."

I stand up and let Jaxon have a few minutes alone with Demon. In the meantime, I head to Olivia's stone and drop off some fresh flowers.

"I hope you and Demon are together," I tell her. "And I hope you'd approve of me and your brother, because I don't think any other woman could possibly love him as much as I do."

I blow her a kiss, and then head to the car to wait for Jaxon, eating Demon's sticky date pudding as I wait.

It tastes delicious, even more so because it was his.

Jaxon slides into the car, and I offer him a bite. He opens his mouth, and I slip it inside.

"Shit, that's good," he murmurs, eyes going wide. "No wonder he liked it so much."

"I know, right? It's delicious," I say with my mouthful.

Jaxon chuckles, and reverses out of the parking lot. "Where to next?"

"Wherever the open road takes us," I say.

"So, home?" he asks, smirking.

"Yeah," I reply, smiling over at him. "Let's go home."

JAXON

Nine Months Later

WE WALK AROUND ROME, hand in hand.

Scarlett takes in the sights, the sounds, just eating everything up like a kid in a candy store. After we lost Demon, we pushed back the vacation because it didn't feel like a good time to go away. There was no escaping what happened, the loss of him, and jumping on a plane wouldn't fix that. The demons would follow us, pun intended. In the past few months I've been healing, and keeping busy with working with the chief of police to bring down all the cops who were on Darren's team. In my own way, it feels like I'm doing this for Demon.

No dirty cop stands a chance while I'm still here fighting.

"I didn't think it would be so cold today," she says, wrapping her scarf around her neck. "This place is so beautiful though. Thank you for bringing me here, Jaxon."

"You don't have to thank me," I tell her, wrapping my arm around her waist. "I love watching you take everything in. You look so happy."

"I feel so happy," she returns, smiling up at me. "I'm glad we finally did this trip."

"Me too," I say, reaching into my pocket and feeling the black velvet box in there.

Time to make her officially mine.